I ONLY SMOKE ON THURSDAYS

georgie nickell

[signature]

Writers Advantage
New York   Lincoln   Shanghai

I Only Smoke On Thursdays

All Rights Reserved © 2002 by Georgie Nickell

No part of this book may be reproduced or transmitted in any form or by any means, graphic, electronic, or mechanical, including photocopying, recording, taping, or by any information storage retrieval system, without the permission in writing from the publisher.

Writers Advantage
an imprint of iUniverse, Inc.

For information address:
iUniverse
2021 Pine Lake Road, Suite 100
Lincoln, NE 68512
www.iuniverse.com

This is in part a work of fiction. Although inspired by actual events, the names, persons, places, and characters are inventions of the author. Any resemblance to people living or deceased is purely coincidental.

ISBN: 0-595-23646-4

Printed in the United States of America

Contents

1. Happy Valentine's Day 3
2. Three Years Earlier: The Night We Almost Never Met 17
3. Back to Reality: Jackie's Book Club 24
4. Finding Out 32
5. The Flight to Mars 42
6. Re-Meeting Bryan 54
7. First Day of the Last Year 61
8. The Next Chapter 80
9. Just Like the Swiss Family Robinson 86
10. Sending a Postcard from Nowhere to No One 93
11. Dustin Dan 96
12. The Time and Place for Everything 116
13. We Had a Good Time… 121
14. Male Female Email. 131
15. Confession 137
16. A Side of Fries and a Large Depression 156
17. No More I Love You's 162
18. Mitchy the Kid 170
19. You Are My Fantasy 179
20. "Look! Up In the Sky! It's the Powerfully Unbearable Boy Annoy!" 186
21. Blah, blah, blah 193
22. Always a Bridesmaid 203
23. JJ Is Pregnant 215
24. Cake 223
25. Why Girls Are Stupid 227

26. Brave New World 232
27. Thursday 242
About the Author 249

Acknowledgments

I thank God for making me the person I was
and allowing things to happen in my life
that have made me the person I've become.

Thanks to my friends who are my family,
and my family who are my friends.

I thank my dad for being the man all men should be.
I thank my mom for paying for my braces, cheerleading uniforms, and dancing lessons.
To my grandparents, Eve & Ed: Your presence in my life will always be cherished.

I thank and appreciate:
Non-verbal love from animals, Prince, the Go-Go's,
the people responsible for making the movie
Girls Just Want to Have Fun,
and Cher.

TO GET ON THIS RIDE YOU MUST BE THIS TALL

You get in
and someone you don't know pulls the bar down,
tells you to hang on and "Keep your hands inside."

Slowly it starts to move
and you think, "Oh, it's fun, look at me…I'm laughing!"
You see your mom down there
and you wave like the whole experience is under your control
but it gets faster and faster
and you start to wonder what you got yourself into.

Suddenly, going higher isn't as much fun
as you thought it would be when you were waiting in line
and there's no ear attached to the person who *isn't* sitting next to you
So you scream and scream with laughter in between
when you realize you're alone
but that's OK
because it feels like you're flying, the next minute you're dying
and having someone there almost wouldn't make the experience
Yours
It would be "ours"
and your dad taught you that Pride of Ownership is half of everything.

The landscape mixes together like all your emotions,
the herky jerks and fluid motion make you sick
and you wonder why you bothered at all.

I Only Smoke On Thursdays

You lose your head and start crying
when you get ripped through a turn you didn't see coming
and the guy operating the whole operation is on a smoke break.

You can't see your mom anywhere
it's all you and a mass of air
whirling around and playing with your hair
and you wish this stupid thing would stop
so you could go back to the safe place,
shrouded in the shadows of things you already know
but with every inch higher it gets lighter and lighter
You suddenly feel warm and can hear your favorite song playing…
somewhere
and you notice that the view from here is really quite lovely
but you're pissed you forgot your camera.

I'm 12 years old and have picked out my wedding dress.

It has beads all over it and a huge bow in the back. It has a very long veil attached to an extra sparkly tiara. I'm going to get married on the top of a skyscraper in downtown Seattle with the lights of the city and the warm June breeze surrounding me like a great big hug. *Oingo Boingo* will perform live at the reception and there will be a huge sit-down Surf-n-Turf dinner. Instead of the usual wedding cake, I'll have a chocolate chip mint ice cream cake. My 12 bridesmaids will wear purple mini-dresses and fingerless gloves. The boys will wear white tuxes with gray cummerbunds.

My husband will be tall with dark hair and wear glasses like my dad's. He will be cute and funny, and possibly some sort of doctor or lawyer (I don't know why that should be important to me, but my mom says it will be *very* important to me one day.) I will have met my husband at a party one year after I graduated from college. I will have a body wave perm and be a professional writer. All my friends will be jealous that I met him before they did. They will refer to him as "the last good one" and look at us with envy as we dance on the multicolored dance floor at our reception. My husband will tell me I'm as pretty as Mork's Mindy, but a little more stylish than she is.

For our honeymoon, we'll vacation in Disneyland (because I've only been there once, and even then I spent most of the time in the hotel room because I got so sunburnt). We'll drive away from the reception hall with our friends and family throwing rice at the car, and as we sink into the plush seats of the pink Cadillac, my husband will look at me and say…

"This is the best day of my whole life."

I'll smile, blink away the tears and say, "Me too."

1. Happy Valentine's Day

I sat on my unfamiliar deck and inhaled the cigarette smoke, letting it scrape and scratch my healthy throat. I almost choked but slowly I took in a breath of cold air and forced it down. I've started smoking again. I know all the facts—how bad it is for you and all that, but at this moment I don't really care. I don't care about anything.

Its been almost a month since I was suddenly dumped by my love of three years. I can't believe that this is the way it is now. I can't believe that I have to accept it and somehow find a comfortable spot within my skin and face my life, the life I thought I was going to share with Him, alone.

I guess you're always alone. Even when you're surrounded by people who love you, you're alone. No one can hear the voice inside my head but me. No one knows what it feels like to be dumped on Valentine's Day.

I can't even cry anymore. I mean full-fledged, falling-on-the-ground, crazy crying. Now I'm in the *Where Do I Go from Here?* phase with *Am I Ever Going to Find Someone?* overtones. How the relationship ended was the worst possible way you could imagine. The process after it is crippling. I'm constantly shaking, even when I'm warm, I'm shaking. I'm shaking now as I sit on this deck, smoking my Marlboro Lights. The only comfort I can find is watching the blue smoke pour out of me in one perfect stream.

I thought I would be further along in the healing process at this point but in fact, I'm worse than the day after it happened. Now it's sinking in... He's not on vacation. He's not coming back. I had to deal with the business part of the split at first: cancel the credit cards, divide the CDs, gather all the pictures and stuff them into a bag hidden in the left corner of my closet.

Right after I read the note He left for me, I called my old roommate. It's funny how strangely rational I was. We would look for apartments the next day; I had to get out of that apartment as soon as possible.

People are calling me "healthy." I don't know how healthy it is to be sitting here saturating my pain in nicotine. I'm not as strong as people think. They say I'm doing so well but they don't know what it's like to sleep alone and empty the last three years of your life into a toilet and flush, when it really didn't need to go. But it was decided for you, it had to go. It was out of your control. There's nothing you can do about it but try to find a way to cope.

My friends are providing countless billable hours of counseling for free. I try to piece all their wisdom tidbits together into a big quilt of comfort I can wrap around my bones for warmth. But let me tell you, it's no fun to lose your craving for Mexican food or to wake up at three o'clock in the morning just to be reminded that He's not there.

Its been one month. A month since I've seen His face or smelled His shirts, but I can still remember what it feels like to have Him rub my back after a hard day or call me "sweetie" over an expensive sushi dinner.

Everything reminds me of Him. Even the air reminds me of Him because I know that somewhere in this world He's breathing air too; maybe the same air I just pushed out of my body. It's too painful to think that he voluntarily gave me up. Me, the one who was there and willing to work through the times that were much harder than this. But He didn't want to fight, and that's the thought that keeps me awake at night, waiting for the sleeping pills to pull me out of consciousness. He didn't want to fight for me. It was easier for Him to just let go.

What's the lesson here? What the hell am I supposed to walk away with? If someone would just tell me why this whole nightmare is happening to me, maybe it wouldn't hurt so bad. I don't have the answers. I don't have anyone. I just have me.

On Valentine's Day morning, I gave Him His card. "You can have the rest of your present tonight, but open the card now. I made it," I said as I sat down next to Him at the foot of our bed.

"Your present isn't ready," He said.

"I thought you got it last night. Isn't that why you said you were late?" He looked at me but said nothing. "I get it. You don't want to ruin the surprise. OK, just open my card now." He opened the juvenile card that I had made out of doilies and cutout paper hearts, and read the poem inside. He read it in silence, interrupted by the tears that slid out of His eye sockets. "Are you crying? Hey, why are you crying?" I asked and hugged Him.

"I don't know."

"Are you *happy-crying,* or *this-is-the-stupidest-card-in-the-world* crying?"

"Happy-crying." Something about it, about Him… I just didn't believe Him. I sat back and looked at this face that I loved and said…

"Do you even want to work this out?"

"Yes."

"Do you still love me?"

"Yes."

Eight hours later, He was gone.

As soon as I opened the door, I knew something wasn't right. It was as if I already knew He was gone. I stayed in the back part of our apartment for at least a half-hour. I made the bed, petted His cat, hung up the clothes. I went into the bathroom and looked in the mirror. I could still see the words He wrote in the shower steam just a few days before; *"I love you."*

I went into the living room and that's where I saw it. I looked away, like it would somehow disappear. I thought that by the time I looked back it would be gone. The colors still clung to my eyes as I turned to look out the windows. The white paper, the red rose, the purple dress I wore in the picture. It was time to face it—the one thing I'd been avoiding all week.

He had acted strangely over the last couple days. Each day I asked Him what it was, how I could help and, "Is there anything you need to tell me?" He always said no. The only thing that He would tell me was that He was extremely depressed. He was 35, didn't own a house, had no savings; was about to lost His job for the second time. He insisted these were the reasons He was depressed. It wasn't me. It was everything else, but not me. It wasn't until Saturday night that I realized it was me.

He asked what I wanted out of our relationship. "I want to get engaged, maybe this year, I want to marry you, have our children, live in a great house, grow old together. I mean, not all right now, just eventually," I smiled.

He sat across from me in the restaurant and continued to look down at his plate. "How can I provide you with all that when I can't even afford cat food?"

"It doesn't all happen in one day. I said *eventually*." I had the most horrible sinking feeling in the pit of my stomach. That's the best way I can describe it: sinking. And that's exactly what I began to do.

We drove home in a saddened silence. I loved this man. I had been picturing my life with this man for almost three years. But I could feel it: He was thinking of letting go.

Back at the apartment, I tried to talk to Him. I said that I knew He was going through some sort of life crisis but we would get through it, together. We had hard times before this and got through. This depression wasn't big enough to destroy us; it just wasn't that tragic. "We have each other. We don't need anything else," I said.

"You don't like to play golf," He said and started to cry.

"So?"

"You don't like to play golf. I like to play golf."

"What are you talking about? You're freaking out because you like to do something that I don't? I don't like golf, but I support you in it. I just bought you a $400 club! I bought you golf shoes last year. A weekend activity isn't enough reason for your depression, I'm sorry, but it's just not. What's really going on? What aren't you telling me?" I could feel I was losing it. I felt panicked, scared, and couldn't believe this was actually happening. There was a crack in my perfectly planned life.

"I'm going for a drive," He said as He stood up. When He grabbed His coat and headed for the door, I said...

"I won't be here when you get back."

"Where are you going?"

"I don't know, but I'm not going to sit here as you drive off to who knows where to decide if I'm good enough for you to stay with. I've supported you mentally, physically and financially for almost three years. I never asked one thing from you, except for you to love me. And now, you're taking these stupid things, like golf and cat food, as signs that... what? We shouldn't be together? I have no fucking idea what's going on but I'm not going to fall asleep alone and wake up without you."

"Where are you going?" He asked again.

"To my parents, I guess."

He was really crying now; big sobs, red eyes, the whole production... I was waiting for the dancing girls to show up. He grabbed my hands and said, "Pray for me. Pray that I make the right decision. I don't know what to do with my life. Pray that I won't do something stupid."

I suddenly felt a sense of calmness rush over me. "I don't need to pray for you. I already know what decision you're going to make. We can get through this. I believe in that. I know I can believe in that. I'm sure everything is going to be okay." He nodded, kissed me, and walked out the door.

I came back from my parents' house the next day and sat on the couch, waiting for Him to turn up. When He finally did, we talked for hours. I fed Him reassuring phrases and said that I would stand by Him through all of the tough times in His life. We agreed that everything was fine between us.

We lived the next five days just as we always had. I still asked if there was anything He needed to tell me. The answer was always no. "Everything is going to be okay, sweetie; don't worry about it. It's all going to work out fine." He said this, and I believed him. But He lied. He never even told me why He lied.

But now it was time to face it head on. And I was facing it alone in our apartment. I picked up the note He left on our coffee table.

Eight hours after He said He loved me and wanted to work it out, He was gone. He said goodbye in a note, with a wilted rose in one of those plastic cone things you buy at 7-11, and a picture of us taken at some wedding last year placed next to it, adding to the drama.

I moved out the next day. I left Him a very short and monotone message on the answering machine asking Him to be gone between one and four o'clock. My parents and brother volunteered their moving services and sat on our couch with blank stares as they watched me simultaneously sort through clothes, pack boxes, and cry my eyes out.

I tore the sheets off the bed that were practically still warm from our bodies and stuffed them into a garbage bag. Hate, disgust, sadness and desperation hurricaned inside my skull as I started to think I was going insane. I forced myself to believe this was a scene from a movie and I was just an actress. *"This isn't really happening,"* I thought, but I knew it was. Someone would have edited this part out.

I thought He would show up and try to stop me, or He would help me carry the boxes down to the car and say, "I just need some time, sweetie. We're not breaking up." But that didn't happen either. I cried all the way to my parents' house twenty miles away. My dad put his hand on my knee and said, "Everything will be OK."

I went to work the next day at 8:30 and acted like everything was normal. But as it neared 8:45, I folded underneath a mass of tears when my boss asked if I had any extra Post-Its. I had no idea where He was or how to get in touch with Him. I had tons of questions but couldn't think of anything that I wanted to know. The only thing I could do was to write Him. I had no way of actually mailing the letters but getting my feelings down on paper had to be a step in the right direction.

All I felt like doing was crawling into the bed in my parents' guestroom and hope I would slip into a very dark coma for 17 years. I prayed that I would suddenly contract a horrid illness that would put me to death in a matter of hours. I wanted to get kidnapped and chained to a wall, with hangnails on every finger that would get plunged into lemon juice every five minutes; it would distract from the pain that was a million times worse.

When that didn't happen, I started to write.

February 17, 1997. [The first letter, three days after; I'm MAD]

If you're actually reading this letter, it means that I'm so mad at you, I felt you must hear me out. You never gave me a chance to say anything and that is something I simply cannot live with. And neither will you.

We had a relationship for almost three years. Years that were hard; harder for me than they were for you. Tell me, when was it that you consciously made the decision to leave me? Was it after my mom bought you all those gifts last Christmas or before I paid for the new clothes you wore to the job that I got for you? Could it have been during the years that I paid your half of the rent and all of the groceries? Let me know, because I'm very curious as to where it was along this well-manicured path that you got bored and decided to fuck up the whole thing. Oh yeah, I should mention that I've decided to blame the whole thing on you.

More unbelievable than imagining that you voluntarily left this kept lifestyle, is the fact that I'm actually upset over you. I can't imagine how I could be upset over a man who willingly chose to have things this way. What really disturbs me is that you don't care enough about me to try to work it out. You ended it in a note with a dramatic setting that... what? Was supposed to shock me? I should thank you for that whole episode. It made me see how weak you are; how unwilling you are to stand up through the down times like I did. For once in your life, be a man, you deceitful bastard. And stop trying to pattern your life after some damn daytime drama that you obviously watched religiously during the extended period of time that you were unemployed.

The decision to forge ahead in a relationship with me should be automatic. *"Do I want to marry her?"* YES. It should go something like that—fast, immediate, quick. If you need to think about what's what and who's who, then you've been wasting your time pretending this was an adult relationship with serious intentions, and that makes you the idiot. You think life and the future is going to happen all in one day but it's not. You're panicking. If you need to run off like a little boy to decide if you want to continue life with me, then your decision has already been made.

It's unfair that you acted like everything was OK this week but ultimately shit on me on Valentine's Day. Congratulations on being the ultimate asshole for choosing such an appropriate day. This way each year I will be able to accurately identify when it was that you ripped my heart out.

I cannot believe this is the way you want it and that *you* left *me*. This is the biggest mistake of your life. You will never have the life I could have provided you. I feel confident in saying that no one will ever love you the unconditional way I loved you.

This wasn't supposed to happen. I'm having a hard time accepting this is the way it is. I can't believe that you think this is the right thing to do. You chose this life for me; left me to pick up the pieces and deal with what you created.

People tell me not to contact you and I won't. I can't let you know how I'm feeling. I want you to think that I'm OK, but I'm not.

February 18, 1997. [The second letter, DISBELIEF]

I haven't cried today. This is the first day that I don't feel sad. I can't believe that you're doing this to me. It's obvious to me now that you've been feeling this way for awhile, yet you continued to use me. I thought every day spent with you was one day closer to the life I wanted, when in reality, it was just another day you put off running away. I never thought in a million years that you would be the one to end it. I thought for sure that I would have dumped you first.

How can you be this incredible asshole? I didn't think it was possible. I thought you were the sweetest thing. I've never and don't ever expect to be so wrong again in my entire life.

Are you still in our apartment? Doesn't it bother you that I'm not going to walk in the door? I think you're going to stay there. That makes me feel even worse; you alone in *our* apartment. Do you just see this as more closet space? Was this whole thing a successful attempt to get rid of all my winter coats and hats? You always hated my green chair. You've efficiently eliminated both of us. Do you wonder what I'm doing? Do you lie in our bed, watching Letterman thinking, *"Just a few days ago she was here"*?

Now you will probably get the job of your life, make a million dollars a year, buy a big house and start screwing some girl. And I got stuck with all the struggle and scrubbing the toilet. Are you going to stay here and torment me with the thought of you with someone else? I want you to be gone. No, I want you to be dead so I won't have to believe that you voluntarily chose to be without me. Why would you want to be without me? Were things so bad that you wanted to be without me *for the rest of your life?*

Everyone is in shock. They don't believe it. They thought we were going to get married. I know everything happens for a reason but I can't figure this one out at all. I want to call you but I know I've got to play the game. I have to give you time to realize your mistake. I have to believe that you don't want this.

February 19, 1997. [The third letter, No Emotion]

I have begun to recite the phrase *"If it's meant to be, it will happen"* over and over, like a mantra soothing me into a lucid trance. I'm considering calling the Psychic Friends Network. The first phone call is free. Maybe some stranger I've never even met will tell me what's going to happen next and how I should start preparing for it. I'm going to start going to church. Maybe God will give me some divine visualization that will tell me what to do.

I find it hard to picture myself doing things without you. Going to weddings, watching movies… I went to a movie last night with my brother and felt sick the whole time.

I don't know what to feel anymore. If I should want you back or just let go. Every day is hard. I'm just trying to make it through the next five minutes.

X. [3/7/97—1:51 am]

Love and hate are fighting like brothers
pulling each other down by the collar
and slamming fists into flesh.

I gave and gave
and gave my heart
I realize now...
I'm realizing
I am the fool
the *blind* fool
that never saw the...
whatever it was
in your eyes that you hid from me.

Why the hell did you do this... this
after all these years
Memories on memories that fill picture frames
mind frames
until there is nothing left
but just "to deal"
deal with what you decided for me
For us.

I gave into your arms
The same arms
that packed up all your shit
The same arms
attached to your wretched body
that will never realize
what a fucking mistake
the mind inside its empty head has made.

You gave up
and I hope you're alone
Alone like I am
People can listen
but no one can feel it but me
Me and the person I once was
Me and the person who's here now that you're gone.

I hope I never see your face again
That I never hear your voice
That you disappear and leave me
alone

But I guess you already have.

2. *Three Years Earlier:* The Night We Almost Never Met

I absolutely hated everything in my closet. I stood in front of my full-length mirror in black jeans and a blue shirt. I yelled over my loud music to my roommate in the next room, "I look like a postal worker!" I knocked on her door. "My hair looks like the Breck Girl, I have nothing to wear and I think I may be retaining water," I said as she stood in front of me in a towel.
"Do I look fat?" She asked.
"Are you honestly asking me if that towel makes you look fat?"
"Yes."
I turned and walked away. "I can't have this conversation."
"Why not?" She yelled after me.
I stopped and looked at her before going back into my room. "Because it means all men are right, and girls really are insane."
After about 30 minutes of clothing and hair trauma, I pulled something together that made me look halfway decent. I stood on the deck of our apartment and smoked. Over the past five months, my life had completely changed. I moved out of my parents' house right after I graduated from college and into this apartment with a girl from work. I broke up with my college boyfriend for no good reason except that he asked me to do his resume for him (that irritated me). Now, I was doing what I always wanted: I lived in Seattle, I was single, I was in the game. I lived on my own, I was dating, smoking, going to clubs… I loved it. At this point in history, I was dating two guys. I couldn't believe it. I felt like the popular girl in school, *"Who should I go out with tonight? Chad? Brad? Neither? Both?"* This was my major dilemma each and every Friday night.

I thought back to the days when I would sit in my dorm room and look out over the wheat fields. I knew then exactly how my life was going to turn out: graduate, live in Seattle, meet a man. He would be older than me and already established in his career. Obviously, he would be very cute (preferably with blue eyes), dark curly hair, and approximately 6'2". He would be artistic, sweet and love sushi.

But while I wanted this perfect person and perfect life, I couldn't help but doubt myself. I mean, who was I? Sure I was dating two guys, but factually, I was a receptionist. I wasn't bosomy or bottomy, not a stick either. Just there, taking up physical space with no real dimension or appeal.

The only real asset I had was my car, which by anyone's good knowledge and appreciation of an automobile, was cool. But other than that, what did I have that would land me this man?... this man that I didn't know but knew I wanted to marry and marry him soon. I was 22, wanted to be married by 25, and have kids by 30. I had a lot of work to do and a limited amount of time to do it in. But, I'm me; I'm nothing special. I'm a receptionist.

I turned around and looked into my living room. Reflected in the glass I could see my cigarette smoking silhouette. For some reason, it hit me. I realized that I was going to *make* myself get all that I wanted out of life. I was going to get this man, and soon, because, yes, I was attractive. True, I had no money, but I did have a cool car, my own apartment, a receptionist job at a local radio station, and all the motivation in the world that I would make it. I was sure that someone someday would be proud to introduce me as his wife. If I was so undeservingly ugly, how was it that I was dating two cute guys at the same time? Because I was hot stuff.

I cocked my head to the side, blew a steady stream of smoke from my lungs and knew tonight I was going to meet Him. And it would be the last night I would ever smoke.

"I'm not going," my roommate said, swinging open the deck door.

"Why not?" I asked, stubbing out my smoke.

"I'm a cow. I have nothing to wear. I'm not going." She turned and sat on our futon.

"You're going."

"No."

"Look," I said, "I'm not going without you and I'm not going by myself; yet I'm still going. So that means that you're going with me."

"Then neither one of us is going."

"I didn't even want to meet his stupid son, you did! Therefore, you are going to meet this clown whether you like it or not."

"You meet the son. His dad thought you'd be better with him anyway."

Earlier that week, the weatherman at the station we worked at told me that I was perfect for his son. This was a situation I hated being in. Here's this man, not my definition of attractive, telling me that I'm perfect for his son. We've all heard that the apple doesn't fall far from the tree and if this was true, then this was one rotten apple with a worm in it. My roommate convinced me that we should meet the son just to get a free meal and expensive drinks out of the weatherman, who generously offered to join us. I told her there was no such thing as a free meal.

Nonetheless, she convinced me to meet the weatherman with son in tow at this creepy pickup place. And now, "You're not going? Get real. Get dressed. You're going."

"I'm not," she said, crossing her arms.

"Free drinks."

"Give me ten minutes," she said over her shoulder as she walked away.

We showed up at the bar and it was an ocean of fakely tanned men, wearing vests with no shirts underneath. "Oh, this is good," I said to her as we stood in the threshold. "This son is a quality person to want to meet us here, right in the very trenches of testosterone."

"It wasn't his idea," she said. "It was the weatherman's. This is one of his hangouts."

"Let's hope he's not doing the shirtless vest look," I said, cringing at the thought. We continued to stand in the doorway, scanning the room to find a younger version of the weatherman. Nothing, nothing… then I see this guy. It was the first time in my life that I actually lost my breath over the sight of a man. A combination of the lead signer from INXS and John F. Kennedy, Jr.; this guy was mine. I sincerely felt all the lights dim, except for one spotlight on Him. He was getting a drink from the bar and turned to face the crowd. Dark, curly hair, corduroy pants, and yes, he was tall.

Now I'm wondering how to ditch the weatherman, the roommate and the unseen offspring and saddle up to this stallion. "Look, there's the weatherman," the roommate said, pointing across the room.

"Girls! I'm glad you showed," the weatherman said.

"Well, this one couldn't find anything to wear," the roommate said, pointing at me. Normally I would have slapped her with a quippy remark, but I had lost Dream Man in the crowd and was performing a frantic search.

"Hon, you look great, you didn't need to worry about what to wear," the weatherman said, rubbing my back.

"I just wanted to make a good impression on your son."

"Yeah," the roommate said. "Where's this infamous son of yours?"

"He went to get a drink at the bar." I looked at the weatherman with serious eyes. No…

Suddenly the seat next to me was occupied. It was Mr. Dreamy. I looked at Him and said, "Hi?"

"Hi," He smiled, blue eyes shining under the track lighting.

"Oh Hon, this is my son…" Jesus, he must be adopted. There was nothing I could do but laugh. So this was the way it was going to happen. This was the story we would tell our kids. This was a great story. It could only get better from here.

On my 23rd birthday, He met me at my apartment with three huge bags full of gifts. I could see Him walking down the sidewalk from my dining room window. He was wearing the most beautiful linen suit. I was arranging the roses He sent me at work and waved at Him. I will never forget that smile.

I buzzed Him in and He burst through my apartment door. "Happy Birthday, sweetie!"

"You angel," I said and kissed Him.

"You got the roses?"

"Yes, all twelve of them. They're beautiful."

"You're beautiful," He said, noticing my barely sheer black dress.

"I love you," I said as I hugged Him, pressing my cheek against His suit, trying to memorize how He smelled, the feel of the linen, and the body underneath it.

"Open your presents!"

I don't know how He did it, but He managed to get me every little thing I said I wanted. I'd never gotten so many presents. Each time I opened one, He would snatch it from my hands and show me how it worked or examined it closely, making sure it wasn't broken. He was quick to remind me where we were when I said that I wanted it. We went out to dinner and a movie. It was one of the best days of my life. All my dreams had come true.

A month later, we moved in together. It was fast, but we started spending every night together and it seemed a little dumb to keep separate apartments.

I always heard that you know The One when you know it. And I knew it. He was everything I always wanted. He was funny, liked to go places, got along well with my family. I knew what He was thinking without having Him say a word. He and my dad played golf together every Sunday and even talked about starting a business together. He was a jewel at family functions. He taught my two little cousins how to play the guitar one Christmas Eve. I stood in the doorway and watched Him with these two boys and imagined this is what it would be like when we had our own children.

I appreciated every day, even days that were nothing special; I appreciated because it was a day spent with Him. I would wait until He fell asleep, listen to His breathing slow down and feel His body fall into unconsciousness.

We would go shopping and He would let me pick out all His clothes. We ate sushi dinners that we couldn't afford and acted like we were the richest people in the place. I loved Him so much, it almost hurt.

About three weeks before our first Christmas together, I decided it was time to get the tree. We walked down a few blocks to a tree lot and He pulled out every tree until I decided on the perfect one. It started to snow as we carried the tree to the grocery store to get some Chinese take-out and eggnog. Then we walked home, with me singing Christmas carols while He provided the lesser-known beat box version of *Silent Night*. We decorated the tree and ate Chinese while watching *It's a Wonderful Life*. I stretched out on the couch with my head on His lap and fell asleep, still seeing the gentle glow of the white lights on the tree. Somewhere around one o'clock in the morning, He carried me to the bedroom and put me in bed. He softly shook my arm.

"Hum?" I asked, tiredly.

"I love you. Goodnight."

"I love you too… thank you."

He laughed. "Why are you thanking me?" I fell asleep before I could answer.

A few months later, we got up uncommonly early for a Saturday. I was making toast in the kitchen as He sat on the couch, strumming his guitar. "Hey, sing my favorite song!" I begged.

He started to laugh. "Why do you like that song?"

"I just do! Play it!" He stood up and started to play *Just What I Needed* by the Cars, but not fast, like it's supposed to be. He would slow it down into a sort of ballad, Musak version. I sat down on the floor in front of Him. He laughed in between the verses and shook His curly head.

About a year after that, we went to a friend's wedding. It was pouring outside as we ran from the car to the reception hall, laughing and holding hands. He left me at one of the tables to get two glasses of champagne. I looked around at all the happy faces and my friend in white and wondered what our wedding would be like. A song started to play that I had only heard a couple of times before. He came up from behind and put the glasses on the table. He started to sing the lyrics of the song in my ear, "*...I look in your eyes...*" I turned around and He smiled as He led me to the dance floor.

"What song is this? Is this Eric Clapton?"

He continued to quietly sing the words in my ear as we barely moved on the dance floor. "*...Darling, you look wonderful tonight...*" I looked into His eyes. "I heard this song the other day in my car," He said. "If I could put how I feel about you into words..." I thought I saw a tear form in His eye. "Well, I just wish I would have written this song about you."

"Then this is our song," I said.

"So it is," He said and kissed me.

3. *Back to Reality:* Jackie's Book Club

One night my mom convinced me to go to her Book Club meeting with her. They called themselves the Book Hookers. Inspired by Oprah Winfrey these women gather, dressed up for one another, eating crab cakes and discussing the sale at Ross Dress For Less. I didn't want to go. There was no way I thought sitting around with a bunch of 50-year-old ladies talking about some trashy novel sounded like a good time. She tried to bribe me with the promise that sushi would be served. I wasn't interested. She told me I would get some good decorating tips from Judy Twishano's living room. I was still not interested. *Oh, how they would love to see you*, she insisted.

"Mom, no one wants to see me right now. I look like shit."

"Oh, you do not! Your eyes stand out more now that you're so pale." Then the mother started to play her little guilt game. She said she was too dumb to go anyway, she hadn't even read the book.

"Just read the back of it. No one will know the difference," I said, pulling the guest bed's covers over my head.

"No, they'll know. I know they'll know."

"Oh God," I said, muffled by the sheets.

"If *you* were there, they could see what a lovely daughter I have. They'd all be jealous."

Slowly, I sat up in the bed. "Stop."

"They would! They would all want to line you up with their sons…"

I flopped back down. "Well, in that case forget it. I'm through with men."

"Please come with me. Just sit there, be cute, eat a cheese puff. Please." There was no point in fighting the inevitable. Once my mom gets going, you're fighting a losing battle. I got dressed and we headed for Judy Twishano's high-style rambler.

When we got there, I was quickly introduced to all the ladies, greeted with a sympathetic handshake. Obviously, my mom had primed them to be aware of my broken heart. It made me want to cry even more.

The first woman I met was Judy Twishano. My mom had known her for years and it was Judy who got my mom involved in this literal cult. She was a short woman who had acquired her ethnic last name from her first husband. Now she was on Husband #4. Everything about her was small: small eyes, nose, hands. I towered over her like some freaky amazon girl. She gave me the sympathetic handshake, her eyes staring into mine as if to say *"I'm with you, sister."* I wanted to smack her.

Her house was very clean with sparse furniture and dark colors. The lighting was that of a museum and she had expensive vases up on pedestals with track lighting that highlighted their shiny exteriors. She scooted me into the bathroom so I could see the *"cutest toilet paper dispenser on the planet"* that she picked up on a recent voyage to Europe. She had stayed with her ex-in-laws while she was there. She still got along with them. "Isn't that amazing? Hate the husband, love the family. Can you just get over that!"

"I can," I said, catching my willowy reflection in the mirror.

"I think the bathroom is often ignored in decorating, don't you? People just think it's just a place to relieve themselves. It's silly, actually, when it could be so much more."

"Like what? Are you going to put a pool table in here or something?"

She laughed. "Oh no, honey. But decorating does not stop in the bathroom." She paused for a moment. "So. Your mom tells me you broke up with your boyfriend."

"That's right," I nodded, looking downward.

"I'm sorry." I didn't reply. "Why did you break up?" Tears jumped out of my eyes. "Do you want to talk about this?"

"No."

She led me out of the bathroom and sat me on her bed. "I know it doesn't seem like it now, but you're going to be OK. When you're in the middle of a tunnel, you can't see the light at the end. But it's there.

"When I was your age, I was already divorced from Mr. Twishano. Immediately after the divorce, I got engaged to another man. His name was Tony, but I call him Needle Dick." I started to laugh through my tears.

"I thought Dick was a wonderful person. We decided to get married in Hawaii. He, of course, had no money so I paid for him and I to go, along with his best friend and my best friend who were going to be Best Man and Maid of Honor. We were going to get married on this huge cliff overlooking the water. I was going to wear this very lovely purple and pink mumu. It was the fashion in those days

"Anyhoo, two days before we get married, Dick tells me that his friend wants to take him out on this little bachelor party thing. So the friend goes. And Dick goes. But Dick doesn't come back that night. He doesn't come back the next day. He never came back."

I didn't know what to say. We just sat on the bed, with the sounds of the Book Hookers murmuring about the quiche in the background.

"I was so upset. I wanted to put on that silly mumu and hurl myself off the cliff we were going to get married on. I didn't eat for days. But thank God for my friend. She extended our tickets and we stayed three weeks. We shopped, tried to eat, and drank margaritas by the sea. And P.S., I looked great in my bikini because I had gotten so thin!

"Our flight home was very small, it was on one of those *Fantasy Island*-type of airplanes, the little ones. The pilot came out and introduced himself to all of us. I married that pilot one year later."

"That's a wonderful story." Tears pushed out of my eyes. "But that will never happen to me. I've never been to Hawaii." I really started to cry then.

Judy Twishano grabbed my hand. "It doesn't matter that you've never been to Hawaii, silly goose! The point is that life goes on. You never know where your future husband may be! This guy was just something to get you from A to B, he wasn't husband material. But maybe this, right now, the hurting and the experience of being with your very own Needle Dick, will lead you to your future husband."

"I don't know," I sighed and wiped my eyes.

"Well, I do. You just dab your eyes and let's go eat some cheese log, shall we? It's going to be all right."

We returned to the others who were grazing around the Jell-O. There wasn't a book in sight and I was beginning to think this book club business was just an excuse to get together. I stood next to my mom and she whispered "Are you all right?" I nodded.

"Jackie, is this your daughter? What a lovely! I'm Robin Swirsky-Warners, this is Connie Hoefacker. Con, have you ever seen a mother and daughter look more alike?"

"Never!" squealed Connie Hoefacker, who quickly popped a black olive into her mouth.

"Do you think so?" my mom said, giving me a sideways squeeze.

"Oh, definitely. My daughter looks nothing like me, at least I hope not," she quietly mouthed. "She's a... what would you call her, Con?"

"A grunge person."

Robin continued, "Can you explain this to me, peach? Why all the flannel? It's not at all flattering."

They all looked at me. "Oh, I don't know. I guess it's... comfortable?"

"If it's comfortable, don't wear it," said Connie Hoefacker, "Comfort is for home. Wear your sweats at home, wear something uncomfortable and cute in public." All three ladies laughed and I tried to remember how I got there.

"Well, I hate to cut to the chase but, *snip, snip!*" Robin made little finger snips in front of my face. "What's the deal, honey? What happened with your beau?"

"No good in bed?" Connie Hoefacker asked, jiggling a handful of peanut M&Ms in her right hand.

"Connie!" my mom said.

Robin leaned in to me. "*Ignore her.* Been awhile, you know?"

"Try eight years," Connie Hoefacker said, dumping the M&Ms into her mouth.

"Why did it end? Honey, tell us what happened."

My mom jumped in, "What does it matter? He was an idiot. Never good enough for my daughter, but I always knew that."

"Let's just get it out there; all men are jerks," Connie Hoefacker said.

"It's true," Robin nodded.

"I don't want to say that…" I started.

"You may not want to say it but we all know it's true. Look at me," Connie Hoefacker poured herself a glass of boxed wine. "Married 12 years, same man. He was great, loved to cook, clean, very handy and *giving*, if you get my drift."

We all firmly nodded.

"Then one day I come home, he's cooked dinner, and right there over the soufflé, he tells me." My mom and Robin exchanged knowing looks.

"What did he say?" I asked.

"He's gay."

"No!" I started to laugh.

"Yes. Bastard tells me he thinks he's been gay the whole time we've been married. He never cheated on me with a man, but he was heavy into the gay pornos."

"Jesus," my mom said.

"You're telling me! It was so hard divorcing this man that I never fought with. We never disagreed. We had it all, except for kids. He was my best friend. But he was gay."

"They still meet for cocktails!" Robin smiled and squeezed Connie Hoefacker's arm.

"Wow," I said.

"I should have known he was gay," Connie Hoefacker sighed, "He loved White Russians." I didn't get it.

I poured my own glass of boxed wine and sat down on a barstool. I sighed, too heavily I guess, because my mom came over to me and put her hand on my knee. "All men are not bad, look at your father and me. Married 30 years."

"True, all men are not bad. I know some pretty awful women," Robin said. "I'm one of them."

"What does that mean?" I asked.

"I'm going through a divorce right now and I wanted it. There's no reason why. It's just over. Time to move on. I'm sad about it, but there's nothing to be done."

"Why is it over? Did you cheat on him?" I whispered.

"No, no. Not that I haven't had the opportunity!" She reached inside her shirt and tightened her bra strap. "If I had a nickel for each time a man hit on me…"

"You'd be in the poor house!" Connie Hoefacker said and reached for another glass of wine. My mom laughed.

"Well, I've had my fair share of indecent proposals, but I'm not interested in having an affair, I never was. Hell, I hardly wanted to have sex with my own husband, let alone some stranger. I've just compromised my entire life. We got married young, I worked to put him through school, then he worked and I stayed at home. We have a daughter but now she's away at college and he's always working. It's time for me to be me. My daughter doesn't need me, he doesn't need me…"

"Your daughter needs you," I said.

"I'll always be there for her, but now it's different. I want to travel and take classes. I've always wanted to take a pottery class, and now I can do it. Both my parents died about a year ago. I have the money to live on my own and do what I want."

"Do you still love him?"

"Of course, but now I don't love me. As long as I stay with him, I'll just be his wife. Without him, I'll just be me."

"Hey, are you going to drop the Warners in Robin Swirsky-Warners?" Connie Hoefacker asked, motioning with a cucumber sandwich.

"I like the Swirsky-Warners. It makes me sound like a corporation." We laughed.

Gradually, Judy Twishano began to corral the masses and some sort of discussion about their assigned reading began. I just sat there and looked at all their faces. Here were all these women and each had their own story. I never realized it before, but that night I started to see there has always been this silent secret group of people who've been hurt. They've all lost the weight, smoked the cigarettes, and wanted to die. But they got through it, whether they went through therapy, talked to friends or drank heavily. They made it through and they all seem to be doing pretty OK.

I'm sure they've had their moments when they feel the bed is too big or the party runs too long. But the point is, they've made it. All these women who look different from one another, act different, have different jobs, have all survived. There was no reason why I wouldn't make it through this either.

The 20-minute discussion broke for a dessert break, and that's when I met Nancy Soupmaker. Soupmaker is the English translation of her Russian last name, but she thought Soupmaker sounded nicer. She was a quiet and plain looking woman, not a stitch of makeup and I could bet she was an expert at macramé and *Double Jeopardy*.

"I'm sorry to hear you're upset," she said, scooting up to me.

"Well, what are ya gonna do?" I said, draining my fourth glass of wine.

"I'm single too. I dated this one person for about five years after we graduated from college. But it didn't work out. I've been alone ever since."

"Great," I exhaled.

"Oh, it's not so bad. I have four cats and they are better company than he ever was," she giggled wildly, and swirled the coffee in her cup.

"You never get lonely?"

"Oh, no. I'm 51. It's too late to be with any one now. Everyone's married."

"No, everyone's divorced. Men your age are ripe for the pickin'," I said, searching my bag for smokes, making sure my mom wasn't looking.

Nancy pulled two cigarettes out of her bag and pointed outside. We stepped out on the deck and she lit us up. "I guess I get lonely, but some people are just meant to be alone. I'm one of those people. I can't have children, I hate to cook, I don't do laundry for weeks at a time. Sometimes I just wear the same thing over and over and over!"

"That could have something to do with your single status."

She laughed. "I know what you're thinking… *am I like her?* You're not. You're young. I hate to tell you, but there are more times like this ahead of you. This isn't the last time you'll be broken-hearted over a man. I made the conscious choice to get out. I don't look for anyone because I was hurt once and that was enough for me. If you want love, you'll find it. You'll be able to make it work with the right person." She stopped for a second and took a very long drag. "You just have to have the stamina to get through the shit," she said, in a very different voice.

My mom and I drove home in silence. It wasn't until we pulled into the driveway that I finally said something. "Thanks, Mom."

"You're welcome," she smiled.

"How is it that you always know just what I need?"

"It's a gift," she said, and gave me a wink.

4. Finding Out

Two months after the breakup I wasn't much better. I lived in a new apartment with my old roommate and felt like the whole relationship never happened. I was right back where I started before I met Him. I didn't cry much any more, but felt sick all the time. I lost 30 pounds and chain-smoked like a frequent bowling alley patron. I had to take two Tylenol PMs every night just to fall asleep and was weak as a kitten each morning. I was convinced I would never have sex again. Twenty-five years old and a sexless existence ahead of me. That was enough to make me lose another 30 pounds.

I had to totally restock my CD collection. I threw all love, sex and together forever songs out in the trash and found comfort in the screaming, accusatory music in Alanis Morissette's *You Oughta Know*. My movie watching habits included such titles as *Thelma & Louise*, *Extremities* and *Steel Magnolias*; movies that involved no men whatsoever, and if there were men in them, they were either shot or tortured. I got into this whole strong female thing and joined a kick boxing class. I cut my long, dark red hair and dyed it blonde, accompanied by obscenely huge platform shoes. I took all the pictures I had of Him and me together and deposited them into a bag full of yellow clumped-up cat litter. The Breakup turned me into a self-absorbed, shallow shell of a person, obsessed with relationships.

Adjusting to the Single Girl mentality was no cakewalk. I had no idea how to flirt. I didn't look any male in the eye and didn't care about anyone. I was totally consumed and convinced no one had experienced the vastness of my pain. Friends would tell me about problems they were having with their family or their job and I would respond, "Well, how would you like to come home on Valentine's Day only to discover that your boyfriend had left you?" I was heavy into the *Top This! Game of Woe*. I always won.

But still, this whole time, I had no idea why we broke up. Neither one of us had actually said, *"I'm breaking up with you."* I just moved out. He said He needed space and I moved out. That was the last time I saw Him. There were no answers, no questions and no closure. I thought about Him all the time and wondered if He missed me. He never called and I never heard anything about Him. It was like the whole thing never happened and He never even existed.

I tried to hate Him because I thought it would make it easier. But I couldn't hate Him. We never fought. We were friends, more than friends; we had fun and we were happy. Of course there were qualities He had that I would have changed (nobody's perfect), but for the most part He was perfect for me. I would have married Him.

But now things were different, I was different. I had to be strong like Tina Turner in *What's Love Got To Do With It*. Like Celie in *The Color Purple*. I needed to muster up the strength to go on. But I wanted to know why my life was forced along this road of misery instead of where I thought it was headed.

Then, one sunny day as I was driving to my brother's house, I got what I wanted via my cellular phone. I got the truth. And nothing would ever be the same.

SETTING: APRIL AFTERNOON, HIGH 60'S, INTERIOR OF RED CONVERTIBLE SAAB, MUSIC AND SUNGLASSES ON, THE MAIN CHARACTER [ME] EXPERIENCING A RARE MOMENT OF TRANQUILLITY, SINGING ALONG TO THE RADIO. THE CELL PHONE RINGS…

Me: Hello?
The Roommate: Where are you?
Me: On my way to my brother's house.
TR: Come home.
Me: Why?
TR: I need to talk to you.
Me: About what?
TR: Please, just come back here.

[I knew it was about Him. No conversation I had with my roommate was ever that important.]

Me: No.
TR: Will you please?
Me: No. I know what you want to talk about and I don't want to hear it.
TR: Yes, you do.
Me: I don't want to hear it.
TR: You *need* to hear it.
Me: No, I don't.
TR: Call me when you get to your brother's house.
Me: I'm not going to call.
TR: Call me back.
Me: No.

THE MAIN CHARACTER ARRIVES AT HER BROTHER'S HOUSE APPROXIMATELY 15 MINUTES LATER.
SETTING: EXTERIOR, A '70s STYLE HOUSE IN A SUBURB, THE MAIN CHARACTER KNOCKS ON THE FRONT DOOR
{DOOR OPENS}

Brother: The roommate has called three times.
Me: Shit.
Bro: What's her problem?
Me: I don't know. Do you have a cordless? I'll just call from out here.

BROTHER DELIVERS CORDLESS PHONE AND THE MAIN CHARACTER PHONES HER APARTMENT, {THE ROOMMATE'S HIGH PITCHED VOICE ANSWERS}

Me: So, what?
TR: Are you sitting down?
Me: Don't get dramatic now.
TR: You should sit.
Me: Get it over with.
TR: He's getting married in three months to a girl that He's been having affair with for a year. She's a waitress at a Mexican restaurant that He went to during His lunch breaks. Hon, she's pregnant. It's His baby.
silence
Me: Oh my God.

TR: I'm sorry.
silence
TR: Are you OK?
silence
TR: Are you OK?
Me: Would you be OK if you were me?
TR: Sorry.

[This was what I would call a Defining Moment. A feeling I will never forget. I sat there, letting the roommate's words sink down into every layer of my skin… deep into the many layers of my heart. My hearing became slightly dulled and my eyes locked on a swing set in the yard across the street. As the swings swayed on this non-descriptive afternoon, I could feel all the hurt and confusion I had stored inside every tiny cell of my body, being released through the very top of my head. It was like some invisible force reached inside my skull and slowly yanked it all out. God took the pain out of my head so I wouldn't have to think about it any more. Suddenly, I could smell my brother's freshly cut grass and hear cars passing on the busy road one block away.

[Everything made sense. The way He said, *"Everything is going to be okay, it's going to be taken care of."* He cheated on me and she got pregnant. He wanted her to have an abortion and she didn't want to. She made Him choose between me and her, and He chose her because of the baby. I believed this so truly that I didn't need anyone to tell me any more about Him for as long as I lived. I knew how His life was going to turn out. I could visualize it. Everything that happened during the last year of my life rolled in front of my eyes like an old movie I saw a long time ago but forgot the name of. I could see Him with her. I could see me waiting on our white couch, waiting for Him to come home after "working late." I could see Him tucking His shirt in as He walked through the front door of our apartment. I could see the look on His face when He was calming me down in the dark after I had another nightmare about Him cheating on me. It was like reading the last line of a book that explains it all. I finally understood. And I could let go.]

Me: *(taking deep breaths, in and out, in and out, and finally....)* OK, then.
TR: OK?
Me: All right. Talk to you later.
TR: Are you coming home?
Me: No.
TR: Where are you going?
Me: I don't know.
TR: Why don't you go over to your mom's house?
Me: Uh, OK.
TR: I'll call her and tell her you're on your way.
Me: OK.
TR: Can you drive?
Me: I think so. I mean... yes.
TR: I'll call your mom.
Me: Sounds good.
TR: My God, what are you thinking?
Me: *(starting to cry)* I'm thinking that I never really knew Him at all. He wasn't the person I was in love with. That person never existed. He's a fake, a liar, and a phony that didn't know how good it was when He had it. I would have done anything for Him, anything...
(crying harder now, for at least 15 seconds then....)...but He's weak and insecure and not even the shadow of a man! I hate what He's done to me. But I don't hate Him. I feel sorry for Him. He got what He never wanted. And He did it to Himself. He chose it and He got it.
(crying slows and softens) He wasn't the love of my life. He wasn't The One. He never was. I just wanted Him to be.
(crying stops) That means the one that really is The One is still out there.
silence
I need to go fix my face. Talk to you later.

Even though I realized that He was slime and I was preparing to move on, I had to take care of a few things. To do a little house cleaning, so to say.

I have a short list of my most unfavorite emotions. I hate being embarrassed, or feeling like someone has pulled something over on me. I don't like people thinking they got away with anything. I'm not a big fan of revenge because I live by the rule that all bad things done will come back and bite you in the ass eventually. There's no such thing as a clean getaway.

Yet having Him slink away, letting me think it was something that I had done, was just too much to take. I could picture Him sitting somewhere with his new, pregnant wife, thinking He was brilliant and had the perfect getaway: there I was, left in the dark, not knowing about His adulterous ways and more than likely, still loving Him. I couldn't live with that. And neither could He. I decided, He *wouldn't* live with that.

I composed a well-crafted letter that I believe captured the true essence of my emotions and forwarded it to His mother's house. I figured she must have some contact with Him. I also sent a copy to His dad's house, just in case. I then proceeded to send a copy of this letter to His sister, His employer and a few nationally distributed magazines and publications. I figured it would be an entertaining read for the legions of burned women that read the *Voices* column in Cosmo. Let all the lies be exposed and have this man own up to His crap. It was up to me to warn women, My Fellow Sisters, of the evil that lurked behind the precious smile of my ex-boyfriend, whom I had begun to fondly refer to as Fuckface, Shitbird, and/or The Waste of Time. The creative titles are too numerous to list.

Now don't misunderstand me, I do not hate men. I love men. I adore men. But I do hate Losers, Cheaters and Liars. There are still many good men in the world (although at the moment I can't think of one...) and

I certainly think that they all are the cat's pajamas. But the others, mainly my ex-boyfriend, needed to know what I thought of His wicked ways.

This is how the modern-day poetry went:

Dearest Shitbird,

I know about everything you've done to me, every lie and every detail. You got away with nothing.

You are such an incredible liar and asshole, I can't believe that I ever loved you. You let people think you are what you appear to be. But what you really are is a miserable person who uses people for everything they have. You're an apparition, a fake, a mental abuser.

I hate you for making me think I was crazy when I questioned your late nights. I hate you for staying with me this last year because you needed a roof over our head, something to eat, and someone to screw when she wasn't available. You may be getting married, but you will never be a husband. You'll just be a deceiver with a cheap-ass ring on his finger.

You ran from me because you knew I was too good for you. I wanted something genuine and you knew that all you could provide was occasional companionship. You will never have anything real because you aren't real. You aren't a person; you're a disease that spreads itself around from woman to woman, infecting them with your infectious ways, making them sick without feeling a symptom. I will never be a man's victim, especially not yours, you waste of space.

But I wish no evil on you. Evil is already on its way. You will receive all the pain and suffering fate has in store for you.

Everything you've done to me is on its way back to you. People like you get what they deserve and you deserve what your destiny will undoubtedly give. Welcome to your life, a place where fuck-ups and self-loathing are dished out on a daily basis. Enjoy your empty marriages to lackluster women who will accept your cowardliness and lack of motivation. And after all is said and done, you will die alone. You may have screwed me out of money and love, but you are just screwed.

Take one minute to look at the best thing that ever happened to you, because you will never have it again.

Never Will Be Truly Yours,

The One Who Got Away

5. The Flight to Mars

It's the oldest question in the world: *Why do bad things happen to good people?* I don't get it. I'm good people, going around doing good things and still this happened to me.

I grew up in a pretty normal family. Older brother, parents still together, no one smoked, no one did drugs… we all ate dinner together every night. We didn't have the problems other families had, like the dad cheating on the mom, or a brother with spiky hair and a safety pin through his nose. I was a cheerleader. I was Class President. I was in the homecoming court. And now, just a few years and a college education later, I'm sitting here with a hole in my heart caused by some idiot man.

I can't believe I've led myself to the position I'm in right now. I've always told my female friends to believe that "You are the prize." Over and over I say "you are the prize," "you are the prize," and yet here I am, thinking that I wouldn't be a prize to the biggest loser in the world.

I was once so happy. I remember thinking nothing bad would ever happen to me. It's easy to see where I got this, coming from suburbia where nothing exciting happens. No one gets raped, no one commits suicide. Things that happened in the real world just didn't happen where I grew up. Every night it was Chili Mack and *The Muppet Show*, then off to bed where I would snuggle down under my Raggedy Ann comforter and in fact, be comforted. I had birthday parties at McDonald's. I had a Sweet Sixteen birthday party with mini-quiches. I drove a VW convertible.

I think everything changed when they tore down the Flight to Mars. It was a ride at the Fun Forrest, an amusement park at the Seattle Center. If you were on the safety patrol at school, you got to go to the Fun Forrest at the end of the year where you could ride all the rides you wanted, as many times as you wanted, at absolutely no charge to your Hello Kitty wallet.

I would think about the joy that could only be caused by a ride on the Enterprise when I was patrolling the crosswalk on 148th. The way the Enterprise flung me around was the closest thing to flying for real, like I did at night in my dreams. My second favorite ride was the Flight to Mars, a Haunted House meets Alien Encounter. OK, yes, it was cheesy, but being guided throughout the horrid freaky scenes of life on Mars was hysterical. I would grab the arm of my very best girlfriend sitting next to me and scream like all the cute girls did when they were scared. It was a five-minute vacation from the math class I hated and my mom who refused to let me get my ears pierced. Now I think of that chipped blue and red car I'd so willingly strap into and wonder, if the Flight to Mars was still standing, would I still be with my boyfriend?

As soon as the City of Seattle decided to tear down the Flight to Mars to build a parking lot in its place, I found out that my friend's mom had cancer. Michael Jackson was accused of doing something other than playing with children. Everything I believed in was being ripped apart with each board they tore off of the Flight to Mars.

The things I heard on the five o'clock news were suddenly infiltrating into my world and I didn't like it. I started to doubt everything, even myself. I wanted to be a writer but started to think it would never happen. I wasn't that different from the little girl on the news whose parents died in a fire on Christmas Eve. I was sure the one bad thing that was destined to happen to me, like the thing that happened to that little girl, was waiting in the wings.

Don't get me wrong, I was no freak kid or anything, I just began to think I wasn't as different as I thought I was. I always entered those *Young Miss Model Search Contests*, thinking that I was as cute as the other girls, but I never won. I was never even a contestant. I did get some *Love's Baby Soft* in the mail as a thank you for entering sort of thing, but that's as far as my modeling career went. I entered poetry contests with my most dramatic work, outlining the tragic life of a thirteen-year-old girl, but I never won. Here I thought my words were so challenging, diverse, so uncommonly profound, and each time I got a short letter encouraging my work but, "Sorry, you didn't win." No *Love's Baby Soft* came in the mail that day.

I always thought I would marry at a fairly young age. Boys always asked me to skate with them at the Snow Ball. I would lie on the floor of my bedroom and take Polaroids of my face, like Madonna did in *Desperately Seeking Susan*, and I thought I was pretty cute. I had a sort of Molly Ringwald thing going. And look at my mom… people always said we looked alike and she got married when she was 21, so I would be married at the same age. If we looked so much alike, why would we be different?

My dad was the perfect man and my mom found him. He was handsome (I always thought he had a Tom Selleck look working for him). He drove off to work every day and came home at six o'clock every night. He tucked me into bed with the same routine. The light would be off, but he'd flick the switch back and forth really fast making a strobe light effect that burned my dilated pupils and totally cracked me up. Then he'd walk toward me to kiss me goodnight and act like he tripped on something and fall on the floor. Oh God, I thought that was the funniest thing in the world. "Daddy, quit that!" I'd laugh.

"I tripped! I think something under the bed grabbed my ankles…"

"Oh, it did not!"

He lowered himself to his knees and picked up my doll and a stuffed animal. "Hello, Raggedy Ann. Hello, Teddy. How are you?" Then he'd change his voice to a high-pitched squeak and move Raggedy Ann's arms and head. "Teddy is driving me crazy. All day long he runs around the bed really fast."

"Hey, you tattletale. Why don't you spill all of our doll secrets, jerk?" Teddy would say in a low voice.

"That's it! You're out of the Doll Club, Ted! We all took a vote and you're through! The others are just too shy to say anything…" Then Raggedy Ann and Teddy would engage in a fist-fight that I thought was comedy at its best.

As cute and innocent as that scene sounds, I think it scarred me. I thought every dad should be as funny as my dad. Every girl had a daddy like mine who made dolls shout profanities at each other, didn't they? But then they leveled the Flight to Mars and I learned that some girls didn't have dads.

I had positive male role models in my life. Obviously my dad was one, but my grandpa was another. He wasn't as funny as my dad, but he always made me feel so special. He died when I was very young, so I only have a few memories of him; like sitting on his lap in the green chair that now sits in my apartment. We would watch TV, not talking at all, just quietly watching *The Wizard of Oz*. I would swipe one of my brother's Hot Wheels and drive it up the stripe of the chair, up Grandpa's arm and park it on his shoulder. He wouldn't move a muscle. He'd just shift his blue eyes over at me and have a little smile on his lips.

I remember walking down the street with him and people would say, *"Hey, is that your new girlfriend?"* and he'd laugh, shake my hand that he was already holding and look down at me. "This is my girl. This is my granddaughter."

He'd take me to this one restaurant where I'd always get a burger and a chocolate shake. I have no idea what we talked about; it was only recently my mom asked if I remembered that he had an Irish accent. I don't remember that, but I do remember going to the restaurant one time and a little girl, just a few years younger than me, choked on a wire that was embedded in her burger. She was choking and someone squeezed her from the back until the wire popped out. That scared the hell out of me. But Grandpa was quick to assure me that there was nothing in my burger and inspected it fully. I knew then that I wanted someone like Grandpa: someone who loved me enough to not want me to choke on a wire in hamburger meat, and who would immediately manhandle my meal to make sure it was wire-free. That was love.

I have always felt closer to men than to women. I never had a lot of female friends as a child; I always got along better with boys. Even now I hate events that require being around a lot of women, like wedding showers or Avon parties. It's all gossip, checking out what the other is wearing and talking about husbands or boyfriends. No one has their own identity. It's always attached to a man's. And while I hated it, I loved it when I had a boyfriend. I was one of two; I was in a relationship that made me fit into the female world. When I was single I didn't fit in because not only did I dislike being around women (and I'm sure that came out in some occasional glance or outward vibe), but I couldn't partake in their discussion of how wonderful their boyfriends were. I know now that was a bunch of crap.

When I met my boyfriend, I thought I found someone who was funny like my dad, caring like my grandpa, and as cute as Jake Ryan in *Sixteen Candles*. But He wasn't; He wasn't even close. He was the idea of the perfect man without actually being it. And I can't believe I fell for the act. I always thought I was more observant than most. But deep down, I'm just as dumb as all the other girls I thought I was superior to. I thought I would never take shit. I thought I would never depend on a man. I thought I would never lose me. But I took it, I did it and I lost me somewhere in the middle.

Tonight I drove by the Flight to Mars. It's a parking lot. I hope the additional room for motor vehicles was worth one girl's sanity. Damn each spot, one through fifty-seven.

The next few months after The Shit Coming Down can best be described as a blur of emotions. There were times when I was amazed by my strength and the *I-don't-give-a-shit* attitude I had acquired. But then, there were times I cried at the oddest things. Things that had nothing to do with anything, but suddenly it would occur to me that I was alone. There would be no messages waiting for me. No hand-holding in the darkness of the Cineplex. I was a cornucopia of emotionally unstable hormones accompanied by the most radical of mood swings.

I thought of myself as a newborn child: I went into my relationship with Him in one form, and came out completely different. I did lots of crying, couldn't sleep through the night, and couldn't keep anything down. I did refrain from wearing diapers though, and from chewing on my car keys.

It takes real talent and inner gumption to go places alone, after almost three years of having a perma-date. I would walk into rooms full of couples and force myself to feel liberated. I would pretend everyone was looking at me with envy as I sashayed into these rooms that brimmed with boring clothes and boring conversations, and I stood out like a bright beam of light. I was Glamourina, Queen of all that is Fashionable and Holy! I was interesting, exciting, and independently wonderful. But then, the music would start, and people would grab their dates and swing them onto the dance floor. I would stand alone and down my fourth glass of champagne in 10 minutes.

I was at this one wedding, alone, and went into the bathroom and stared in the mirror. What was wrong with me? How could it be that all these chubby, flower-print-dress-wearing cheesebombs had someone to sleep with and I was in the bathroom talking to myself? Was I that ugly? That misshapen? That unbearable to bear? This chain of questions always led back to the strongest link, the one question that no one could answer, not even me. Why did He do this to me?

Although I hated what He did to me, I didn't hate Him. The truth was that I felt nothing for The Man Formerly Known As My Boyfriend. I didn't love Him, hate Him, miss Him… nothing. The revealing of the truth evaporated every emotion I had for Him and just left me completely empty.

I would see people who had someone, and I would miss being with someone, but not Him. He was gone and every day I got more and more used to the idea. He wasn't The One, just A One. This whole thing was meant as a challenge and educational procedure.

I was so naive before it all happened. I thought my life would go the way I planned it. Graduate from college, live on my own, meet the man of my dreams and get married. It's so easy to create this Map of Perfect but the truth is, no one ever sits down and *plans* on having a fatal car crash at the age of 18, or sets an appointment to have their grandmother die of cancer. Things happen and you don't know why, but you have to handle it the best way you know how.

I know everything is temporary. I've started believing that all those clichés you hear in movies and read on greeting cards are actually Survival Guides direct from God. I started to pay attention.

Every Christmas when I was growing up, I would work myself into a pretty good case of stress hives over what Santa was or was not going to bring me. Through puffy eyes I would stare at the tree and pray I was good enough to get that special Barbie with the miraculous suntan lines.

I would reach toward my dad with rashy hands and beg him to tell me if I was going to get that damn suntanned Barbie I wanted so badly that I would have practically killed for her. He would look down at me, pat me softly on the back and say, "Waiting is half the fun." I hated it when he said that. Twice a year I heard those cryptic words come out of his mouth (Christmas and my birthday) and would want to scream so hard that my teeth would fall out.

I wanted the whole fun right then and would run to my room, dramatically flop on the bed, hoping my dad would get hit by a bus before the next gift-giving holiday. But now, twenty years later, I sat on my deck, smoking one too many cigarettes, and began to think he was right.

Life is like a movie with soundtracks, actors and bad lines, the whole bit. And you sit there and watch this movie and think, *"God, this is slow. They could have taken this part out"* or *"Why was that person cast as the leading male? Why is she getting so upset over that loser?"* What type of movie is this anyway? Action/adventure, romance, comedy, horror? How's it all going to tie in and how's it going to end? If your Life Movie was all romance or horror, it would be pretty boring. You might get up and leave that theater to sneak into the next one over.

My life up until this point could be categorized as an R-rated After School Special. I never really did anything too bad, too adventurous or too scary. The Shit Coming Down was the first rise of conflict or challenge that I had. I was unknowingly cast as the lead in this, The Movie of My Life, and I had to do an Oscar-worthy performance. I had to jump from the small screen to the big one and make the audience sit up and take notice. I had to deliver the great lines I created, have wonderful timing and be prepared to cry at any given moment. That, and try to always stand in filtered light.

I am going to live my life like a modern-day Scarlett O'Hara, and as Scarlett so beautifully said, her blue eyes brimming with tears, framed by Max Factor lashes: Tomorrow is another day.

Life is a series of steps. Sometimes you can take three at a time, sometimes you're too weak to even think about heading toward the staircase. When you break up with someone, you never realize there are about a million little steps to be taken to move back into normal, single, dating society.

It's almost as if everyone has to go through this ritual before they're allowed back in. Let's take a look at the mass sufferings that must be accomplished before you are Officially Single.

First, you go through the pain of the actual breakup. The crying, the carrying-on, fighting the inevitable fact that it's over and this person no longer wants to be around you. That's rough.

Then there's the Moving Out or the Exchanging of the T-shirt, depending on the level of your relationship. If you live with someone, it's harder because not only are you never going to see this person again, you're never going to see the apartment again. This leads to the whole apartment hunting process, which everyone knows is excruciating, and then the ceremonial Packing of the Boxes. The sorting, the throwing away, the revelation that this is seriously the end. Never fun.

If you don't live together, it's not as bad but still there's the sorting process and returning his T-shirt you've been sleeping in for the length of the entire relationship.

After this, comes my most unfavorite part: releasing the information to the general public. Sometimes this process can take over a year.

At first, you're a rumor... *"Is it true?" "What happened?" "Here's how I heard it..."*—that whole scene. Then you get with your people and come up with an official statement: "I cannot confirm or deny the allegations. I can only say that it's over and both parties wish each other well." You spread that little lie around but of course it doesn't reach your relatives and a year later, you're at the Yugoslavian picnic with your great Aunt from Walla Walla and she asks, *"Where's So-'n'-So?"* That freshens up that emotional wound faster than the speed of light. Thank you, Aunt Whateverhernameis, and suddenly you regret that second helping of macaroni salad.

The next couple steps can be called Various Sufferings. Hearing his favorite song on the radio. Thinking you saw him with some girl at Safeway. Finding a note in your glove box that he stuck under your wipers in happier days... ouch. If that doesn't drive you to drink, become bulimic or seriously consider Drug Addict as a professional occupation, there's another toughie: Looking at other guys.

At first I felt like I was cheating on Him (God forbid!). It felt so foreign to rotate my eyeballs in the direction of a hot-blooded young male. I'm not trying to be saintly when I say that when I was with Him, I never noticed other men. I mean, I knew they were out there, making up the other half of society, but I never wanted them. I had a man. Why did I need to look? But now I find myself forcing my gaze to that cute construction worker. I have to start picturing myself with someone else.

Chances are that I will "do the business" again. I can't be bankrupt yet. I'm not out of business. I'm still very much in the business world, meeting new clients, taking meetings. But it makes me physically nauseated. What would it be like to kiss someone else?

And when I picture a naked man, I picture Him. I'm scared to see new parades. Parades. That's what I call the male genitals. It's nicer than the other P-word. You can talk about parades when you're riding a bus or when your mother is the room. No one cares. No one is offended by a parade, so how would people know that I'm not talking about a parade when I *am* talking about a parade?

I just can't believe I'm never going to see the same parade ever again, and now I have to get all psyched up about a new parade that I know nothing about. What kind of parade is this? Three kids pulling their mutt in a three-wheeled wagon down a country road? The Macy's Thanksgiving Day Parade with two Santa Clauses on a 72-degree day? You can guess which one would be more popular.

Yet, I can accept looking at other guys and knowing there may not be any good parades left in the world. But even after you go through all the steps in this twisted form of hazing, people still say you're not over it.

"You can't be over it. The amount of time it takes to get over a relationship is two times as long as the relationship lasted."

Where did this logic come from? Who brought Math into Feeling and Emotion? So if I was with The Waste of Time for almost three years, and it ended when I was almost 25 years old, it will be six years until I'm fully healed? When I turn 31 I'll graduate into Over It status and have this odd sense of enlightenment that will show on my face? What about someone who was in a relationship for 12 years? Twenty-four years later the person is emotionally ready to go to a movie with a member of the opposite sex? Give me a break.

If you ask me, you're ready to enter society when you can listen to "*Mandy*" by Mr. Barry Manilow and not want to eat glass. Other requirements include being able to eat chili, see a romantic comedy and come out inspired rather than suicidal, and feel the urge to see a parade. If you can do all that, but especially hurdle *Mandy*, you're going to be fine.

Lots of harder things have happened in history other than having your boyfriend leave you on Valentine's Day. It couldn't have been fun to be in World War II. Slavery was no picnic. Husbands have left wives after 22 years of marriage for the babysitter. Life is not easy and what you think is going to happen never will, so you better begin to see that nothing is predictable.

There's no such thing as rhyme or reason. Life is made up of random acts of tragedy and happiness with moments of lust in between. You're going to die one day anyway, so as long as you're here, why not have a good time? Make the most of it. Life goes on.

As for me, I will go dancing. When I was a kid, I would fantasize about going to dance clubs whenever I wanted. One o'clock in the morning, five at night, it didn't matter, because I could go dancing and I *would* go dancing. When I dance, I forget all the problems of the world. I just close my eyes and dance.

I have always wanted to live in my own apartment with a gray cat named Pinkie. I want to have sex with a random man on my living room carpet and purposely not ask his name.

And now, I can do it.

Now, I WILL do it!

I will travel any place in the world I want to go and see things only I want to see.

I will spend four hours in a museum and not worry about someone else being bored.

I don't have to call anyone back at 7:30.

I don't have to make dinner for anyone but me, and if I feel like having chip and dip for dinner, that's what I will have.

I will sleep in my very own bathtub and not have a reason why.

I will never rent another action movie staring Bruce Willis, ever.

I will never watch another golf tournament.

I am not responsible for anyone else's happiness but my own.

And I'm ready. I can handle it. Give me your Assholes, your Cheaters, your One Night Stands, I can take it. Deal me a hand of Top Ramen for dinner five nights a week because I can't afford anything else, and I will survive. Treat me bad, tell me lies and I will laugh and move on, stepping over the shrapnel in my black, plastic platform boots with zippers on the left side.

There is no one better than me. There is no one stronger. Glamourina rises again with a vodka tonic in one hand, and a cigarette in the other!

I am here.

I am now.

I am moving on.

6. Re-Meeting Bryan

I was trying to look busy at my desk when this man from Accounting came up to me.

"There's some guy in the lobby for you."

I looked up from reorganizing my pens. "Oh?"

"Yeah, I was just walking through the lobby and a guy is waiting to see you."

"OK, thanks." I put the pens down and watched Accounting Man walk away. What guy could be here to see me? It must be John, boyfriend from the college-post-college era. I talked to him a few days earlier and he said he might drop by.

I could see into the lobby from my glass office door and saw the back of a tall man. *John,* I thought as I started to open the door. *No, not John.* This person had wavy hair; John had straight hair. Perm? Forget it. I pushed my glasses farther up the bridge of my nose, shut my near-sighted left eye and took a serious look. Tall, wavy hair, wearing a plaid shirt. My heart fell to my kneecaps. It's Him.

Oh God, what the hell is He doing here? Five months later and now He wants to face me? Did He have a testosterone transplant or defy nature and grow another set of balls? Who does He think He is? He shows up here and I'm supposed to listen to Him tell me about His wife and child and... what? Am I supposed to congratulate Him? *"Blow it out your ass,"* I muttered under my breath and walked away.

But then, I stopped. Was it really Him? It was almost impossible to believe. Even He couldn't be stupid enough to think that I would actually want to see His miserable face. Back at the doorway, I took off my glasses and sized up this tall glass of water one last time. After all, I had nothing to get back to. Something was very familiar about this person;

something I couldn't quite figure out. He turned and I could see his profile. I knew this man; how I knew him I wasn't sure but there was no doubt I knew him.

Before I was aware of what I was doing, I opened the door and said, "Hi."

His response was a huge, curious smile. I was still clueless as to who this person was. Did I go to college with him? Why did I come to the lobby? "Can I help you with something?"

"Yes," he confirmed and slowly extended his right hand to shake mine. "It's very nice to re-meet you." It was then that I finally caught on to his Italian accent. Who do I know from Italy?

"Oh my God... Bryan."

When I was 15, I met Sophia. She was an exchange student from Italy and we hit it off immediately. I had never met anyone from a different country and was easily fascinated by her foreign ways. We became the best of friends. She went back to Italy at the end of the school year but we kept in touch through letters. She would write and tell me her older brother thought I was hot. She sent me a picture of the two of them together and I taped it to the mirror in my college dorm room.

Just like any other friendship, we slowly lost touch. That is, until I was out of college and in my first apartment. One night she called. She was in Seattle with her brother and invited me to meet them. Three hours and seven years after I first heard about him, I met Sophia's brother. His name was Bryan. (How Italian is that?)

We danced, drank and didn't talk for three hours. But that didn't stop us from making out in my car at the end of the night. Sometimes, there's no need for words.

I wrote him once. He wrote me back a month later. I didn't write back. I can't remember what he said in his letter but something made me not want to respond. I forgot about him as easily as I met him. He was there and then he was gone. I didn't even notice. Three months later, I met the Asshole Formerly Known as My Boyfriend.

That whole day after Bryan came in, I had a smile on my face. This was what I wanted. Something and someone to be excited about. I had been alone for five months, and while that doesn't sound like a long time, it seemed like forever after spending every day for the past three years with someone. I wanted to be with someone else—as if being with someone else would prove that I was over and done with the trauma that happened in February.

He wanted to go out that Friday night and I was looking forward to the male companionship. He was only in town for three and a half weeks. He probably had people to see and things to do and I certainly didn't think that I was that magnetic of a person that he wanted to spend every day with me.

This was a distraction, an interruption, an innocent episode. He very well could have a girlfriend back in Italy and just wanted a tour guide. Why not look up his little sister's American friend? It was harmless enough and I wasn't making more out of it than it was. I wasn't fantasizing about a brief and torrid affair with this foreigner. I wasn't nervous about our date. I wasn't fooling myself.

We had dinner with his family that I hadn't seen in years, and years of questions were aimed at me over the dinner table. I laughed the whole time. I never knew how interesting my boring life was. I stole little peeks in Bryan's direction; he never seemed to catch me in the act.

After a few hours, we took off in my convertible with the intention of seeing a movie. But while I was parking my car, Bryan said he didn't want to sit in a movie theater. We sat on a dock on the waterfront instead.

We talked about whatever floated into our heads. Questions took up much of Bryan's brain capacity. I'm all for inquiries, but a barrage of questions has never been my favorite conversational tool. A question should be used with the intent to get the conversation going; leave it up to the person to reveal what they want to.

But Bryan was a *What Is Your Passion?* Man. You know the type. He asked questions that made him seem really in touch with cosmic forces in the universe. I almost told him that I'm not comprehensible by answering yes or no to twenty questions on his *How To Make A Babe Think I'm Deep* questionnaire.

At this point, I'm thinking there is nothing between us but air. Not only does he stab me with a bazillion questions, he proceeds to launch into this story about a girl back home. They had this highly sexual, flirtatious courtship that lasted for weeks. He spews detail upon detail about how she could turn him on like a common household appliance. I think to myself, *"Why am I here?"*

He was so not interested in me that I couldn't believe that I wasted good lip-gloss. I pulled all the tricks out of my hat and nothing worked. I smelled good, acted charming and was sitting on a moonlit dock. I got nothing. No vibes, no moves, no advances. Nothing.

We decided to get some coffee. The only place I could think to go to was this all-night diner that required smoking. I needed the nicotine. I quit trying to be sexy, put on my glasses and stopped caring about what he thought. It was only after I put my glasses on that I started to see something brewing, and not just the stuff they were passing off as coffee. Something behind his eyes changed and I started to think that I was, in fact, the It Girl. He casually traced the outside of my leg when he talked. This action alone is enough to get things going, but combined with the accent? I don't care who you are; you're a goner.

"Look," I interrupted him, "I'm not talented enough to listen to you talk and have you touch my leg, so it's either one or the other." I can't remember what he said after that. Doesn't matter. Something was starting.

Driving back to his sister's house, I was getting The Vibe, big time. But I noticed that The Vibe had a little disclaimer on it that said if I wanted some action, I was going to have to take action. I was tired of being the action figure, so I turned to him and said, "You're going to have to make the first move. So if you're waiting for me to do something, you're going to keep doing it. Waiting, I mean." I never claimed to be shy, and Lord knows you can't wait for a man to take initiative.

He kissed me, in an awkward, clumsy, innocent way. I felt it run through my body like a warm breeze. I thought I would freak out when I finally kissed someone new. Up until that moment, The Crap Talker had been the last person to touch me. I almost felt like it was this invisible type of branding that meant that I still belonged to Him. Now, that was gone. I was thinking, *"This isn't Him, this isn't Him,"* and it didn't make me sad. It was almost like regaining my faith. To have someone kiss me passionately, hold the back of my neck, touch my face… it was amazing. I never thought this would happen five months after I thought I was going to die without Him.

"I want to see you again," he said in his sister's driveway.

"You will," I smiled.

"No, I mean I want to see you tomorrow, and the day after that, and the day after that. Every day until I leave."

"You shouldn't commit to that right now, Bryan. I'm sure there are other things that you want to do…"

"No, I know what I want to do. I want to spend every day with you."

And he did. We crammed a mock-relationship into a brief three-and-a-half-week period. We did it all: had fun, fought, got on each other's nerves, made up, made out, and had long talks about the world as we knew it.

Our second Saturday was the best. We spent the day touring Seattle. I showed him all my favorite places. We came back to my apartment and I got dressed for the evening as he stood, looking at the city from my deck. I walked out to ask where he wanted to go for dinner. "You look beautiful," he said.

"Oh, Bryan, thanks. Where do you want to go?"

"No, wait. I just want to look at you for awhile." I stood uncomfortably as he looked at me in a way that no one looked at me. It had been too long since anyone looked at me like that. I missed it.

We went to an Indian restaurant that was decorated completely in white except for individual pink roses that stood in delicate vases on each table. I looked at him from across the table; he was so different. Yes, he was foreign, but everything about him was foreign. The way he actually took an interest in what I said, the way he complimented me and the way he would kiss me in the middle of a drug store, not caring who saw. He was the complete opposite of You Know Who. And I wanted to grab him.

After dinner we sat outside and drank coffee. I couldn't help but chain smoke with the hope that I would burn off some of the pent-up energy that had been slowly building all night. We walked to my car and as I unlocked his door, I did it—I grabbed him. What followed was 25 minutes of heavy breathing against the car. It had been years since I'd experienced a passionate exchange like that. Cars would drive by, we didn't care. Time would pass, we didn't care. There were no expectations, no limits and no inhibitions. We had three and a half weeks. We were living in the here and now.

That night all my doubts about my romantic future were eliminated. Bryan wasn't my first, and he wouldn't be my last.

I was leaving for New Mexico in three days and by the time I got back, Bryan would be gone. This was for the best. I wanted to be able to get on a plane, have a good time in Santa Fe, and when I came home, have things back to normal. I could go back to being me, alone.

The last day he was here, we drove by the water, singing songs louder than they played on the radio. We drank wine on my deck and I sat on his lap as we looked at the skyline. I soaked up the sound of his voice, his accent and things he said so I could replay them in my head. We laughed about movies we'd seen and talked about our life aspirations. I told him about books I'd read and about Georgia O'Keeffe; he told me about his job and described Europe in great detail.

I left the next morning and wondered what the purpose of the last three weeks was. Was it a lesson or a joke? Was it real or was he faking the whole time? The pain of Valentine's Day had made me an extremely cautious person and I wasn't ever going to try to understand a man again. They simply are different creatures.

I spent six days in the desert, in museums, restaurants and old churches. Bryan would make his way into my thoughts and I debated whether or not I should call him. I didn't call. The Sunday that I was coming back to Seattle was the same day he left. For some reason I was consoled by the knowledge that he was in the air at the same time I was.

I've been back for two weeks, talked to him three times, and received one letter. He wants me to visit him in Italy and I'm deeply considering it. I don't know why we re-met three years after I met him after seven years of hearing about him. But I don't want to figure it out. It's not up to me. Fate, God and what's meant to be is something beyond human control. Maybe it was what I wanted: pure distraction from the life I was trying to rebuild. Maybe it was something more.

7. First Day of the Last Year

I met John, my college/post college boyfriend on the first day of my last year of college. It was a broadcasting class held in a TV studio on campus. There were about 20 desks set up when I walked into the studio and they were all vacant, except one.

"Is this Broadcast 455?"

He looked up as if I interrupted him doing something really important. "Yeah?" he said, more like it was a question instead of an answer.

"Oh." I sat down next to him. "Good. I've never been in here before. I thought I was lost. Right when you think you've seen every inch of this building, a TV studio pops up and you never even knew it was there." I was rambling, I know, but something about the way this guy was looking at me made me not want to stop talking.

He had the qualities I'm usually attracted to: dark hair, glasses, tall. Maybe he would be the next man in my life. I looked down at his long legs stretched out in front of him and imagined getting tangled up in them. What did he look like without those glasses? Does he wear them in the shower? He could make this year-long class very interesting indeed. We could be a couple; he looked like someone I would be with. He could so easily fall in love with me; I could just see it. A few perfectly flirtatious eyebrow raises on my part should do the trick with this one. I hope he didn't have some weird last name like Clikenheimer or Ass-Wipe. I'd have to keep my last name. I hate it when married couples have different last names. It's always so confusing for the kids.

Pretty soon the studio started to fill with people I recognized from last year and I was caught up in *What did you do this summer?* chatter.

That same day, I met Dee in my speech class. She had a quiet coolness about her that I immediately recognized as potential friend material.

She invited me to her house that night for drinks and then we'd go dancing.

By the time I got over to her house, Dee had developed an extreme headache. We still proceeded to have a few cocktails along with her roommate, Claire, but as far as dancing went, Dee was writing a rain check. But there wasn't a cloud in the sky, and I had my boogidy boogidy shoes on.

"Why don't you and Claire go?" Dee asked when Claire was in the bathroom.

"I can't go with her," I whispered, "I hardly know her."

"You hardly know me! Just ask her. Jesus, it's not like a date or something," Dee said with a swig. I didn't have a vibe on Claire yet. I wasn't sure if she liked me even though we had already experienced some semi-drunken bonding. "Claire, I don't really feel like dancing but why don't you two go?"

"If you don't want to go it's no big deal," I said, off-handedly. "But the stress of the first day of school is pretty brutal. You can't let that sort of thing build up."

"You're right," Claire said, "Let's go."

We had to hit at least one bar full of fraternity guys before dancing; it was a college requirement. "So," Claire shouted over the bar talk, "Do you have a boyfriend?"

"No, no boyfriend. I had one this summer but he was a lot older than me. The College Girl status was a little uncomfortable for him," I said and lit a cigarette.

"Ah… not the same as Nordstrom-shopping wife."

"No, but that's OK. I think he's going to sashay out of the closet any day now." We laughed "You?"

"What?"

"Got a boyfriend?"

"Oh," Claire said, clearing her throat, "Yes. John. Hey, you might have a class with him. He's a Communications major too."

I slowly shook my head. "I don't know any Johns."

"I bet you know him; he's a really good artist. He's always submitting things to the college paper… comics and stuff; really funny."

"Don't know him."

"Dark hair, glasses, tall?"

Oh, shit. I took a very long drag off my cigarette. "I know him."

Claire and I became fast friends. We saw each other almost every day. It was amazing we got so close so quickly; I never had a friend like that before. She was the kind of person you felt like you knew your entire life the moment you met her.

My first-sight crush on her boyfriend, John, had faded. Soon we all started hanging out together. John was funny, smart, artistic and witty; I could see why Claire loved him. But something about seeing him and Claire together wasn't right. In fact, it made me sick. I liked him but at the same time, he was incredibly annoying. It was obvious to the world that Claire loved him, but I knew he didn't feel the same. Don't get me wrong, I thought he cared for her, but not to the same capacity. When he and I were alone together, walking to class or having a drink as we waited for Claire to join us, I would ask him if he really loved her. He would never answer me.

As the year pushed on, my relationship with John began to change. He began to bug me to no limit. We would fight almost every time I saw him. He drove me absolutely insane. I had never met anyone like him before. He thought he was so funny… he would laugh at his own jokes as I stared at him blankly. He was overly confident and would talk for hours without stopping to take a breath. He would throw these stupid one-liners at me that I knew he spent the whole night before making up. I grew to almost hate him.

Finally, I think it was in January, John broke up with Claire for no apparent reason. It was hard on Claire. It was more than a breakup for her; she was so close to his family, mainly his brother, Jeff. Them breaking up meant that she wouldn't see either of them. She made her whole world around these two boys and when it ended it meant she had to rebuild everything she had already constructed.

John, on the other hand, didn't seem too upset. I still had class with him three times a week and he acted just the same as he always did. A big talker, everyone's pal… it made me hate him even more.

It all came down to this one Wednesday night. A bar called *Study Hall* was home to Reggae Night: $3.00 pitchers and enough reggae to guide you into a drunken stupor you'd feel three days later. I was there with Claire when Jeff and John came in. When they approached us, Claire still looked at John with the same adoration that she always had. He looked away and eventually walked away. I followed him outside.

"What the hell is your problem?" I asked.

"Stay out of it."

"Why are you such a shit to her? What the hell did she ever do to you except put up with you and your whole bullshit routine? Why did you break up with her?"

"It's none of your business."

"I'm making it my business. Claire is my friend and I can't stand to see you treat her like this."

"You have no idea what happened, so drop it."

"You're right, I have no clue. Every time she tries to talk about it, she just starts crying. What did you do to her?"

"What did *I* do to her? Try, what *she* did do to me."

"What could she do to you, John? Smother you with affection?"

"She got together with some guy."

"Bullshit."

"You don't have to believe me. Ask her."

It turned out to be true. I couldn't believe it. It meant nothing to her and I almost didn't blame her for it. I knew John cared for her, but as far as love goes, I wasn't sure. I thought there was a chance they would get back together. No girl would put up with as much crap as Claire did. She laughed at every joke he told, a feat that proved she was not only a good girlfriend but also some sort of comically patient saint.

Even after this ugly little truth was revealed, Claire refused to confide in me. I knew she continued to experience some sort of loss over their relationship, but I was not the ear she wanted. We would still go out together, to bars or movies, and out of the corner of my eye when she thought I wasn't looking, I'd see her scan every room for John. We never saw him.

Finally, after too many vodka tonics, Claire told me that she thought John was seeing someone else; that's why she did what she did with the mysterious stranger. I told her she was crazy. If there were anyone else, I would have known about it. John would have let something slip when we were walking to class or when a bunch of us went out for drinks. I always keep my eyes on him, searching for some devious detail he would whisper to one of our friends about a new love interest. But nothing. If anything, he would see me watching him and give me a little wink like he was onto me, the recently self-appointed Nancy Drew. He wasn't smart enough to keep something from me. Or so I thought.

John and I had a Love/Hate relationship. One minute we were getting along fine; the next, I wanted to stab him in the back of the kneecaps with a fountain pen.

He just had a way about him that was so charmingly annoying, it drove me insane. He was the Bill Murray of our broadcasting class. It was like a Comedy Central marathon, line after line, crack after crack.

You had to take a nap after one conversation with him, he was that tiring. You'd have to load up on carbohydrates before class just to maintain the stamina it took to be around him.

Before John and Claire broke up, he had some kind of surgery on his hands and couldn't do things like make dinner, tie his shoelaces, or bathe. I was over at Claire's house with her and John. She had made him dinner and was about to give him a bath. For some reason, this totally pissed me off. I felt like he was taking advantage of her or something. In all actuality, I was probably jealous because he was getting all the attention... or because she was.

"John, is it really necessary for Claire to give you bath? Are you a child?"

"Excuse me, but if you haven't noticed I don't have working control over my hands."

"Yeah, I've heard that one before; but it's usually on dates."

"I'm totally serious."

"So am I," I said, craving a cigarette.

Claire helped him off the sofa. John said, "It's hard for me to maneuver in there."

"I think you can wedge a loofah into your mangled claw. You don't need the use of individual fingers to take a bath so unless you want to pick your nose or something, you should be able to manage."

"I don't mind, I want to do it," Claire said to me, eyebrows raised. Point taken.

I didn't think they belonged together. She was entirely too good for him. I adored Claire. She was funny and cute and very possibly the best girlfriend on the planet; somewhere in between a cookie-baking girlie girl and just one of the guys. She helped him study and never got mad. She would buy him presents and make mix tapes for him.

John and Claire continued to date, despite my hope that they would break up any day. I continued to have classes with John and if we had to be partnered up in class, I was always stuck with him. I dubbed him Big

Talker. He was the kind of guy I could see either being a corporate sales schmooze or managing a used car lot.

We somehow developed this weird game of matching wits. He thought he was so clever and me being me, I had to take him down a peg or two. People would watch our conversations take place like a tennis tournament. Heads moving back and forth as he tried to leave me speechless; me lobbing a well placed yet graceful slam.

One day, this guy from class came up to me after witnessing another fun-filled round of *Who Will Get the Last Line*, and asked if John and I were dating.

"Dating? Oh God no!"

"I thought you were."

"Why would you think that?" I asked.

"A lot of people think that. I thought I heard someone in class say you guys were together."

"John happens to be dating one of my best friends."

"You'd never know it by looking at you two. Lots of Chemistry going for a Communications class. Think about it." And I did.

Why was it that John pissed me off so much? Why was it that I wanted Claire to break up with him when she so obviously cared for him? Why would it make me mad to see the two of them together? Did I really like John and just hadn't realized it? Why were we always sitting next to each other in class? If I was late, why would he save me a seat next to him? Was it possible, plausible, even comprehensible to think that I really, truly wanted him in the worst way?

It couldn't be. It wouldn't be. I hated him, plain and simple. All that arrogance, the so-called wit he tried to wow me with. The way he tried to stare me down at any given opportunity, or how about the way he called me *Darling* or *Sweetheart* whenever possible? The way he thought he was all-that-and-then-some made him a contender for the *Most Irritating Person I've Ever Met* title.

True, when I first laid eyes on him I thought he was fairly cha-cha, but those days and thoughts were far and gone, replaced by the knowledge and confirmation that he truly was a major league jerk. There was nothing romantic happening there, just dislike and the ability to match wits. That's all. Nothing more.

The following week, John and I were paired up on yet another project. We were assigned to shoot a promotional commercial for one of the student-produced shows that ran on the cable station. We decided on an MTV/Denis Leary type of ad, having John dress like a redneck and smoke cigarettes next to a big bonfire with an old rusted car in the background. He would talk fast and pace back and forth. The whole thing was unscripted, just us two idiots making up stuff as we went along. I was shooting the whole thing. John, of course, was the on-camera talent.

It was a horrible day: freezing, pouring down rain. I carried the camera equipment, light kit, tripod, battery pack (with two extra five-pound batteries), cords and tapes from the Communications building to the location we scouted a half mile away. John, of course, met me there.

He was dressed perfectly, just how we'd planned, complete with a carton of Camels. We shot this 30-second spot for three hours and laughed the whole time. I was laughing so hard that the camera shook something awful and the mike was picking me up. Eventually, I just set the camera on the tripod in one standard shot and he walked in and out of the viewfinder. I stood ten feet away with my scarf in my mouth.

Looking at him through the black and white screen, I got an unhealthy twinge. He was hilarious and tall to boot. I started to picture us *together* together. But Claire's sweet face popped into my brain and I told myself to stop.

John felt nothing for me; this I was sure of. I could always tell when I was wanted and I was not wanted by him. There were no vibes, no signs that concretely confirmed that he had some sort of attraction for me. I was nothing more than his girlfriend's friend and fellow broadcasting student. Plus, I was dating someone at the time, nothing serious but, you know. It wasn't nothing, it was something. Nothing is never nothing, it's something even if it isn't everything. This John-thinking had to stop.

But it didn't.

We had to storyboard the whole promo out the next week. This meant more time with him. Alone.

Behind closed doors in his studio apartment, his wicked waterbed silently watched us from a darkened corner. Taunting me. Torturing me. John torturing me. John kissing me, me kissing John… wait a minute. No, that's not what I meant. Need to think of clear water and a white beach. That's right. Me in a white bikini, John with no shirt on. John walking toward me and pulling off my bikini. No, me in a turtleneck bikini made entirely out of wool, on the white beach, reading… the Bible.

"OK, I guess the first shot is the only shot. This whole thing is continuous, so this is going to be pretty easy." I pulled a sketchpad out of my bag and looked up at him. "Right?"

"Yep," he said, staring at me.

"What's going on?"

"Excuse me?"

"What are you doing?" I asked, pushing my hair out of my face.

"Nothing."

"My hair looks bad, I know. It started to rain when I was walking over here."

"No," John said, "I was just looking at your eyes."

"Why?" I said, wiping invisible eye goobers from the corners of my eyes.

"Why was I looking at your eyes? What do you want me to look at? Your chest?"

"OK, shut up."

He moved his eyes to my chest and leaned in closer. "Is this better? Does this make you more comfortable?"

"That's enough, Big Talker."

"Because I'm perfectly willing to stare at those things if you'd like. Really, it's fine with me."

I put my hands on both sides of his face and pulled him toward me. "Eye to eye contact is just fine, John." I left my hands on his cheeks just a second too long and suddenly the air between us changed. When I noticed it, I pulled away.

"Let's get to work," I said, but that time I knew. I was definitely getting a mutual vibe. And Claire was going to end up hurt.

I'm in love with my ex-boyfriend.

Bryan just left, and it could be me looking to fill a void, but I think I may have loved my ex, John, this whole time and have subconsciously built a roadblock to stop the feelings.

What made our relationship exciting at first was the fact that it was forbidden. He was with Claire as you know, and she was one of my best friends. I really don't know why I chose to start this thing between John and me all those years ago. After all, I started the whole thing.

It wasn't until the night before we were graduating from college that I really started to get The Twinge so bad that I couldn't ignore it. It was so late, probably around three o'clock in the morning, and a bunch of us were playing Hide and Seek around campus. It was this big drunken game, which was completely ridiculous; we were all so drunk we couldn't find the bathroom door if we tried, and here we were, running around campus like a bunch of yahoos. John and I were hiding in a group of trees by the Communications building. I wanted to kiss him, right there in the trees. At the time, I rationalized the situation by thinking I was drunk, and when one is drunk, the random kissing of people does tend to occur. I suppressed the smooch by knowing it was wrong to even want it. I knew Claire still loved him even though they broke up a good four months earlier.

The next morning was graduation. There we all sat, all the people I had hung out with for the last four years, and me and John, side by side. Somehow a wicked game of "I Spy" whipped up when Professor Nosehair took the podium. John was acting strange. I asked if he was upset about something. He looked at me with serious eyes and shook his head. Somewhere in the middle of that incredibly boring ceremony, I realized that I had looked forward to seeing John in class every day since the first day that I met him. I discovered the reason why he bugged me so much was that I liked him… I cared about him. He challenged me like no other guy had. He wouldn't let me push him around. He did the one thing no other guy ever did: he made me laugh. Laugh hard, with full-bodied HA HAs… and I loved that. But maybe I was being emotional, afraid to let go of him because everything was changing so fast. It was time for me to be an adult, and who wants to be an adult? Let's face it, it's not fun.

That night there was a big party at someone's apartment. We all brought our parents and John, accompanied by his brother Jeff, showcased his comedic talent. All the parents laughed. All the graduates laughed. It was the last night I spent in my small college town.

After Mom and Dad went back to the Motel 6, I found myself sitting on a veteran couch with Jeff. Claire had tried to line me up with Jeff a few times that year. He and John were brothers so I guess Claire thought it would be cute; her and John, me and Jeff. Somehow, it never really panned out. I can't remember what Jeff and I were talking about when the conversation turned to John. He asked me if I ever thought of John in *that* way.

"Oh, no… I don't think so," I said, trying to hide my recent revelation that just came to me 13 hours and eight minutes ago.

"Why not?"

"John drives my crazy. I can't stand him; plus, you know… him and Claire…"

"They aren't dating any more," Jeff interrupted me.

"This I know." We both took a sip of our obscenely strong drinks.

Jeff leaned back and crossed his long legs. "John has liked you since the first day he met you. In the beginning he actually considered breaking up with Claire to go out with…"

"Stop," I said. "I don't want to hear this."

"He came home from that very first day of class and said he met the most beautiful girl he'd ever seen."

"No, Jeff. Don't say any more."

I was at a loss for words that you would not believe. Could it be true? There's no way. This whole time? Nine months of liking and he never said a word? He would have said something, wouldn't he? Now everything was different. I just realized my liking for him yesterday, and he knew he liked me and he hid it? I thought back to all the time I spent with him, and the whole time, *the whole time* he was thinking this? Was I somehow part of the reason why John and Claire broke up?

I looked across the room at Claire, who, of course, I brought to the party with me. Did she know he liked me? No, if she knew she would have killed me by now. This was terrible. This was really, *really* bad. It was bad because as I sat there, reeling from the news, I discovered… I was happy. I was ecstatic and flattered. I was out of breath.

Claire caught me looking at her and smiled. I was screwed.

"So what do you think of that?" Jeff said.

"Oh God, Jeff, what are you doing to me?"

John looked cautiously in the direction of the couch. He walked over, in slow motion it seemed. I had a major crush on him from the get-go and it never stopped. I wanted to smash my mouth onto his and spin around his leg like a stripper spinning around a pole. I needed a cigarette.

"What are you two talking about?" he asked.

"Nothing." I shot Jeff a look.

"It sure looked like something."

I stood up; "It was nothing." I patted him on the shoulder, real friendly like, as I walked past him and over to my good friend Claire.

Needless to say, the whole night I was completely distracted. I kept looking at John and wondering. I was leaving in the morning; it was too late for anything to happen now. If we had another year of school or something then maybe, but now? This was one of those out of control situations that had no solution. Or did it? I had to do something. I had to do something fast.

"Wanna take a walk?" I said behind him.

He turned. "Sure."

We walked to the back of the apartment complex and stood by the pool. Steam rose from the aquamarine square as I looked at John and said, "Jeff told me some pretty interesting stuff."

"Oh yeah?"

"Yeah. Anything you want to share with me, John? Anything I should know about?"

"Not that I know of," He shook his head.

"Hmmm," I leaned toward him and whispered, "I'm kind of giving you a chance here, if you'd like to take it."

"Take what?"

Was I making a total fool out of myself? Jeff did say that John liked me, right? Or did he mean that John used to like me? Did I misunderstand him? No, I was not wrong.

"Shit, John! Say something!"

"What do you want me to say?"

"You have nothing to say to me?"

"No." He looked embarrassed.

"Nothing at all?" I asked, taking a step closer, hoping I looked sexy.
"No."
"John, take a chance! Look at me! I'm taking a chance and making a complete ass out of myself in the process. Say something to me! Do something to me!"

In one swift movement, he grabbed me by the shoulders and kissed me. Everything was quiet except for the blaring realization that this had been building up for nine months. I couldn't stand still. He was calmly kissing me and I kept shifting from one foot to the other, arms stretched out from my side, fingers wiggling for some odd reason, as if I were experiencing some sort of odd tick for the first time. My breath escaped in quick, short hums.

We stepped back and looked at one another.
Claire walked around the corner.
Claire saw us standing there, turned and walked the other way.
I went after her, leaving John by the aquamarine square.
And that's how it began.

Claire and I stopped being friends as John and I started being more than friends. The next weekend after graduation he visited me in Seattle and we went on our first date. He even brought me flowers. I still felt a little weird. Just the week before we were friends and college co-eds. Now we were living in the real world. I guess I got over it soon enough, because we dated for seven months.

I don't know why I broke up with him that following winter. I think I ended it because I wanted to get married soon and I knew I wasn't going to marry him. I had gotten my job at the radio station and was moving out of my parents' house. He had no ambition. Everything was a joke to him and I stopped thinking he was funny. I knew something and someone else was out there waiting for me; I had to see who it was. And, he asked me to do his resume for him. That really annoyed me.

One month after we broke up, John visited me in my new apartment. We were trying to make the fantasy of being "just friends" come true. He thought that we would get back together but I couldn't do it. In the short amount of time we'd been apart, I started dating three different guys. I wanted to be single.

I didn't see John again until December of the next year. He showed up at my work looking all dapper in a suit. He had gotten a sales job at some company. I had been promoted to a position in the newsroom and told him that I had met the most marvelous man (Fuckface). He had gotten back together with Claire, a little tidbit he chose not to tell me until I walked him out to his car. I said I was happy for him, but I wasn't. I was jealous. I tried to convince myself that they were meant to be together. I hadn't talked to Claire in over a year, but I knew she loved and would always love John. She could forgive him but not me. But I was in a serious relationship after all, I had moved in with The One Who Shall Go Nameless that past July. John deserved some happiness too.

I didn't really think of John again until that summer. Somehow I had become obsessed with him. I was in love with my current boyfriend so much so that I was convinced Shitbird and I would be engaged by the next Christmas. But Shitbird never gave me flowers. I couldn't see the love in his eyes the way I was able to see it in John's when we were together. I never thought I made a mistake in breaking up with John, I just missed him.

I think I was scared. I thought I was about to get married and on some level it scared me. I started reminiscing a little too much. When you face the fact that the person you're with is the person you want to marry, you have to let go of the past and accept that there will be no more stories. You're committing to this one person and that's all there is. For the rest of your life. All the old stories become old tales you tell around campfires. The night you met your ex-boyfriend is always a little more romantic than it actually was. All your boyfriends become fables who live in a shoe.

Then one day, two years after I broke up with him, I saw John. He was parked in the lot in front of my apartment building. My pulse quickened when I saw him. He was walking from the front door to his car. I yelled his name but he didn't hear me. He got in his car and drove away.

My relationship with Shitbird ended horribly that following February. Just two months later, I tracked John down at the same place he was working the last time I saw him.

The relationship that started from here is hard to define. This time, he was living with his girlfriend; not Claire but a different girl he had been dating. We had lunch together pretty much every week. At one point during this lunching relationship, I decided I was going to tell him that I thought about him when I was living with Shitbird. And now that I was single, I thought about him all the time.

But I changed my mind. I couldn't do that to this poor girl—the nameless, faceless object of his affection. She was like me. I began to think she was me. Here she was, living with this guy she loved, and some bitch comes in and starts screwing him? No. I just had that done to me; I couldn't do it to her.

But then he started to tell me that he was thinking of leaving her. She wanted to get married and he didn't. Genuinely, I was concerned for him. I didn't secretly want him to leave her. OK, I did want him to leave her, but I tried not to think it. I didn't want him to be sad; he must love this girl a little bit. So I bit my lip (wishing I was biting his) and said nothing. I wanted to see what would happen next.

What happened was that he decided to move out. He said something about still dating her but I didn't bet on it. You can't go from living together to just sharing popcorn and a box of Milk Duds on the occasional Saturday night. But before I get into all this, I have to tell you about the day that I can't stop thinking about.

John and I were lunching at this restaurant just a few weeks ago. I found The Vibe especially electric that day. I had to remind myself that I wasn't going to pursue him because of the poor girl who at that exact moment was probably calling his office to say that she loved him.

But he was pushing my limits of protecting my fellow sister. He was looking at me like he used to. Getting through this lunch was not going to be easy. I had to think of a way out of the neon karma.

I started talking about Bryan.

Talk about a fire extinguisher! He clamed up. It was a dirty trick, an old trick. He hated it when I talked about other guys, even when we were still in the "just friends" category. I had to pull that little cutie out of my pocket before I started to spill the beans about my rekindled feelings for him.

I told John that Bryan had all the physical qualities I looked for in a man. "Like what?" he asked.

"Tall, dark hair, glasses…" I stopped when I realized that not only was I describing Bryan, I was describing John. He started laughing when he realized it too. I decided I had to spill, what the hell.

"John, I have to tell you something. I know you're in a relationship and I'm happy for you. You will probably end up marrying this girl and you'll invite me to the wedding. I'll be sitting in the back row, wearing some fabulous hat, and even though you'll be up there marrying her, I'll still have a thing for you."

He didn't say anything.

"John, I'm sorry. Have I completely screwed up our new friendship?"

"No."

"Good, because I would hate that."

"It's OK," he said. I felt better. I said what I had to say, and yet I didn't change anything between us. Look at me, all worried for nothing.

"It's OK because I still have feelings for you too."

What? "What?"

"I'm just saying what you said."

"I know, but you have a girlfriend! I don't."

"I'm just saying I'll always have a thing for you, that's all."

I couldn't speak as he drove me back to work. It was amazing that all my body functions were functioning. Where did this leave us? Here I'm single, he's not, but he may leave his girlfriend. Is he going to leave Girlfriend #2 for me?

I got out of the car and said, "Well, it was fun."

"Yeah," he laughed.

"Hey, maybe next time you just want to get a hotel room or something?" I teased him.

"You bet."

And that's the conversation that I can't stop thinking about. Later he called me and said that we should get together again soon. I wasn't sure if he meant for lunch or *lunch*. Two weeks go by and he calls me to say, "I've decided to move out on my own."

"John, I'm sorry."

"Don't be. As you know, I have been questioning things for awhile. So…"

"So…" I say. "We should get together sometime."

"I know," [Pause.] "OK, gotta go. 'Bye."

What's going on here? For someone who was involved in this love triangle, I sure had no idea what the hell was going on. Oh God, help me. Only a person in love could be as stupid as I was at this very moment.

I'm in love with my ex-boyfriend.

HE & ME MAY NEVER BE. [Date? 6:15 pm]

The Thought reached in...
But I shooed it away
... this unwanted stray
although the thieving thought
snuck in the back window
stole my confidence
shattered my dreams
and hocked my hopefuls at the seedy moral pawn shop downtown.

What if it never happens?
all this praying and prodding
is simply time wasted
and the part of the fool
is exclusively Me
while Fate sits and laughs amusedly
shaking her head at my sad, sad performance.

I'm so afraid
of the wickedly possessed thief...
that I take offensive action
and lock out Impossible,
weaponing my wardrobe
against all factual possibility
that NEVER
will he love me
and I will always
be

alone.

8. The Next Chapter

John called late in the afternoon the same day we were going to get together for drinks after work. "I can't meet you tonight."

"Why not?"

"I'm still with my girlfriend." I was silent. I tried not to act shocked but don't think I hid it too well. My voice was shaking when I said, "So what?"

"I don't think it would be right if I met you for drinks while I have a girlfriend."

"I don't know how you interpret having drinks, John, but it's consuming a beverage, not rolling around in some back alley," I said.

"A drink is more than a drink when it's with you."

"What makes you say that?" I said, starting to get irritated.

"Lunch is one thing. My girlfriend has no problem with us meeting for lunch. But meeting for drinks is an entirely different thing."

"Oh, right. Because people only have sex at night. It's physically impossible to have sex when the sun is up."

"You know what I mean."

"No I don't," I said. "This is stupid. Are we friends or not?"

"We're friends."

"Did you tell your insecure girlfriend that we're friends?"

"Yes," he sighed.

"Well, I'm not sure if you know this or not, but friends go out. They meet for drinks, have dinner. That's what friends do."

"I cannot go out with you and feel good about it when I have a girlfriend."

"Bring her along! Why don't you just bring her? I can't exactly jump you right in front of her, can I? I'd have to wait until she went to the bathroom or something."

"You know it drives me crazy when you talk like that."

"Tell me, John. Why are you with this person? You obviously still like me. You can't handle it when I say anything remotely sexual. You call me. You are the one always asking me to meet you for lunch. Why are you together?"

"I've been with my girlfriend for a year."

"That's your answer? You've been with her for a year and that's why you're together? You think if someone asked you why you were dating your girlfriend you'd say, *'Because she's nice'* or *'She's beautiful, fun to be around'*—something like that."

"How would you feel if you and I were dating and I met my ex-girlfriend for a drink?" he asked.

I hesitated. "I wouldn't care."

"Yes you would."

"I would not. There was a point in my life when I wouldn't have liked it, yes. But… I've changed. I've been the Insecure Girlfriend and where did it get me? My last idiot boyfriend cheated on me! If you act like you don't care, there's no cheating. Act like a paranoid freak? Bring on the cheating. It's the Forbidden Fruit Syndrome."

"I still can't meet you."

"You still *won't* meet me."

"Whatever."

"I don't care," I said.

"You don't?"

"Nope," I looked down at the outfit I had spent an hour picking out for that evening.

"I guess I'll see you later," he said.

"When? I'm never going to see you. We can't be friends."

"Yes we can."

"How? Are we going to have long conversations at work because you can't call from home? I can't believe what a wimp you are. When we were dating, if I told you to do something, you'd do the exact opposite."

"That's a lie," he said.

"You're right. I never told you what to do. I wasn't your mother, I was your girlfriend."

He apologized and hung up. I was mad. I just wasn't sure who I was mad at. I was mad at *her* for telling him what to do, and knowing I *would* have put the moves on her man. I was mad at *him* for making *her* more important than *me*. Who was this girl? I dated him first! I've known him longer. She had no right to be more of a priority than me. I was mad that he put her feelings before my own. I hadn't seen him in months and this little creep has a temper tantrum and I'm tossed aside like an old shoe? I'm the old shoe that's going to kick you in the ass, bitch! Watch out, sister, I'm coming to getcha!

And what's with this whole *Girlfriend* thing? Did you notice he didn't mention her name, ever, not once? Like he's afraid once I know her name, I'll track her down and slash her tires or something.

He never asks if I have a boyfriend. Not that I actually have one, but I could. I could be dating some guy and still want to see John, but does he think of that? I could so easily have a boyfriend and cheat on him with John. I could be a Roll-Around Sally. I could be a slut. Not that this is such a great goal, but I do have the power. I could be a sleaze if I really wanted to. Not that I want to; but I'm wanted by men, aren't I? I must be. I am. I have to be.

Actually, I was mad at myself. How could I let me do this to me? I've been doing so well, kickboxing and acting like Tina Turner. I put everything into this guy and got nothing in return. I was the typical woman, getting all jacked up over some jackass and getting the jack. I was some sort of an idiot. Why didn't anyone stop me? I'm an out of control locomotive with every car filled with little Johnny fantasies that were never getting off. I wasn't even getting off.

I'm not going out with him again. No more occasional lunches. I don't care if she decides it's OK for us to meet for drinks. It's over. This spineless bastard is no longer a part of my life. Anyone this beige is a waste of time. Why I've held a candle for this guy for so long, I will never know.

He must be afraid of me. I broke up with him and he can't get over it. If we got together again, I may break up with him again and that is just too scary. This little mousy girlfriend isn't scary. She's probably some meek librarian type that couldn't get a decent man if she walked around with her shirt off and hundred dollar bills falling out of her pockets. A no-talent, unexciting, milk toast pansy with only one request: don't meet your ex-girlfriend for drinks.

Of course, he'll oblige her one pathetic request. It's just one stupid request. She'd do anything for him; she would never break up with him because he asked her to do his resume. He has to do want she wants so she will do whatever he wants. It's like some sort of a sick trade off, a legal version of boyfriend-girlfriend slavery.

I've got this whole relationship all figured out. Another reason why he is and probably should be scared of me: I'm like a whip; smart and quick, possibly causing some pain. Don't try to fool me with your lies and half-truths, Glamourina can smell the bullshit before the stench hits the air. This sort of power has got to be intimidating. Hell, it frightens me! All this power, all these smarts, stored inside one perfectly groomed head of hair.

Then again, I could be way off. What if this whole girlfriend excuse was a lie? Maybe there was no girlfriend at all. Maybe he didn't want to see me because he doesn't like me. He wishes I would just go away and leave him alone. I was old news, I was the pathetic one. He was just trying to be nice, pawning me off with this whole girlfriend thing.

He's probably single. The only reason why he talks to me is that he feels sorry for me. I once was so cha-cha and now I'm through. It's sympathy that makes him call, we did date for almost a year. There's no girlfriend at all. He just doesn't want to see me.

I'm such a cocky asshole. Thinking he still has a thing for me. I cannot believe I said that on the phone. He was probably gagging himself on the other end of the line. I hope he thought I was kidding.

I didn't sound like I was kidding. Oh God, he's laughing at me. He's telling all his friends that his heifer ex-girlfriend wants him in the worst way, and the whole time he wants to send me out in the fields to die a slow, painful death and have buzzards peck me to pieces.

Depression has set in like a recurring nightmare.

I retreated to my apartment, clad in extra large sweats, comforted by a lone carton of cigarettes. Whatever version of the story I chose to believe, it was still over. I was never going to see him again.

I felt very alone. I'd always had the thought of John to fall back on and now that he was gone, I just fell back. It made me miss my old relationship with Shitbird. That bastard went right from me to someone else. Hell, He was already with someone else when He was with me. He went from me to her without even stopping for gas and a pack of gum.

Letting go of someone you've held onto for so long isn't easy. Especially after you realize that this person isn't the person for you at all. It's like saying your favorite color is red every time someone asks you, then one day you realize you hate red. You like blue.

You convince yourself of one specific thing and believe in it so certainly. You think about it, dream about it, plan the future around this one stupid thing that you don't really want, but you've convinced yourself that you do. But it was never there to begin with. It was a mirage you pieced together with your own craziness.

I don't think I ever really wanted to get back with John. I just thought of him fondly, I guess. He treated me better than any guy I'd ever dated and I wanted to be treated that way again. I wanted to feel pretty. I wanted to feel wanted. But he's different than he was when we were together. People change and he was people.

Now that I realized the fantasy was over, the badness came back. The sick-sick feeling; the feeling you get when you look around and see there's no one there to say *"Bless you."* You won't be bringing a date to the wedding. Now that the person you've clung to is gone, you have a damn gaping hole that sucks the air right out of you and you don't know what to do to feel better.

The easiest thing to do is to shift that affection to someone else. But there was no one else. Who was I going to like now?

9. Just Like the Swiss Family Robinson

I have decided to construct a new society. A society where women are free to live in peace and clean carpets. A place where the toilet seat is always down and there are no reading materials in the bathroom. A sacred homeland where people replace the toilet paper roll and reimburse others. I know you must be sitting there thinking this sort of society can never be fully realized and I do admit it would be a lot of work. But it is entirely possible, if we all work together.

This is my idea: break apart these huge, bulky continents and make a series of mammoth islands. On this series of islands you would find one island where all the straight women live, an island for all the gay men, an island for the straight men, and lastly, Lesbian Isle.

Right off I can see the benefits. There would be no racism. We're simply split in four general, non-color issue groups. And these groups would all individually benefit from being assigned to these islands.

First of all, I know that the gay man's society is one where it is hard to find a suitable mate. By keeping them all one island, it makes it so much easier to find a boyfriend. It eliminates any need at all for personal ads.

Gay Man Island would be very clean and well thought out. Their cities would be carefully planned and every home, restaurant or retail establishment would have a good view and manicured rooftop garden. The outrageously themed dinner parties would obviously be fabulous, with tons of food and drink. Every home would smell good and the dry cleaning industry would be very well supported. So would the gym. If Cher, Bette Midler and the Pet Shop Boys ever went on tour, all the shows would be sold out on Gay Man Island.

All the lesbians would be put together as well, and let's face it, they just want to be left alone anyway. Lesbian Isle would be strictly no frills.

No stupid lace curtains, no cow print kitchens; it would almost be hippie-like. The scent of patchouli would fill the air and no one would ask if their pants made them look fat.

All the straight men would be put together on their own little island, which is really where they want to be. No one nagging them about how they never do anything. They could lie around with all their friends, burping and scratching themselves, not giving their non-opinion on wallpaper patterns they don't care about. They could sleep in as long as they like, eat all the junk food they want, and never have to send out Thank You cards.

This would be the land of dirty cat boxes and empty milk cartons. Countertops would be continually sticky and beds unmade. Movie theaters would only show action flicks and pornos, and typical gift giving holidays would be completely ignored. The major motives of transportation would be motorcycles and ridiculously expensive SUVs. Wardrobes would consist solely of things that never need to be ironed, ever.

The land of the Straight Girl would be a mystical oasis. It would be clean and well-decorated. Plants would be planted and gardens would grow. Target stores and day spas would be everywhere, not to mention a Starbucks location every couple of miles. We would invent cars that would never have to be filled up with gas and if there was any need for repair or automotive detailing, we would put our cars on one big ferry and ship them over to Straight Man Land. There would be throw pillows on every couch and no one would say, *"Why are there so many damn pillows on this couch?"* Cupboards would be stocked with Snack Wells and diet Coke. Sheets would always be clean.

These islands would not be completely without interaction. I propose once a month sex romps. The gay men and lesbians don't have to worry about this because they have access to nookie 24-7. But once a month, we would fly all the straight men in and have one hell of a mixer. It would be a dance-drink-screw extravaganza where it is expected that you have sex with as many men as you possibly can.

There would be a Male Order Service where you could order any kind of man you want and in any capacity you want him in. If you wanted someone to impregnate you and wanted to be sure the child was smart, you could order some doctor or computer genius to come in and give it to ya. If you wanted a little romance, you could order that too. It would be a guaranteed Pain-Free relationship. You could program him to call when you wanted him to call or make sure he sent you flowers on Valentine's Day. I'm not sure if these men would be robots or just really well-behaved from living on that stinky island.

If you chose to get pregnant, life would be really easy. Your women friends would be supportive and helpful because they know what it feels like to shove a human out through the center of your body. All the women would raise the baby together. Of course the mother would be the primary caregiver, but women would live like gypsies—in one big old wonderful house, each teaching the child her own individual gift, like a bunch of damn Fairy Godmothers.

You could get married but you wouldn't live with your husband. He could come visit for awhile; you'd get a visa that would allow him to stay for, say, a month or so, but then he would have to go. If there was some sort of a way to be assured the marriage would be without fail, then you could get permission from the Board of Directors and move to your own little private island. Actually, no. Forget that. Allowing people to go off and live on their own would totally screw up the whole island society. It could be like asking for anarchy and mayhem, when this is a completely chaos-free zone. I think it's best to stick to the original plan. Men could visit on certain occasions but only for a minimum amount of time. But it's not like I'm proposing totally separate lives, just minimum contact. It's for the best. Believe me.

There would be twice-a-month get-togethers with Gay Man Island. I figure we would have a mid-week Dinner & a Movie night. We'd watch some old Bette Davis thriller or major league crier like *Ordinary People*. The dinner would be a finger food theme: Little Smokies and mini-pizzas. Then later on in the month, we would have Drunken Dance Night. On Straight Woman Island, we'd construct entire cities of dance clubs specifically for the purpose of this one night. Gay boys and straight girls would all get wasted on tequila shots and grind on the dance floor, laughing so hard we'd spit all over each other, accidentally burning each other with ultra-light cigarettes.

I'll have to wait and see if there would be a Lesbian night mixer. The girls and I will have to take a vote on that one.

I actually think this island idea is very smart. Human society would be so much more efficient. Think of the things that would get done! Companies would grow, houses would be built... I think the suicide rate would definitely decline and crime rates would be cut in half.

Ideally, I would like to live on my own island. I would have no problem living alone in my own personal paradise. I could always hand pick the people who can visit my island, and if I really liked them, I would invite them to live with me. I would have a gigantic, well-decorated castle, with tons of guestrooms. I would send out an open invitation to the other islands when I wanted to have a party and felt like meeting new people. But for the most part, only certain people would be blessed enough to be on my list. My friends, my family, a handful of past co-workers, certain men with the sole purpose of being my sex slaves. There would be a small list of celebrities who are always welcome: Cher (obviously), Janeane Garofalo, Angelina Jolie, Geena Davis, Drew Barrymore... only the coolest, A-list Hollywood vixens; no stick-bitches allowed.

The celebrity men who can come to my island any time they want to are Johnny Depp, Mike Myers, Jeremy Piven, Vince Vaughn, John Cusak and Jon Stewart. These men are my idea of perfect. If I could wad them all up into one tiny ball and put them in my pocket, I would do it. If I could keep them in a little treasure chest where I could peek in on them or attach them to a key chain, I would surely do it. These are the men I want to date, *or* I wish I was currently dating, *or* I wish I could find someone like them and *then* I would currently date them. If any of these men asked me to have sex with him within the first five minutes of our initial conversation, I would make a mad dash for the nearest flat surface.

Johnny Depp. He reminds me of someone who would be one of my brother's friends. I fantasize that he is the kind of guy who would beat the crap out of anyone who was mean to me. I love that. Any man willing to take a major blow to the head for my honor and good reputation has got to be a keeper.

Mike Myers is always invited to my castle because I love his Canadian accent and I believe him to be a good dancer. I think he would be good at a party. He would talk to people and let them be funny, knowing the whole time that he is funnier than all of them put together. He has certain looks that make me fall in love with him. He has soft brown eyes and seems to be very loyal. Very puppy dog-ish. Love puppies. Any guy the slightest bit canine is one to keep tabs on.

After saying the name Jeremy Piven, I immediately want to scream out, *precious!* In the movie *Very Bad Things* he became very hunkalicious and I wanted to lick the screen whenever he was on it. I always thought he had good eyes and a nice smile, but the sex scene with that hooker in the bathroom caused some severe wiggling around in my chair. Oh, why couldn't I have been that hooker?

Vince Vaughn is invited to my island for sexual purposes first, personality second. His personality only adds to his attractiveness. I know *he knows* he's finger lickin' good, and I'm attracted to that confidence. I want to get drunk with him and make out against a brick wall or have sex on the hood of a junkie car. He's that kind of guy. The Bad Guy. Love the Bad Guy. My mom would warn me about the Bad Guy; she'd tell me not to trust him. But I would love him because he could kiss the seeds out of a watermelon and make sexual comments on the phone that would make my toes curl. I would sit and smoke too many cigarettes with him, just so I could look across the table at him and imagine all the things that he would do to me later.

John Cusak is the only person out of this select group I have loved since age fourteen. We're talking years of devotion here. Any movie he is in, I have to run out and see. At some point during these years of devotion, I have convinced myself that one day, we will be married. I am sure of it. I know we have a lot in common. I've seen him kiss girls in his movies and observed that he is one hard kisser. Love the Hard Kisser. Grab the back of my neck and kiss me like a mad man, you passionate bastard! He could come to any of my island parties and I would welcome him with open arms and legs. I'm almost sure my mom would approve of him.

But if you are forcing me to pick one person out of this group of angels to have permanent residence on my island, I would have to say I would take Jon Stewart in sickness and in health, for richer or for poorer, as long as we both shall live. He is my ultimate idea of the perfect man. He's cute as a bug's ear for one thing. Funny for two things. Sweet, kind, not obnoxious, good dresser, sweet to old people (not that I've seen him with old people but I'm sure he's polite). I can think of 23 attractive qualities right off the bat, and I haven't even started talking about the lovely streaks of gray in his hair.

Jon is a fairly new crush for me. I've known about him for years but never really thought of him for me and my island life. That is, until just recently. I think he has a very small shyness aspect to his personality and I adore that. His funniness comes naturally, without deep thought or rim shots. He is clearly smart and would go up and talk to people he doesn't know when at a party. I think he's the type of guy who buys Girl Scout cookies and soccer candy from kids because he remembers what it was like to sell them. And that is why he has the corner, room-with-a-view, luxury suite in my castle.

Where to go from here is a difficult thing to say. It's not like I can take a jackhammer and start splitting up the continents. And I don't think this is something you start with a petition. Hell, let's face it, this idea is never going to get off the ground. People will fight me over this issue, guaranteed. And you just know that there's going to be one rebel who's going to chain himself to something large and immovable just to make a point. The media will have a field day. I really don't want to start hitting the talk show circuit to try to convince people to move to a big island in the middle of the ocean. Someone is destined to fight the system.

I still believe in its thought and premise but no one is going to listen to me. Can you imagine trying to coordinate this project? *Complete nightmare.* Maybe one day my island society will come true and it will be the end of war and the beginning of peace and sanity for all women. Until then, life will continue on as it must and will inevitably do. It's a shame.

10. Sending a Postcard from Nowhere to No One

I'm in a state. Not Nevada, not Iowa; I'm in a state so bad that I would actually consider suicide if I weren't so afraid of pain and bleeding. Not to mention the fact that my mother would never forgive me. And there's going to be a really good movie on TV next week that I want to watch.

Too much happened today. My car won't start. Now tomorrow I'll have to walk to work. It's not far, it will probably only take me a half an hour but still, you know there will be torrential rains or something. I have a horrible cold that makes it painful to blink. I feel as if my entire head is filled with slush. I can't sleep. I'm not hungry. My skin is painful.

OK, right there is enough incentive to OD on a prescription drug but let's throw another couple of logs on the fire. My mom gave me this really beautiful candleholder, a big silver ball with stars all over it, and I put it right on my kitchen table. I smashed it. When I got out of the chair, I shook the table and the ball rolled to the linoleum. I smashed it. It broke into four big pieces and about one million tiny ones. For some odd reason, this unfortunate mistake led me to muscle up the nerve to call information to get John's number. I talked to his roommate and asked if John might be available for cocktails. John wasn't home and wouldn't be for the rest of the night. Immediately I think he's with her, as he should be, I guess. She is, was, his girlfriend after all. He has no way of knowing about my love for him and how could he?

How *couldn't* he? I asked him out for a drink! I suppose there are lots of different levels that could be taken on. A drink could be casual. A drink could be romantic. A drink could be catching up on old times. How was he to know that this drink was a life changer, or at least, a status changer from single to non-single?

What am I doing? I get myself all wrapped up in these fantasies and for some reason I think they're going to turn out exactly the way I want them to. They never do. Looking back, everything I thought was going to happen, never happened. It's always the exact opposite. Keeping with that theme, now that I'm single and John is somewhat single, I won't be with him. *Great.*

Everyone has someone but me. Most of the time I'm pretty OK with it, in fact I like it, but everything in my life right now is in the shitter. My car is broken, I hate my job, I smashed a special gift from my mother, and I have no love life. I can't help but think that if I at least had a nice boyfriend, all of these other shitty things wouldn't seem so shitty. I can't even say that the dates I've had lately have been bad; I've had no dates to be bad. It's a pitiful existence.

I've just taken a strong muscle relaxer and had a vodka tonic to help me see the purpose of my life. Nothing yet. I'm waiting.

I'm waiting.

OK, I've just had a cigarette and figured out the meaning of life.

It's meant to be hard. We struggle and we struggle, but there is *no meaning.* It's a test to see if we have any balls, any gumption and I don't know if I have any.

I've repaired the silver ball candleholder. I've decided that this candleholder is much like my life. If you look at it from across the room, it looks OK. Once you get close to it you see it's all held together with tape. The back parts are still missing (they were too small to put back together). It does its job, it can successfully hold a candle, but I should probably get a new one.

ALL I CAN DO. [*I don't know the date, 3:37 am*]

Depression seeped in through the obvious cracks,
flooding the basement and ruining the carpet.

The smell of stagnant water and unfiltered air
filled my room and made me sick.

All the windows are jammed shut
Forcing me to lie
down
and try to think of a way out.

But I can't think
or see
or feel
because the stench is real
and all that I can do is cry
and wish someone would save me…
or, I could save myself…
pull myself "up by the bootstraps"
and walk out of this place where everything stinks
but all I can do
is hope
one day it all will stop.

11. Dustin Dan

I met these two guys in the same bar on the same night and since then, have been dating these two during the same period of time; but not on the same nights. Actually, I did do that once, but it was too much. I was trying to pretend I was the popular girl in school, but I couldn't keep one conversation with one of them separate from another with the other.

I met them at *Fruit Fly*, the bar I usually go to on Thursday nights with my friend, Scottie. Actually, I met Dustin a few weeks before. He came up to me at two o'clock in the morning when I was getting my jacket from the coat check. I thought he was gay; his freshly scrubbed face, gelled hair and pleasantly pressed vest were dead giveaways as to which team he was on, or so I thought. But when he asked for my phone number, I guessed it wasn't to talk about eye makeup.

But (and you knew there was going to be one of those) he was so not my type. I was a good three inches taller than him, but what the hell. Something was definitely said by him having the guts to talk to me and I figured that confident quality should be rewarded and encouraged. But alas, there was no pen and me without a business card. I said I would just have to catch him the next week when I was prepared with a pen.

The next week, I was back at *Fruit Fly* and putting my only New Year's resolution into motion. I resolved to smile at any and all cute, attractive men. I hadn't really done that before. When I see a cute guy I usually do one of two things: look away, or turn bright red. Sometimes I do both; most of the time I do both. But this year, the entire year, I was going to push all of my insecurities aside and smile like I was the most attractive, sexy Cheshire cat in the whole pet shop.

So, there I was, at the bar with my usual gaggle of gorgeous friends, smoking too many cigarettes around a sticky table, when this guy I had never seen before walked by. Dark hair with glasses; he stood out from the mass waves of white tank tops and half shirts. He walked by again and I smiled. He walked by again. Yes, I smiled. Even though he was looking at me as if I was a freak, I stuck to the resolution. I would not, should not, could not waiver from it.

Somehow he roped his way back over to our table and commented on my ring. "Is it an antique?"… was his opening line.

"Actually, no," I said.

"Where did you get it?"

"My parents and brother gave it to me when I graduated from college."

"Oh yeah?" He took my hand and inspected it further. "It's really beautiful."

"Thanks," I smiled (again with the smiles). "Not only is it beautiful, but I find it's a good conversation starter."

He laughed. "You're right. It worked."

"And," I continued, "a good excuse for some guy to randomly hold my hand."

We talked for about 45 minutes. He was easy to talk to. He had a nice laugh. His name was Dan.

After all this conversationing, Scottie, my usual dance partner, was getting antsy and wanted to dance. I didn't want to leave Dan so I invited him to join us. Now this was a big test. It wasn't intentional, but as we walked toward the dance floor, I realized I shouldn't be doing this. One of the quickest ways I can lose interest in a guy is seeing him dance, or should I say, seeing him dance badly.

A bad dancer is bad news. Not only does it mean that if I end up dating this person on a semi-regular basis, we cannot and never will go dancing—something that I feel is almost medically necessary. Not to mention that one of my biggest pet peeves in the world is riding in a car with some guy who cannot correctly bob his head to the beat of the song playing on the radio. He may be right on the beat to some song playing somewhere, but in this car, to this song, he's completely lost. This theory of mine also works in the opposite direction. There could be some guy that is just OK looking or even stepping over into the borders of ugly, but if he can dance, I want him.

But surprisingly, Dan could dance. He's not a real hoofer but he passed the test. After an extended version of *Dancing Queen*, Dan and I headed for the bar. As we sat, he said he should check on the friend he abandoned earlier on in the evening. I lit up another unnecessary Marlboro and congratulated myself on a smiling job well done. Look at me, smiling and attracting a man like this, on my very first attempt to be irresistible. Then, I see him, not Dan but Dustin, the guy I had met the week before. I smiled (of course), "Hey… Dustin. How are you?"

"Good; how are you?"

"Very well, thank you." [Dramatic drag on the cigarette.]

Dustin produced a pen from nowhere. "I came prepared this week."

"Getting a lot of phone numbers, are you?"

"No, just yours… that is, if you still want to give it to me," he said.

I laughed and saw Dan was returning. My smile powers had gotten me into a bit of trouble. Dan burst into our conversation and leaned toward my ear. "I have to take my friend home, he's a little drunk."

"OK," I said, thinking *"Shift One is over, and Shift Two is about to clock in."*

"It was great meeting you."

"You too," I smiled, oh no, got to watch that.

"I guess I'll see you around?"

"Yes, you will."

He hesitated. "OK, take care," and he walked away. I watched his retreating figure and really thought he was a nice guy. I wondered if I would see him again.

"So, can I still get your number?" I had almost forgotten that little Dustin was still at the table, looking at me with eyes that belonged on a stray dog.

"Yeah, sorry about that…" I said, and waved at the spot where Dan once stood.

"No problem." Well, he was certainly bright-eyed. I wasn't sure what this guy saw in me. Didn't he pick up on my lack of interest vibes? Like I said, I was taller than him and by the look of that little boy face, more than a few years older than him. Oh well, the secrets of attraction are not for me to define.

As I jotted down my seven digits, here comes Dan walking back. He pressed a little folded up piece of paper into my hand. "I'm sorry if this is too forward. Is this too forward?"

I shook my head "no," again with a smile.

So there it began, two guys, one night, and one me.

Dustin the Duck

Dustin called me the next day. My first reaction after hearing his voice was disappointment. Not in him really, but in me. I knew I had no real interest in this person. I thought for sure that I would have to do all the talking. Inevitably, it always ends up that way. Men always seem to have a verbal handicap when it comes to conversing on the telephone, but Dustin was quite the wordsmith.

We talked for over an hour about a myriad of things: sorority girls, places we've been, the significance of bumper stickers. I was pleasantly and unexpectedly surprised at how well we got on. It was as if this person wasn't the same guy who approached me in the bar. It was hard for me to picture this voice and these words coming out of that little boy mouth.

The thing that really won me over in the Dustin Department was something he awkwardly told me in the middle of our conversation about sponges. "How long have you been going to that bar?" He asked.

"About a year. A little less than a year, I think."

"Yeah, that sounds right."

"What do you mean?"

"Well, I don't want you to think I'm a stalker or something, but I've been admiring you from afar since you first started going there."

"You have?"

He laughed. "Yeah, I'd see you there but you were always dancing with your friend…"

"Scottie?"

"Yeah, and you were just so… I don't know. I would say to my friends, 'Look, there she is again,' but I never had the guts to come up to you. All I wanted to know was your name. I wondered what your voice sounded like… stupid stuff like that."

I was shocked. No one had ever said such things to me. Admiring me from afar for a year? It was unheard of. No one admired me. I tried to think of all the Thursdays I had gone there and wondered if he ever saw me do anything stupid, wear something unfashionable or just act like the basic idiot that I really am.

Wait a minute, was this a line? Something that would get him in good right at the beginning? It could be. It could be a big lie. To flatter me, to make me feel special so then he could move in for the easy squeezy. Was that the game? But something about the way he said it, so openly, so honestly, so unprovoked; I almost believed him. I believed him more than I didn't believe him. Plus, that little boy face? There was no way that face could spin tricks like the rest of the male hootchies.

That did it. The information revelation and genuine honesty got me hooked. We agreed to meet for cocktails that Monday night. I was excited to see him. I was the Smitten Kitten.

We talked and drank for almost five hours. I can't remember the specifics of our conversation but I do remember that somewhere in the middle of the evening I felt the urge to kiss him. He had nice lips and that little face! It was precious! Adding to my budding smit was that physically Dustin wasn't my type. He was young (just turned 21), well-scrubbed, short, and he wore a necklace, breaking my cardinal *No Jewelry* rule. He reminded me of Ducky from *Pretty in Pink*. Because he was so wrong, it felt right. It was like taking a test drive in a different sort of car that you never considered buying.

He walked me to my car in the pouring rain. I got in, started my car with the door still open and he said, "We should get together again soon."

"Yes, we should, we will, I hope," I said with an uncomfortable smile. I always hated this moment. "This is the moment I hate."

"Why is that?" he said, with a smile that knew exactly what I was talking about.

"What do I do? Sit here and will your lips in my direction, or do I shut the door and drive off?"

"Well, I'm thinking about kissing you."

"Sounds good," I said as he leaned again.

I saw Dustin a lot over the next few weeks. I discovered that we had little if nothing in common. I tried not to let that bother me. We went to a furniture store and he had the uncanny knack of picking out all the furniture that I hated... not that we were shopping for "us" or anything. In the car, he would fast forward over all the Tina Turner songs I liked.

He liked himself, a lot. He told me that he recently went to a job interview and all the women loved him; that they swooned over him. Yes, he said *swooned*. He claimed to look like Bailey on *Party of Five*; I didn't tell him that he looked more like Ducky.

He was not a good drunk. Not that there are good drunks, but people who cannot hold their alcohol, or at least have an air of dignity and style as they throw up, have no place in my life. One night we went to a party at his friend's house. Dustin always had his arm or hand somewhere on my body and that did win him some big points. (I always feel it's important for the date to feel like a date.)

I didn't actually see his vast consumption of beer, but we were standing by the keg so I guess it was just a matter of time before he was completely trashed. When we arrived back at my apartment, little Dustin didn't feel so cha-cha. In fact, he turned an unflattering shade of green and scooted his way into my bathroom. I sighed as I heard him throw up. He was young. I think a great sign of maturity is knowing when to say no to beverages.

Dustin slept on my bed, apologizing for his drunkenness. I told him it was OK as I secured a spot for the bucket. He passed out soon after that and I sat at my kitchen table, smoking and wondering what the point of dating was.

Dating is a crazy thing. If it's not one thing, it's another. There are all these questions: Does he like me? I don't know. OK, yes, now we spend time together. This is this, and that is that, and should we or shouldn't we do the business? I stubbed out my smoke and looked at the city lights with the confirmation that everything happens for a reason. I should enjoy this as long as it lasts.

It didn't last long. The following Friday he came over to watch a movie and make up for the drunken night. When we got back from the video store, he offered a back rub, which I never turn down, so the rub begins and it feels good, blah blah blah. Then the rub gets slower and slower; the *I'm-Falling-Asleep* kind of slower.

"Dustin!" I flip over and see that his lids are drooped and he is about to fall asleep.

"Yeah?"

"Are you sleeping?"

"Nope." [yawn.]

"You are."

"I'm not."

I gave him an uncertain look. This is not good. Here I am, the girl he's been admiring from afar for almost a year, and he's sleeping? This situation is very telling.

1.) He's sleeping with someone. If a person was horny and not getting any, no "*I had to get up at six o'clock this morning*" would get in the way of some nookie.

2.) He's gay. This is very possible. I thought he was gay the night I met him. Maybe he's led a straight lifestyle all his life, fighting the urges of gayness and I'm just a roadblock.

3.) He's stupid. Here I am being passed up for some unaccountable Z's? I've been tired. I've been so tired that I feel like my head is nailed to the pillow, but when the person I'm lying next to gives me the slide of hand, a touch in the right direction, I'm up, baby.

The next morning, I was embarrassed as hell. I couldn't believe I got the snooze. I wanted him out as soon as possible. I can put up with the difference in furniture preferences. I can put up with fast forwarding through my songs. I can even put up with the drunken night spent in my bathroom. But this was it. I couldn't do it any more. Just weeks after it had begun, it was going to end. But how would I do it? I hadn't broken up with someone in years. The big breakup I went through wasn't one person ending it, it just ended. This was different.

I could do it on the phone. We hadn't been together that long. I realize breaking up with someone on the phone is tacky if you've been with them for awhile, but this was a few weeks we're taking about. I decided it would be on the phone, what the hell. But I waited for him to call me. I gave him two days to call. If he didn't call by then, I would call him, and leave him a message saying it was over.

He called. "Haven't seen you in awhile," he said.

"I know."

"What have you been up to?"

"Oh, nothing, Everything. Somewhere in between nothing and everything."

"Are you OK?"

"Yes," I lied. "Why do you ask?"

"You just sound a little different."

"Yeah, I guess I do."

"Why?" Before I could answer him he said, "So when are we going to get together? I need to see you."

"You *need* to see me?"

"I'd like to see you."

"What for?" I asked, cautiously. Was he going to beat me to the punch?

"How about Thursday? I'll pick you up and we'll go dancing."

I thought about this. Should I end it now and spare him the effort and the five bucks to get into the bar? Maybe I should wait and see how Thursday went. If it went well, I wouldn't end it. If it went badly, then it was back to the original plan.

"OK, that sounds good."

"It's a date then," he said, with a vocal smile.

I took three hours to get ready. Tonight was a night of big decisions. If the evening went bad, the whole thing was off. In that case, I wanted to look really good so he would have a good mental picture of me when he was crying for the next several weeks. If the evening went well, then we are back on. In that case, I wanted to look good so he would look forward to the next several weeks of us continuing our budding relationship.

He called me at seven o'clock to tell me the meeting he had to go to after work was running late. "Can I just meet you there? Would that be OK?"

"That's completely fine," I said.

"Are you sure?"

"Of course."

"I'll meet you there. Can't wait to see you," he said. At this point, I'm fine. Not picking me up was no big deal. I would get a ride from one of my friends and see him there.

I got to the bar at 10:45 p.m. and started scanning the room for that little face. He wasn't on the stage like he usually was. He wasn't at the bar. Now this struck me as odd. At this point, I'm a little concerned. Did I misunderstand him? Was he going to pick me up later at my apartment and I just stood him up? No, I was sure I was doing what I was supposed to. His meeting probably ran late and he would be here within the hour.

An hour goes by. No Dustin. At this point, I'm more than concerned. It's 11:45 and he's not here. Maybe he got into a car accident. What was this meeting that he went to? A late night counseling session? Maybe he had an emotional breakdown at his shrink's office and they were locking him in a padded room as we speak. Was he bleeding all over the interior of his car? *"No,"* I decided. *"I'm not going to worry about this. Here I am, at my favorite bar with my friends. There is still a good time to be had."*

Now it's two o'clock in the morning and the night is over. As the house lights go up, I realize what's happened. I've been stood up. At this point, I'm mad.

That little bastard! Who does this duck think he's messing with? I'm not going to be treated like this. This was a date. He said *"It's a date then"*—therefore it's not a matter of him running late or getting tired and going home. He stood me up.

This is a good point to talk about boundaries; internal, moral boundaries that we all have. I can't let anyone I care about, friend or otherwise, tell me to *"fuck off"* or sincerely call me a bitch. That's a cross over the line for me. I cannot let some 21-year-old punk, who is already skating on thin ice, stand me up.

Maybe something did happen and it was physically impossible for him to make it. *"OK,"* I decided. *"If I have a message from him on my machine when I get home, I will not punish him."* He had to leave me a message of course, I mean, wasn't that common courtesy, even for Stander Uppers?

There was no message on my machine. Not only that, I did not receive a call that entire weekend. A call the next day was still in the margin of forgiveness. But a call on Monday, which is what I got, was too late. The boundary had been crossed and Dustin was on his way to Mexico with a burrito in one hand, and walking papers in the other.

"Hi there."

"Hello, Dustin."

"This is a good sign," he said.

"How's that?"

"You didn't hang up on me."

"Give me a minute," I said.

"You're mad."

"I'm not mad," I said.

"You're not?"

"No," I sighed. "Disappointed? Yes. Mad? No."

"Why are you disappointed?"

"Because you're stupid enough to ask my why I'm disappointed." This was not going to be an easy conversation for him. The nasty, cruel and spiteful core hidden deep in the inner caverns of my soul doesn't come out too often. But slowly I could feel the core inch its way out and attack through vocal cords, slicing him with a slam and slaying him with sarcasm.

"Are you going to give me a chance to explain?" he asked.

"No."

"Why not?"

"Dustin, there's nothing to talk about. It's no big deal. I'm not mad."

"You're not?"

"I already said no."

"Good. So I guess everything is OK then."

"Oh, I'm sorry. We're not seeing each other any more."

Dustin said, "We're not?"

"Did I not say that before?"

"Why?"

"You stood me up and didn't call for four days. Hi, it's over."

"I did call."

"You did?" I was surprised. "I didn't get a message from you."

"I hung up after three rings."

"Well, I have this high tech system at my apartment. It's a new thing called an answering machine. This little beep goes off and you can actually record your voice. It's really quite advanced."

"You're mad. You always get sarcastic when you're mad…"

"Dustin, don't act like we've been together for five years, it's been a few weeks. We're not exactly breaking up, because I didn't consider us boyfriend/girlfriend so what this is, is just a stopping of dates. I know it's not a big deal to you."

"Why are you saying that?" he wailed.

"If this so-called relationship meant anything to you, you would have called me Thursday and apologized for not showing up. You would have been forgiven. You could have called me Friday and you would have been forgiven. But four days later, you're not forgiven. If you were going to meet a friend at a bar and you didn't show up, you'd call the next day but you didn't even do that. Standing me up is on my list of things that I cannot accept. I'm sorry but those are the rules."

"Can we please get together and I'll explain?"

"I hate drama. I know it's a way of life of for you, but I think it's best if it just ends this way."

"You have to let me explain. Please let me see you. Meet me this afternoon."

We met that afternoon. Dustin tried to amend his ways and I admit it was kind of sweet watching him sweat. He was chain smoking and shaking. I wasn't sure if it was because of the nicotine rush or because he knew he was waist high in shit. Then he gathered up his courage and said, "I've been seeing my ex-girlfriend. I was with her that night." I decided to indulge his dramatic sense by pausing for a long time before I replied.

"I don't care if you're dating your ex."

"You don't?"

"No, in fact I'm kind of relieved."

"Why?"

"Because I thought you were getting too attached. I'm glad you're seeing her. That takes some of the pressure off of me."

"If you're not mad about her, then why aren't we going to go out any more?"

I took a sip of my vodka tonic. "I'm probably the only girl in the world who doesn't care that you're dating your ex-girlfriend, let alone encourage it. But if you're going to date two people at the same time then you have to alternate nights with us. You shouldn't have planned something with her, if you had plans with me. You need to get organized. Trust me, I know what I'm talking about." I lit a cigarette and looked at my watch.

"You and I really didn't have plans. I just said I would see you there."

"No, Child," Glamourina said quietly, "You said it was a date and you stood me up. You lied to me and told me your *meeting* was running late. Lie. Then you didn't have the courtesy to call to apologize for not showing. That's why we're not going to see each other any more."

"I want us to keep dating."

"Sorry."

"Come on! You can't turn off your feelings that fast."

"Well, Dustin, I didn't have too strong a feeling before. Therefore I can turn it off, easily."

"You can't do that."

"I just did," I said and blew a puff of smoke in his face.

That was five days ago. Depending on what day is, I change my mind. One day I'm glad it's over because he was driving me crazy. The next day, I miss that little boy face. Today, I'm not sure.

I just wish I could find someone I liked. Someone taller than me. I don't think I'm going to meet this person at the *Fruit Fly*. One of my friends told me I should go to a bar and have fun with the people I go there with, not try to meet men. In a bar, people try to impress each other by creating this illusion of who they are. Sooner or later the exterior will start to rot and you'll see what they were trying to hide in the first place. I don't know where to meet quality people. It's not like there is a place where designated jerks go and a place where saints go. If it were that easy, no one would go dancing on Thursdays.

Dan the Labrador

I may look like I'm 25, and be housed in a 25-year-old female body, but in all actuality I'm a little girl who always thinks that this one is going to be The One. Right when I think this, I should realize this is a sure sign that he isn't The One. I don't know why I haven't learned this by now. You'd think I'd be so completely jaded and fucked up by this point that I wouldn't have a positive-thinking bone in my body. It's amazing how I've dodged insanity in a most successful way. All I am is a shallow bitch; I got off easy.

As you know, I met Dan at a bar on one of my usual Thursday night romps. I called him the following Saturday and he promptly asked me out for coffee Monday at three o'clock. Come Monday at 2:30, I was a nervous wreck. I swallowed two painkillers with a chug of wine and walked down to the café.

I remembered him being cute and was sure that my extra coat of mascara fooled him into thinking that I was cute too. But he'd figure it out soon enough. I can only hide my true colors for so long before the façade starts to crack.

I arrived at the cafe before he did. I should have been late. What does this make me look like? Eager, desperate? This was bad. I started to stand up and eyeball the record store across the street (that should kill some time), but then I saw him. He was wearing a beige sweater and the leather jacket he was wearing the night I met him.

"Were you leaving?" he asked.

"No. I was going to… grab a paper but now that you're here …" We talked about random stuff for hours. He was intelligent and cute, but something was a little off. I discovered that it was me. I was turned off. He turned me off. It was so odd. Although I did find him attractive, I felt no sexual chemistry between us at all. Why was this happening? It made no sense. He was cute, he was smart, but the thought of rolling around with Dan was just so unappealing, unwanted, and unimaginable.

I continued to date him. This little lack of attraction thing had to wear off sometime. Maybe after I kissed him I'd be attracted to him. I'm a big fan of kissing. He had nice lips, he could dance, he must be a good kisser.

He was the worst kisser I've ever encountered. I realize this accusation sounds a little harsh and I openly admit to that. But just between you, me and Connie Chung, he was the worst kisser on the planet.

How hard is it to kiss someone in a desirable way? We've all had some time to prepare for a lifetime of kissing. Am I the only one who paid attention to all those kissing scenes in movies and music videos? Research! You have to do research, study for the test. I'm known to boast about my kissing ability. I have big lips, big lips for a reason I figure. Why else would I have them? Are they just supposed to sit there on my face and occasionally wrap themselves around a stray cigarette or Popsicle? I think not.

Dan's embarrassing kissing ability was such as shock to me that I thought I imagined it. I had to kiss him again. I was obsessed with discovering the truth. It was like a UFO sighting: I had seen it, I was sure I had experienced it, but I had to go back for evidence. Plus, no one believed that Dan was kissing disabled.

"He's entirely awful. I cannot believe this guy is 30 years old and somehow schlepped his way through those crucial kissing twenties."

"He can't be that bad," my friend Richard said.

"He is. It's frightening to kiss him," I said, exhaling a steady stream of smoke dramatically into the phone.

"No way."

"Richard, I'm telling you at one point he grabbed my face and licked me from chin to cheek, cheek to nose and back to the chin. He's like the hybrid mix of a man and a Labrador!"

Richard sighed into the mouthpiece. "There's no way he can be that bad. He's sexy."

"You think he's sexy."

"Sure."

"Really?" I asked quietly.

"Yes. Don't you?"

"You know, it's weird. I do think he's attractive but for some reason I'm not getting tingles in parts. There are no irrepressible urges; no roll around want or need."

"Maybe there's something wrong with you," Richard said.

"Me!" I shouted, "There's something wrong with him. Maybe he's gay or something. It's like you and me; I think you're attractive but I don't want to screw you, because you're gay."

"Thank God," Richard muttered under his breath.

"Just hear me out: You know how for some chemical reason gay men don't send Sex Me vibes to straight women? There are no pheromones within you for women, but for other men, yes."

"Do you honestly think Dan is gay?"

"Not gay. Gay-ish."

"He's Gaelic?"

"I'm not saying he's gay per se, but like a gay man he sends out a non-sexual vibe that I can't ignore. You can't avoid stuff like that."

"You're nuts," Richard said.

"Oh, no," I gasped.

"That's just my opinion."

"No, Richard… maybe he's not attracted to me. Do you think that's it?"

"He's attracted to you."

"How do you know?" I asked.

"I see the way he looks at you. He totally wants to sleep with you."

"Normally, Richard, I would take that as a compliment but right now it just depresses me."

Dan treated me wonderfully the whole four weeks we were together. I could feel that he wanted the Roll Around but I couldn't force myself to do it. He took me great places and bought me wonderfully chocolate desserts, but I still couldn't do it. There's a line between appreciation and desperation, and that line is very thin.

The kissing situation did not improve. It got worse. He continued to lick my face. I would try to act all erotic when he did it, but the maneuver just grossed me out and I couldn't even muster up a moan. Plus, I began to see a pattern with Dan. A sweater-and-leather-jacket pattern. All the time, sweater-and-jacket, sweater-and-jacket. Every time we went out it was sweater-and-jacket. I was beginning to think that I was dating that damn sweater-and-jacket, like it was part of the Full Dan Deal. I couldn't take it; the poor demonstration of kissing, the introduction of this licking thing, and the sweater-and-jacket combo pack.

He called me at two o'clock in the morning after dropping me off from one of our dates. I got into bed with all my clothes on and wondered why I didn't want or crave a sexual relationship with this man. It was beginning to be cruel, to both of us. To keep seeing him knowing that there was never going to be a physical confrontation was wrong. I knew what he wanted, what he expected, what any guy would expect after a month of dating. The cruel part for me was that I was beginning to think that I'd spent so much time hanging at the *Fruit Fly*, I was no longer attracted to men. I could very possibly be standing on the threshold of lesbianism. I don't want to be a lesbian. I didn't want to start buying sports bras and making them a major staple in my wardrobe.

I told him on the phone that night that kissing him didn't seem entirely… "natural."

"You mean you think of me as your brother or something?"

I actually thought I had more sexual attraction to my brother than this guy. "No, of course not. I feel like you want a *girlfriend* girlfriend and do things that you would do with a *girlfriend* girlfriend and I can't really provide you with those things."

"Oh."

"I really enjoy being with you and would still like to see you, but I understand if you think that's unfair."

"Uh-huh."

"OK. So I guess I'll leave you with that. Have a good night, a good sleep, whatever." What the hell was I supposed to say? I know what I was thinking: *"Shoot me, shoot me now."*

"Sweet dreams," Dan said and hung up. He was a gentleman right down to the end. Not that I knew this was the end. I honestly didn't think that I broke up with him.

"You broke up with him," Richard said.

"Are you serious?"

"You told him that it didn't feel natural to kiss him and that you weren't going to have sex with him."

"I did not say that!" I said, switching the phone to my other ear.

"Basically, yes. You said that you couldn't be his *girlfriend* girlfriend. You broke his heart and you dumped him."

"Oh my gosh, I think you're right. Shit, Richard. I thought he was going to be The One."

"Forget about it. Let's go have a drink."

"I should stay home."

"You have to go out tonight," Richard said.

"Why?"

"You have to find the next guy to write about."

I'm 17 years old and have picked out my wedding dress.

It's powder blue and super short in the front with a long train in the back. Instead of a traditional veil, I'm going to wear a pillbox hat like Jackie Kennedy with a veil that pulls down over my face in the front. I'll get married by an outdoor pool on a spring night with candles and flowers floating in the water. The reception will be immediately following, and some sort of glass structure will cover the pool so we can dance on top of the water. The music will be DJ-ed by a hip spinner from the hottest dance club in Seattle. The caterers will serve my mom's lasagna (because it's the best!) and there will be tons of pink champagne fountains everywhere… even in the bathroom. Instead of a cake, we will have chocolate cupcakes with our frosted initials on the top. My five bridesmaids will wear dusty rose, simple dresses that have mini-straps and hang straight down. They'll wear hats like mine (but not as pretty). The groomsmen will wear black tuxes with tails.

I will have met my husband in a bar, a year or so after I graduated from college. He will have long curly hair and a tattoo on his back. I will be totally funky and have a job as a writer. He will slowly move to the rhythmic sounds of Terence Trent D'Arby at our reception and say that he can't wait to go to France in the morning and take a picture of me in front of the Eiffel Tower.

When the clock strikes midnight, we'll run out of the reception with our friends and family blowing bubbles into the air and all around us. As we slide into the back of the horse-drawn carriage, he'll take my hand and say…

"I can't wait to spend our lives together."

"Me too," I'll whisper.

12. The Time and Place for Everything

My single girlfriends are always asking me where to meet good men. This question asked directly to me is very bizarre since we all are very aware there are no sport deodorants or foreign toothbrushes being stored at my place. I think women ask me this question because I am, at all times, very aware of my surroundings. I can tell you how many attractive men are in the room within the first five minutes of me entering it. Call it a useless talent.

Women are looking for some traditional place to find men like at church or the grocery store. But that's not where the treasures are. Grab your maps, ladies. The secret location is about to be revealed. The place to go for men is… wherever you are. Men are all around you. You're just looking at the wrong time of the day! You no doubt look for men at night and this is your single biggest problem. At 10 o'clock on a Saturday night, all sincere good men have already morphed into the player they think their friends want them to be. They're all together, feeding off each other's insecurities and hiding their true self under a veil of beer and exposed chest hair.

If we lived in the opposite of worlds, people would go to nightclubs in the morning and then everything would be different. Men would be fresh, rested, and more than likely alone, without the bastard influences of their friends. These Morning Men would be too fresh in the day to act like anyone else so they'd be forced to be themselves.

But alas, we do not live in Backward Land. Therefore the time and place to meet good men is anywhere on a weekday morning. I see so many cute men in transit in the mornings, I don't think I can even count that high. And I can bet that the jerk ratio of these men is very low because they obviously have jobs meaning they are somewhat responsible and mature.

On workday mornings I see them in droves: three-piece suit wearing babes, Friday casual studs in skater jackets... you name the type and I see it on the morning drive. There they are, waiting for a bus, walking down the street, riding their bikes, driving cars. You can actually get pretty specific in choosing one to your liking. The whole sex is on display.

Are you an environmentalist? Go for a guy on a bike. He's obviously conscious of the environment, which is a good indication that he's a caring person. This is a guy who would never forget your birthday. And of course there's the added bonus of him being physically fit. Riding to work, legs pumping, muscles flexing... ouch. Certain people were made for Spandex.

I see many cute bike messengers on the way in too, if you're looking for that free-spirit sort of attitude. Every bike messenger I have ever run into (not literally, of course) has been very friendly and cute in a nose-ring, tattoo-ey sort of way. Girls who are into that type of guy should try to frequent downtown latte stands in the morning, or work in an office where you have to send a lot of packages by courier. UPS or FedEx men are totally separate from the Messenger Boy. The Messenger Boy is going to be alternative, the Delivery Man is a completely different breed. I hear a lot about how FedEx guys are usually cute but I'm not attracted to anyone required to wear an issued outfit, head to toe. This covers all men in the fast food, package delivery, or postage handling industry. The exceptions are doctors in their white coats and surgeons in scrubs. And men who load trucks. I'm sorry but when I see the man who carts the beer kegs out of the truck in the morning, I do tend to sigh. I think it's the whole strong man, hard-worker sort of thing. It's easy to pretend it's me he's throwing down on the bed of a truck and loving me like a real man should.

Let's talk for just a moment about men who ride the bus. They are also environmentally aware, but in addition, they are efficient and conscious of money. I see these men waiting for buses and they tend to cover the whole map. You got the Conservatives, the Alternative Boys; your bases are covered at a bus stop. To meet these men, take a bus. Or you could do the one thing that I've always wanted to do. Drive by a bus stop and pull over to some wonderful dark-haired stranger and say, *"Hop in, Sexy."* It's just so modernly Mae West, I adore it. The guy gets in the car and there you have a wonderful story to tell your kids.

The men who walk to work are often Professional types. I have to say this is my favorite man in transit. I adore the way they stand on street corners, waiting to cross with a to-go cup in one hand, briefcase in the other. They pass in front of my car like a herd of real-life models strutting on a catwalk. This method of scoping men also provides an excellent opportunity to check out their walk. I cannot stress enough the importance of a walk. For me, it's as essential as the way they smell. If either one of these two things is unpleasant, you're looking at real danger.

Lastly, there are men in cars. It's harder to spot them as they speed by, but if you happen to be at a stop light and glance over at them and they're looking back at you, there's nothing better than that electricity you'll feel through your knee caps.

Car flirtation is a difficult thing because obviously you are captured in entirely different vessels. I consider it tacky to crank down the window and yell your phone number over the horn honks and bus burps. I haven't yet found a way to break through the barriers and obstacles of car flirtation. You should just chalk the whole thing up as a self-esteem booster. And that's something everyone needs once in awhile.

Now you know my secret time and place to meet men: during the weekday commute. Now, let me tell you some key clothing articles that will tip you off to the sort of man you want. All this is determined by who you are and what you're attracted to. But for me, there is nothing like a man in corduroy pants.

What is it about these pants that always makes me feel a heated rush? Is it the texture? The bumps, the ribs, the ridges? The heavy warmth of the fabric? It could be the way they hang off a man's body in such a way that shapes are implied but never stated. Whatever it is, I know that the gravitational pull is always stronger when a man in corduroy pants is near. These pants are my own personal cryptonite; they get me every time.

This seems to be an appropriate time to talk about the controversy of tattoos. I am very much for them. On Alternative Boy it's practically essential. But what's more cha-cha than that? A tattoo on the suit-wearing Conservative. It is a badge of his artistic, crazy side dying to break out of its reserved shell. A tattoo on the upper part of an arm? Build me a coffin, I'm dying. Just picture yourself ripping off their bold tie and crisp, white shirt only to reveal the flamed heart tattoo on their upper arm. It's the stuff of midnight fantasies and morning masturbations.

On the other hand, something that will automatically trigger my gag reflex is a man wearing a black button-up shirt with a white tie. There's something about this horrible combination that makes me queasy. I cannot find the words to even talk about this horrible Fashion Don't that continues to defend itself. Yet it lives on from generation to generation, causing a wake of disgust streaming behind it. Someone put it out of its misery!

Besides clothing, there are certain occupations that attractive men are attracted to. I'm sure if you searched every industry on the planet there would be several attractive people in every occupation. But personally, I don't think I'm ever going to be physically attracted to the guy who performs the autopsies at the morgue. I'm sure morgue workers nationwide are completely heartbroken by this declaration, but I cannot get past the idea of him and that little rib cage drill. Nothing is a bigger turnoff than bone dust.

This is totally sick but I do find myself attracted to the high school and college boys who work at car washes. I hate to say it because I feel a little like Mrs. Robinson here but it's true. Not that I would ever act on these animal instincts. But there is something so sweet about these boys. *"Come here, little boy, let me give you the education you can't get in high school."* Here are these 18- to 22-year-old boys, young enough to be fairly innocent but old enough to care how they look and actually to do 8-Minute Abs every day. By the time men reach age 32, that tape is a coaster instead of a fitness utensil.

The moral of the story is: *Timing is everything and there is a time and place for everything.* There's a time for a meaningless roll in the hay and a time for something more. But whatever it is you're looking for, it's all a matter of time before you get it. And you'll find it on a weekday morning.

13. We Had a Good Time…

I went to this one bar just because it was called the *Cha-Cha Hut*. Not only is "cha-cha" a frequent in my nonsense vocabulary, "hut" is right up there with "toasty" as one of my favorite words. "Pillowy" is another good one too, and now that I think about it, I do have a strange fondness for the words "extravaganza" and "effervescent."

I went to the *Cha-Cha* feeling relatively cha-cha, thanks to the vodka tonics I downed at some company party Scottie took me to just a few hours before. The drinks were free at Scottie's work event, which made them taste even better, hence the reason why I downed six of them in approximately two hours. (The glasses were small.) So here we are, at the *Cha-Cha* and I say to Scottie, "I'm dangerous tonight."

"What are you," he laughed, "A USA Movie of the Week?"

"For real, Scottie. Watch out! I'm bad ass."

"OK, Leather Tuscaderro, what are you planning to do?"

I signaled the waitress over. "That's just it. Plan on something unplanned to occur. I may do an Irish jig right here in the middle of the *Cha-Cha*. I may start singing Nina Simone tunes…" I looked around the bar and started laughing. "I may even go up to that retro boy who looks strangely like Chris Isaak and introduce myself."

"I dare you."

"Why are you daring me? Don't you think I would normally do that?"

"Would *you* do it? No. Would the eleven drinks you've had go up to Chris Isaak? Yes." He lifted his beer to salute me.

"I'm going to talk to him just to spite you."

"Do it," he laughed.

"I will. I'm going right now, you bastard." I looked over to the place where Chris Isaak was sitting, looking too cute to actually be single. "I'll do it, right after I finish this cigarette."

"I knew you wouldn't do it."

I stood up, crushed out the smoke and exhaled. "Watch and learn what a real woman can do." I marched myself right up to Chris Isaak and said, "Hi, Norm."

"Excuse me?"

"I just figured your name was Norm, sitting right here on the corner seat of the bar."

He laughed, "It's Brandon."

"Brandon, has anyone ever told you that you look a lot like Chris Isaak?"

"I get Elvis," he lit up a cigarette, "but not Chris Isaak."

"Young Elvis?" I asked.

He stopped for a second. "God, I hope so."

I took a sip of my drink and said, "Actually I hate it when anyone says you look like a celebrity. You never know if it's a compliment or not."

"Who do people usually say you look like?" he asked, sizing me up.

"Oh, anyone with blue eyes. Anyone who happens to be starring in a movie at the time."

"I see," he said.

"Would you like to join me and my friend?"

"Is that your friend?" Brandon asked, pointing at Scottie.

"Yes, that's my friend; just *friend*."

"Sure, I'll join you."

"Great." We were walking over to the table, when I suddenly got even braver and whispered in Chris Isaak's ear, "Jeez, you just come in for a quiet drink and some chick starts picking up on you."

"I know. I'm minding my own business and this redhead starts dropping lines."

I stopped walking. "Some redhead was picking up on you? Who was she?"

He laughed and touched my hair. "You."

We went on a date about a week later. He suggested this quiet bar downtown and I met him there. I was nervous that I wouldn't recognize him or maybe he wasn't as cute as I remembered. But he was. And he recognized me too—always a good sign.

He bought me a few drinks (which means that he knows the concept of dating: *Girls get everything for free*). Brandon was interesting and as far as I could tell, pretty close to the person I was looking for. He was quiet and shy which is a good match for someone like me. Not only did he have a full-time job and go to school, he was a contributing writer for some big magazines, and the lead singer of a band. HELLO. I always thought it would be cool to date someone who was in a band. You could go to these smoky bars, watch him perform, lean back against the bar and say, "Yes, that is my boyfriend. I have seen him naked."

We moved on to another bar that Brandon said had some severely tacky lounge singers. There were five people in the entire place. It being such a small crowd and me with a few cocktails in me, I started talking to everyone. We're all laughing and talking about how much we all hate first dates ("But this one is going pretty good," Brandon said), and I started to feel a little toasty.

Brandon walked me to my car. "I had a really good time," he said.

"So did I."

"You did?"

"Brandon, yes."

"Maybe we can do this again sometime?"

"I'd like that."

"I'll call you next week," he said. Then he leaned over and kissed me. And what a pillowy kiss it was. At this point in time, only one other person had been my kissing ideal. It was this one guy who liked to quote movies all the time. This is what he thought was funny, quoting funny movies. I'm all for recycling, but not recycled humor. I felt like every time he opened his mouth, the Library of Congress would arrest him for copyright infringement.

Kissing Brandon was a close second. It was great; more than great because he was someone I could actually see introducing to my parents. Ever since The Breakup, I never introduced my parents to the guys I was dating. Before Shitbird, I did it all the time. But maybe Brandon would meet my parents. I could see him walking up to my dad…

"Nice to meet you, sir."

"Nice to meet you," my dad would say, looking at me with a smile.

"Mom, this is Brandon."

"Brandon, our daughter has told us so much about you!"

"Oh," he would shyly laugh. "All good stuff, I hope."

"Nothing but!" I would say, as I slipped my arm around his waist.

"Well, come sit down. Brandon, we hear you're a writer, much like our own daughter here," Mom would say, giving me a little wink.

"I am a writer, I go to school, sing in a band and work full time."

"Good grief," Dad would chime in. "I guess there's no questioning that you're a hard worker."

"I pride myself on making things happen on my own; putting myself through school and all that. It's taken a long time but I'm glad that I saved up and can do this for myself."

"Mom, isn't it funny that he's a writer too?" I would say, resting my head on his shoulder.

"It *is* funny. And he looks a lot like Chris Isaak. It seems as if you two were made for each other!"

We all would laugh.

"Hey, Brandon," my dad would say, "How about you and I go out in the driveway and wash the car?"

"Great, sir, I'd love that." He'd turn to me, "Do you need your car waxed too, honey?"

"Why not?" We would all laugh again, much like Scooby Doo and his friends after they have solved a mystery.

I opened my eyes and smiled at Brandon. "OK, talk to you next week." I drove home with the biggest effervescent smile on my face that my face has seen in awhile. Could it be that this was the beginning of something worthy of something? What if I just kissed, for the first time, my new boyfriend? He was so sweet; I loved the way he would say something and act all shy but then follow it up with a bold move, like his hand on my leg. How many men have I gone out with who were either too dumb to open up their mouths, or too scared to make the first move? This was the first guy that I didn't have to encourage to kiss me goodnight. And it was a good kiss: not too long, not too short. I loved the way he moved his hand up to the back of my neck when he was kissing me.

I rolled down the car window and lit a cigarette. Could things actually be turning around for me? Could this be the last boyfriend I'd ever have? I looked in the rear-view mirror and caught myself smiling at me.

Don't be such a girl. You'll talk to him next week, you'll go out again, and that's the way things will go. One day at a time, phone messages blinking and waiting to be heard when you get home.

This could be the beginning of a dating extravaganza.

…Why Didn't You Call?

The following week the euphoria continued, filling me full of hope and excitement for what I thought was about to begin. I was as cool as could be. My friends said, "It's Wednesday already and he hasn't called. Aren't you getting nervous?"

"It's only Wednesday, there's no need to be nervous. He still has four days to call." And I remained this cool until Sunday, when I woke up with a lurch.

He didn't call.

Why didn't he call? We had this great time! He gave me the *I'll See You Again* kiss. One just can't go around kissing people like that if it's not true. It's not fair, ethical, or morally right. If you want to kiss someone just to kiss someone, make it trashy and against the wall. But placing that hand on the back of my neck and kissing me slow is not the proper procedure for a *Thanks for the Fun, But I Never Want to See You Again* smooch.

I continued to lie in bed and mull this over. I'm logical. I can sort this one out. Let me think here for a minute. Let's go over the possible reasons why he would not call:

1. He was busy. Very possible. This man leads at least five different lifestyles; calling someone when he says he will call them is probably a very difficult, yet seemingly easy task.

No, I'm going to refuse this one right off. If I'm this excited about him then there's no reason for him not to be as excited about me. Therefore, he should be excited to go out with me again. Therefore, he would call me posthaste to schedule another date. The busy excuse is not valid.

2. He lost my number. Again, very possible. People lose things all the time: phone numbers, email addresses… their minds, from trying to figure out why someone does not call when they say they're going to call.

3. He is a snake. A snake that goes to bars, sits alone looking all cute, and some idiot [insert ME here] talks to him, they go out, he gives a kiss that promises something, yet it means nothing. He gets bored and moves on to the next idiot. This is a very snappish judgment to make about someone whose last name I don't even know.

I rolled over and grabbed my cigarettes from the nightstand. With one hand resting behind my head, I put the cigarette in my mouth and lit it. Big inhale. Big exhale. What else could there be? Busy is ruled out, losing my number is still a candidate in the running, being a snake is an option. What if he has a girlfriend?

The girlfriend could have been out of town for a couple of weeks. He meets me, we go out, but now she's back. He doesn't know if he should break up with her or me; or he could have been screwing around on her just for kicks.

Maybe he's decided to break up with her and he just wants to be on his own for awhile. After all, he's been with her for five years. It would be nice to be able to pick out the movie once in awhile. Hell, I can relate to that! The way she continually checked her machine for messages and bugged him about wearing jeans to fancy restaurants was irritating. He just wants to be himself, without criticism or spare Tampax stashed in his pockets because they won't fit into that tiny purse she always carried. God, how he hated that purse. When she was nervous, she would click the snap open and shut, open and shut, until that *click-click-click* sound made his skull numb.

Why am I getting so upset about this one, misplaced phone call? Here is this great man, trying to rebuild a life of his own and here I'm bitching about a phone call. After dealing with Ms. X for so long, this man is trying to be a voyager into the unknown depths of his soul. I finished my cigarette and smiled at the way I so thoughtfully figured it all out.

Except for the fact that luminous reasons Number Two and Number Three are still hovering in the corners of my morning stupor. How did I actually turn the lack of a phone call into a John Waters movie about "a young man figuring out what he wants and making it his own"? Where did this imaginary purse snap addiction come from?

Girls are insane. Genetically insane I figure, but these men filter into our lives and speed up the hysteria. If you don't want to call, don't say that you're going to call. What are you guys trying to do? Make dating into some sort of sick game show? *"Wait and see if you'll get the call! Or take what's behind Door Number Two?"*

Men get freaked out and claim to have no idea what's going on when girls go slightly mad. You started it! True, women must learn to control their actions, but who can blame them? You never want a cat to scratch you but you know it has the ability. If you back it into a corner, starve it and don't clean out the litter box, that feline is going to go nuts and a scratch is coming; bet on it.

I rolled over and faced the wall. What should I do? I hate this situation. Much like a *Choose Your Own Adventure* Book, I never know which way to go. Should I call him? "Hi, Brandon. I haven't heard from you and wanted to make sure you still had my number."

"I threw it away."

"You what?"

"I threw it away."

"Why would you do that?"

"Listen, Kid, it's over."

"How can you say that, Brandon? I thought we had fun together."

"Think again, Innocent." *Click.*

And then depression sunk in. The heroine of our great novel hung up the phone and downed a full bottle of muscle relaxers, slipped onto the cold, hard, bathroom floor while hitting her head on the well-scrubbed toilet and focused her eyes on the ceiling. Slowly, one million tiny spiders crept from the crack in the white ceiling, making it black. She silently screamed as the spiders lowered themselves with clear, silvery strands down to her face, with her not knowing the spiders were actually hallucinations caused by the pills. She shut her eyes and began to imagine she heard that damn kid in the *Teletubbie* sun laugh his wicked laugh while she lost feeling in her left foot.

"Hi, Brandon. I haven't heard from you and wanted to make sure you still had my number."

"I'm so glad you called. There was a horrible fire in my building three days ago. Everything was destroyed, except for my cell phone. I transferred all my calls to this number. I'm sorry but your number went up in the flames."

"Brandon, that's horrible. Are you all right?"

"I'm fine. I wasn't home, I was out with my girlfriend."

"I get it..." I would start to say.

"No, I don't think you do. I was breaking up with her. I've been with her for five years; it's been going downhill forever. I've just been too scared and too stupid to end it. But when I met you, I knew that there was something better for me out there... you. I want to be with you. I want to look out from that stage, see your face and know that you're there for me."

"I will be there for you, Brandon. I'll always be there."

"Come over here, right now. I want to hold you. I want to kiss you. I want to see you naked."

I really don't want to call him. He said he would call, he should call. I guess I could call him once and hope to get the machine. That way, the ball is still in his court. But if he doesn't call back, I look like an idiot. But do I? What's idiotic about calling and saying something totally generic like *"Hi, Brandon. Just calling to say hello. My number is..."* That seems pretty safe. Assertive and not asinine. I sat up in bed and put a pillow on my lap, with the phone on top of it. I'm going to call.

But what if I lose my cool? You can go into a message-leaving situation and think it's going to go one way, and then it goes horribly wrong and you're in the land of rambles and mumblings. I often think I'm in control of my thoughts and the English language, when all of a sudden I pull a Farrah.

Women think about things over and over, stress out about meaningless shit, and you know what the man is thinking? *"Is it called Macaroni and Cheese, or Cheese and Macaroni?"* He's going to call when he wants to call and I say go on with your life in the meantime. If you really like this guy this much, take a chance, call him and say, "Do you want to go out with me again?" If he comes up with creative excuses for his endless busy schedule, then you'll know he isn't interested in you. Be thankful you don't have to waste time on this one. Every relationship is one step closer to the one you're supposed to have; the one that will last forever.

When I see him again, I won't be rude. I'll be nice and say, *"Nice to see you."* That sort of thing. He will start to think that he should've called me back, and wonder if it's too late to do so.

I never like to say I'm sorry for anything I've done. I try to behave in a way so that no apology is needed, ever. You should behave in a way you're proud of and realize that everything is temporary. If he is meant to be more than one date, he will be. If not, then this whole thing was a lesson; try to think of what you got out of it. I went up and talked to a guy I would've never talked to. That's something I've never done before. I went out with a guy who wasn't a friend of a friend, an old high school classmate or former boyfriend. Progress is being made within me and that's something to appreciate.

Glamourina made a pot of coffee, had a few more unnecessary smokes, and called him. I got the machine.

"Hi, Brandon. I haven't heard from you and wanted to make sure you still had my number…"

This was a message to feel good about. If he doesn't call, I'll be OK with that. I enjoyed meeting him, but bon voyage! Let's have some champagne and go dancing. I am bettering myself every day.

14. Male Female Email.

Recording my answering machine greeting is one of the most stressful things I encounter in life. I voluntarily put myself through this every couple of weeks because I want the message to sound fresh. There's nothing worse than calling someone on a semi-regular basis and hearing the same message over and over.

I think the answering machine greeting is very important. If the person sounds like a dud, no one is interested in leaving a message. On the other hand, when I call someone and their message is trying too hard to be interesting and creative, I want to vomit. "Leave your name, number, and one reason why life is wonderful, and I'll call you back. *Beep!*" Life is wonderful because I can hang up on your stupid machine and frustrate you with the question "I wonder who called me and left that rude message on my answering machine." *Click!*

The stressful aspect of recording a greeting is deciding which audience you want to appeal to. If you're looking for a job and a potential employer may call, you probably shouldn't have the ten-second musical interlude of Prince's *Sexy Motherfucker* before you say, "Leave a message." I hate greetings that try to be clever; like voice impersonations of Jimmy Stewart saying the person isn't at home, that sort of thing.

I always try to have a well-blended combination of sexy breathlessness and innocent girl next door (sort of Ginger the Movie Star meets Mary-Ann). I like to keep the greeting short. It sounds easy enough to record a greeting but it takes me about two hours to get it right, and even then I eventually give up because I'm sick of trying to be Marilyn Monroe. I always try to make my message appealing to the potential male caller. My mother may be the only person who leaves messages on my machine, but I'm always hoping for a mysterious man to call, and when he does, I want him to hear the voice of a seductive angel dwelling right in his very own area code.

I've never admitted this before but I occasionally save messages that men leave on my machine. I even save calls from male solicitors because I want to listen repeatedly to my name being said by a male voice. I once saved a message from some guy calling for donations to the blind simply because he said my name twice in the message, each time with a quiet raspiness that made me itchy. I've stopped dating men months before, but still have the messages they left me, like audio skeletons of our brief encounters.

I don't save messages that are too sexified because I'm not at all into phone sex. First of all, I don't understand it. I can get frustrated enough on my own, I don't need someone whispering wants to me so I get all twined up like a ball of yarn. Why would anyone want to voluntarily get worked up into some sort of fit and then just hang up the phone, only to be left with frustrations?

Oh. I get it now. I can't believe I just got that, right now. This is probably the reason why I'm single. I'm completely clueless about certain things. It's kind of like when I was 18 years old and finally realized that a tuna fish sandwich was actually made from a type of fish; it wasn't the given name of this particular sandwich. Hey, a Ruben sandwich isn't made out of Ruben is it? Give me some slack.

Nonetheless, I'm still not a good phone sex candidate. Now with all the email conversations that commonly get exchanged all day long… a new breed of sex has been born. I'm not at all into the sexual emails either.

I met this one guy at a wedding and thought that he was the bee's knees. Totally cute, good job… the only bad thing about him was that he lived in a different state. Thus began an email relationship that lasted for months.

I've heard about people who meet over the Internet and end up getting married, but I don't know how it works. The thing that's great about dating is learning about the person: how their voice sounds when they laugh out loud, not LOL. I love getting acquainted with the quiet way someone speaks when they talk about their favorite song or how they sound when they're tired. Email is read the way you want it to be read. If you think someone is being bitchy to you, no doubt you will read the words, *"Hope you had a good night last night"* as bitchy and not the polite way they were intended to be.

Out-of-State Boy began to practice his creative writing skills in the form of sexual emails that made me cyber-blush. The way he said he wanted to kiss me from head to toe was pretty sophisticated language from a person whom I'd met once five months earlier. Every day it was a new message saying how he wanted to have sex with me for hours. Once, during an Instant Message conversation, I told him I didn't want any more sex-mails.

OUT OF STATE BOY: can't wait till I see you again so I can find out if UR double jointed☺

CYBER SISTER: How you can talk to me like that is truly unbelievable, seeing as you probably can't even remember what color my eyes are.

OOS BOY: I know what color your eyes are… they are Beautiful!

CYBER SISTER: Nice dodge but no sale.

OOS BOY: come on, give me something to keep me going till I see you again!!!

CYBER SISTER: Check out the Adult section of your local video store.

OOS BOY: ☹

This email relationship went on for many months and when I finally did see him again, he was nothing at all like his virtual persona. That's why I hate email. It's too easy to pretend to be what you want to be without being anything close to it. There are enough deceitful relationships in the real world; I don't need one in the computer world.

When the emails stopped, I began to think that I was too real for the real world, thus the beginning of a new neurosis, the one where I start to think inanimate objects are looking at me. Like the computer. Here I was, typing away to Out of State Boy, looking at the screen when I started to think it was looking at me, recording me and my every keystroke.

Are we really watching TV or is it watching us? Laughing at us? Learning from us? Who really invented television anyway? Maybe aliens from outer space dropped it from the sky and we just adopted it as our own. But as we sit back and relax in the easy chair with a diet Coke and a bag of Baked Lays, the TV is taking inventory of our lives for future knowledge, thus leading to the overthrow and eventual destruction of the earth.

I've noticed lately that Leif Garrett has been on a lot of talk shows, which I'm sure is a sign that he is an alien and/or controlled by alien-like substances. He has been on TV so much that I've developed an odd obsession for him. When I was younger I liked him OK, but now that he's all rehabbed, I'm beginning to fantasize about him. The way he constantly chain smokes in all the interviews makes me have something dangerously in common with him. His devil-may-care attitude and fondness for cocktails is luring me into his faded appeal and new, nostalgic fame. I must have him.

Obviously, I'm watching way too much television. Thinking the TV is looking back at you is a pretty clear indication that your TV habits are out of whack.

But before I forget to tell you, I saw this *Biography* on Elizabeth Taylor and the narrator said, "Her sexual talents were said to be considerable." I want that to be said about me. I want it to be engraved on my headstone: *Here Lies a Woman Whose Sexual Talents Were Said to be Considerable.* Something about the way those words flow together appeal to me in such a way that sometimes they float into my head at the most inappropriate moments, just to remind me that I've stored them there.

These thoughts are too complex for the rainy Saturday morning that it is. I'm going to have a smoke. I never get tired of sitting at this kitchen table and looking over the rooftops toward Puget Sound. The ships come in and the ships go out, and with each one I think of the complexities that make me who I am and wonder if anyone will truly know me.

Being single at times is great and at times bad. The double-edged sword is that you have tons of time to discover who you are, what you like to do, and whom you want to be with. But sometimes discovering new things about yourself is something best left undiscovered. Maybe if I would have gotten married at a young age all my psychotic episodes and random thoughts could have been avoided. I'd be too busy thinking about how I'm going to take Susie to soccer practice, pick up Tommy from band rehearsal, and be home in time to make appetizers for my husband's business dinner at our duplex.

Starting into my ninth cigarette this Saturday, it dawns on me that the HOME ALONE kid got married before I did. I know something completely wrong when a damn child star is picking out china patterns and I'm smoking out some kitchen window, with my cat, Pinkie eyeing my habit like a watchful mother.

It would have been so much easier if the relationship with Shitbird would have just worked out. That's how I think of it now. I wouldn't have had to move out, move in with my old roommate only to move again into my own apartment just a few months after that. I wouldn't have to go to parties alone and tell my relatives that no; I'm not dating anyone right now. It would have totally kept with the plan that I mapped out when I was 12 years old. Everything was going according to that plan until one day he decided to have Mexican food for lunch. I could have had stretch marks by now. But I don't. And I never knew that I wanted to learn how to speak French. I never would have thought those years ago that I would go to New Mexico and dance every Thursday night until I collapsed from the heat. I would have never discovered that I like doing crafty things and meeting friends for coffee. I would have never known that I love treating myself to M&Ms for breakfast one Saturday morning a month and this was my Saturday to have them.

I stubbed out my cigarette and dumped the M&Ms on the table. On the wrapper there was some sort of contest going on, *See inside for more information*. When I turned it inside out, I read the words YOU ARE NOT A WINNER.

I laughed out loud.

15. Confession

I went on a lot of dates. I would meet random guys at random; in bars, friends of friends. But not a one held my interest for more than two dates. If you figure the usual date lasts about four hours, that's about eight hours of interest that I had in one man. That's not long. You can't even watch the entire *Thorn Birds* miniseries in that amount of time. In the amount of time it would take the average viewer to watch the damn *Thorn Birds*, I've already tossed aside some nameless man.

Sadly, the only person I continued to stay interested in was John. I had no idea why. I definitely did not see him on a regular basis. It was on a very irregular basis. But the mind is a powerful thing. I started to picture all the wonderful things I was sure would happen in the somewhat near future… him and me in France, him and me going to the movies, him and me. Period.

When you think about something every day, you can almost convince yourself it has already happened or you firmly believe it will definitely happen in the future. I knew he had a girlfriend, but was sure it was just a distraction or a simple waste of time. We had such good times when we were together; he was everything I wanted. I was such an idiot for breaking up with him in the first place. I broke up with him because he asked me to do his resume. What kind of a reason is that? He asks for my help and I get so irritated that he can't do it himself that I break up with him? What is that? But everything happens for a reason. My destiny was to waste almost three years with The Blue Eyed Devil to see what was really meant to be. John and I were meant to be.

I don't want to make it seem like I was about to boil rabbits or anything, but I thought about John all the time. It got so bad that even if I went out with a half-decent guy, I wouldn't even give him a chance because he wasn't John. No one could compare to him. I would have dreams at night about him that were so real. When I woke up, I expected to see him making breakfast.

The Logical Me knew I had to figure out a way to end this. Either get it all out and tell him that I thought I was still in love him, or call the whole thing off and get on with my so-called life. Both options were not appealing. Either way, I knew the reality of the situation would never live up to the perfection achieved in the fantasy. The Emotional Me was scared. I didn't want the sick-sick feeling to come back. I was safe here in the Land of Make Believe. I liked it here. Just little old me and my little old thoughts, swirling around me like a lovely pink, rose-scented cloud. But the only true way to get rid of a fear is to face it head-on and see who walks away, and who walks away with a severe limp.

I turned to the movies for guidance on what I should ultimately do. I figured everything usually turns out OK in the movies and even if it doesn't, there is a 60 - 40 chance it will eventually lead to something better. I know how frustrating it is to watch a movie where two characters have feelings for one another and they never say anything until the very last scene where they finally spill the beans and end up getting married. I wanted that ending: maybe not the whole marriage thing right now, but marriage potential in a few years' time. I always walk out of a movie theater and think to myself, *Why can't I be more like that girl? Not afraid to look like an idiot, and get those feelings out there in the open.* It always seems like movies give fairly OK advice; if it were crap advice, they wouldn't include it in the film.

This one decision could determine my whole life's happiness. Everything that happened to me for the rest of my life would branch off from this one decision. I could tell him I think I love him and he could say he felt the same way. Then we have greatness. The music swells, the lights get dim and I'm happy every day for the rest of my life. Everything would only get better from here. I'd have this fantastic man in my life, great in-laws, 2.5 children and a picture-perfect house, with a picture-perfect life happening inside of it.

Or, I could tell him the truth and he could say, "Buzz off." The very next day I'm carted off to a padded cell where I live out the rest of my days making leather wallets and multicolored potholders, talking to my imaginary friend I've named Mitzi. The State will decide that I need to have a lobotomy in order to be allowed to re-enter everyday society. But, then who knows? It could be that the doctor performing the operation turns out to be my future husband, thus leading to a relatively small ceremony by a pool full of floating candles and a reception featuring an all-you-can-eat sushi bar. Now that isn't so bad. It goes along nicely with my whole *meant to be/will happen* philosophy. But then there's always the other optional ending that has me back in the padded cell, surrounded by wallets, potholders and the Myth of Mitzi, eating lime flavored Jell-O and dying alone.

Deciding to tell him was like planning a party for a group of people with Turret's Syndrome. It could go well and thus lead to a fun-filled event where everyone loves the chocolate cake with cream cheese frosting. Or he could start spewing an avalanche of obscenities. I have no idea how or where I should tell him. In a bar? On the phone? Another casual lunch? I definitely think that in person is the way to go. If I call him with this little bomb, I can't see his face; therefore I have no idea how he is reacting. He could have this vocal smile but in reality he's clutching his throat and giving me the finger.

In person it was. And since he was so fond of the safe lunch, that's what it would be. What kind of food should I eat? I think no pasta. I could be right in the middle of my declaration; then I suck up a noodle drenched in red sauce and it slaps me alongside the face. Then I'm sitting there like a two-year-old with a noodle streak on my face and sauce in my hair. That is no charmer. Japanese? A little too manual. No burgers or sandwiches, I'm risking a green thing stuck right in between my two front teeth. I think salads are safe (with the dressing on the side, mind you) or some sort of shellfish that you can use with that little fork. Except that the little fork makes you look like you have severe man hands. The size of that fork makes the whole shellfish experience into some sort of odd optical illusion; your hands are suddenly magnified to twice their normal size and you look like a bad drag queen. I strive to appear small and meek at all times. On the other hand it could be perceived as cute… the little woman with the little fork. A normal size fork is just way too big for my delicate hand bones. I have to have a Barbie fork in order to function.

There was a restaurant right next to my office that had a wide variety of safe foods. And it had a good view too, therefore giving me a good excuse to avert my eyes. If we go to some place like Denny's, the only visual diversions are asphalt, traffic and the occasional sobbing street person. No one thinks that's interesting for more than 15 seconds. But a good view on the water, there's a world of possibilities. A ferry coming in, seagulls, boats… a myriad of distractions to choose from.

As far as clothing, I think no short skirts. Too obvious. A nice v-neck sweater is acceptable paired with dark colored, semi-fitting pants. That will show him just a little of what is on the menu without serving him from the hootchie buffet.

The final decision was the hardest. What was I going to say? What words do you use to express that you *may* still have feelings for a man you haven't dated in four years? I mean, how do you tell someone something like this when you know chances are that he will not reciprocate? It's a destiny of disaster. I am asking for pain. He has a girlfriend. If he felt something for me he would have dumped her by now. But there is the very real possibility that he doesn't realize I am feeling more than friendly toward him. That could change everything.

Who am I kidding? Being with me would mean a major lifestyle change for him. Maybe I'm just missing the past and want to recapture a bit of what was. Maybe what was isn't possible any more.

But could I live my life with a maybe? I hate the maybe. A definite Yes, a definite No, now that was the way to live a life. No gray areas, no safety zones. Live life in the fast lane, say what you feel when you feel it. Take a chance, life is a gamble, take a hit, live on the edge, live each day as if it were your last. That's got to be a good way to live. It's the Rambo approach to life. And I want to be Rambo. Who wouldn't want to be? With that whole headband thing? Please. It's high fashion and fierce.

In choosing what exactly to say, I decided I must be clever but honest. I'm going to write it all down. That way I can edit it to say exactly what I mean to say, instead of just blurting out like a high school girl, "I like you!" Writing it down was a good idea for more than one reason. I can take the dumb stuff out, leave a couple of things open for his interpretation, or I can wimp out at the last minute and keep the confession trapped in my leopard print bag and simply enjoy a pleasant seafood salad.

The obvious drawback to the letter idea was that I wouldn't see his reaction or give him an opportunity to reply. But I don't want him to reply. This was it for me and I had to end it. If it was going to be nothing it was nothing, if it was going to be something, then… you get the idea. I needed to end this stupidity that I've been carrying around with me for years. Even when I was living with The Waste of Time I thought about John and wondered what it would be like to be a couple again. I needed a mental enema and this was it. This is the very last time I will see him. No more teasing lunches, no more occasional phone calls. I need closure and damn it, I am closing the door.

But now that I think about it, writing this grown up version of a love letter is pretty high school too. What am I doing here? Am I going to slip it to him in the middle of math class? Ask my best friend JJ to stick it in his locker? I'm an idiot. A spineless, freak-out idiot that is still resorting to high school behavior when I am in my mid-twenties and supposed to be mature. Pathetic.

I reflected back on the idea that I didn't really like him, but the *idea of him*. That's all very possible. More than possible, probable. I was just lonely. I had been on my own for awhile; maybe I just wanted someone with a pulse. It's so easy to fall back in love with old boyfriends. They're a comfortable bed to sleep in. It's not scary when you're with them, it's easy. There is no risk; they already know that you hate peanut butter and adore free samples.

Suddenly, it didn't matter what he said. I was sure it would be bad. After I give him the letter, I will never call him again. This was the end. He and me weren't meant to be. It would've happened by now if it was meant to be, I'm sure of it. This is the big kickoff to the rest of my life. If I happen to meet him somewhere down the road, then that's the way God or fate or whoever planned it to happen. Who am I to question it? A mere mortal! A stupid pseudo-adult woman who has been letting her college crush crush her. I'm through. I'm washing my hands of the whole thing and allowing myself to be alone, in the truest sense of the word. In order to meet the one that is The One, I need to be completely free and clear. Until I do that, I will continue to pine away for this guy for the rest of my life and watch him marry this dumb girl who has been unaware of my existence the whole time.

I sat down and began to write. It took me five hours to get it exactly right. When I was done I put it in my bag and called him. We're going to meet next Wednesday for lunch. This is it. I just hope that I will have the nerve to pass him the note without suffering a massive stroke.

John,

I have these moral codes that I try to live my life by: *Say what you feel when you feel it*, and *Do what you think is right*. I tell this to people who come to me for advice. I feel a little like Yoda or Kermit the Frog when I say it, but I honestly think it's very wise.

I've struggled with something, a question, for years now. An inner battle between my head and heart not knowing what to do. Do I say something now, take the chance of not speaking to you again after I say it, or should I shut my mouth, not say a word, and keep you in my life?

I made a list of pros and cons. I've thought about this list a lot, talked about it with my friends, and finally, come to a decision. I don't see you too often so I guess not having you in my life isn't too devastating. I decided it was a small price to pay for some mental and emotional purging.

I was with someone for years and honestly wanted to marry Him. But for some reason, in the back of my head, in the back of my heart, I thought about you.

I think about you now. I have dreams about you that are so real… they're not especially sexual, they're just about you. I can never remember what the dreams are once I wake up, but I know that I've seen your face.

I don't regret the fact that you and I broke up. I had to experience things, good and bad. And looking back, I wouldn't have changed a second of the past four or five years. I needed it to happen, it was meant to happen, and it did.

I don't want to interrupt your relationship, but I couldn't sit back and continue with these occasional lunches without telling you that I think I love you. I don't expect this to be a big shock or create a huge difference in your life. But if I were in a relationship as you are, I would want you to tell me how you felt about me. I would want you to be honest. I think you can be in love with someone and still having feelings of love for someone else. I know this because I was in love with someone yet loved you at the same time.

Maybe I'm being ridiculous. I mean, how can I possibly say this four years after we broke up? How can I think this about someone I haven't seen in eight months? And when I do see you, it's not like we have this ultra-romantic date or something, we have lunch and talk like old college friends.

Sometimes I think I'm confused. Maybe I just think I love you because I want someone much like you. I could be over-indulging in the details of what it was like when I was with you. It's all very possible my romantic vision has allowed these details to get a little fuzzy.

There are so many movies and TV shows about a girl who loves this guy who's now in another relationship or married or something. Somehow this tension is enough to carry the movie through two hours, or the series through six years of one person finally getting the nerve to say something, but then the phone rings or some convenient distraction pops up that prevents the truth from coming out. It's all very cute and entertaining to watch, but I don't want to live it.

I have no idea how you feel about me, or should I say, how you feel about me now after reading this letter. I'm sorry that I felt that I had to do this, but this whole thing was a setup. I wanted to see you, have lunch, and, if I was brave enough, slip you this letter as you walked away.

I think I know what will happen next. You'll go on as you think you should, but you deserved to know. Most people have someone they will always love and could have been very happy with. You are this person to me.

Well, I guess I followed my moral codes. I didn't tell you how I felt when I felt it (I'm about four years too late) but I had to let you know, and do what I thought was right.

Now I can feel good about this and move on. I'm sorry I was never really able just to be your friend. I always wanted the John that I had when I had him. I'm glad things happened like they happened. I want your life to be what you want it to be. But I think I love you, John. I'm shaking as I write this because I think I'm crazy for saying it, but here I am, saying it in spite of it all.

I always hate drama and here this letter sounds like Chapter 17 of a Harlequin Romance novel. I'm sorry. If I could have thought of an easier way to tell you, I would've done it that way.

I gave John the letter. I was debating whether or not I should give it to him because when I saw him, I didn't feel like I had in the past. I wasn't nervous, shaking or freaking out like I usually do. I think it was because I had written the letter a few days before and once I had those feelings on paper, I didn't have to feel them anymore. It was as if I released them somehow; gave them away.

He was different. He wasn't the John I had known and loved. He had become *her* version of John. It wasn't so much because he was wearing a tie and had a pager, it was everything. He wasn't as crazy as I remember him to be. I was sitting there in the restaurant, looking at him over my seafood salad, and I saw someone who looked a lot like my John, sounded a lot like my John, but it wasn't my John.

He had become… boring. He was very corporate. I have to believe that you can be corporate and still be crazy. You don't have to trade in your funny bone for a cellular phone.

Another thing that bothered me was the way he always mentioned her, as if to remind me that he was taken. I didn't need to be reminded. Maybe he was reminding himself. I was in a serious relationship at one point in my life and still acted alive. I trusted myself to have a lunch date with someone and not want to roll around in the coat check room with them.

I asked him what he did on the weekends: did he still like to play basketball or go out drinking with his friends? His new idea of fun was going out for pizza on a Friday night and possibly (if he was feeling wild) drinking a pitcher of beer. I swear, all he thought about was acting like an adult. He lost his sense of whimsy. He had become someone that I wasn't; someone that I never wanted to become. I think there's nothing wrong with wanting to do something immature and stupid once in a while, like eating dinner in a bowling alley or going on a roller coaster. Childish or not, it's just something that should be done once in a while. I'm all for being an adult, but if being an adult is all finances and couples' card games, then I don't want to be one. I'm going to start running in the opposite direction.

I gave John the letter as he walked me back to my office. I figured I had put so much thought into it, I should hand it over. At least he would know how I felt about him for the past four years. And as I watched him walk to his car, I knew it would be the last time I would see him. When he rounded the corner, he was gone. He was really gone.

The hard part came later that night, when I discovered that I was alone in my head and in my heart. Even when I wasn't actually dating anyone, I still had John in my mind. I still had someone to get excited about, someone to motivate me out of bed to go jogging on the weekends. *"I have to look good so when I see him"*… that sort of thing. Now, I'm not dating Dustin or Dan, and I don't have anyone on the back burner. I don't have a crush on anyone. It's just me.

I don't like it.

Now it's the day after and I still don't like it. I'm almost tempted to call Dustin and have him over for a romp or something. I know I don't want that, but I don't want what I have either, which is nothing. Who wants nothing? You always want something.

I called Scottie last night and told him that John was no more. Scottie said it was a good thing, now I could go on to something and someone else. He said that it would be no time at all until I was excited about someone new. I know he's right. I'm experienced enough to know that there's always another one on the way in. But that doesn't make The Now any easier. And Scottie, even as he's relaying these words of wisdom, he's sitting next to his current love interest. Saying there will be someone else is easy when the revolving door of relationships in *your* life is always motion.

Sometimes it's tiring being me. Having people ask, *"Are you seeing anyone right now?"* or *"Who's the latest?"* Not only is it tiring, it's pathetic. I hate being the one with these two-week episodes, entertaining my committed couple friends as they laugh at me with other people's arms around them. I don't want to be a sideshow freak anymore.

They laugh when I tell them I dated this one guy who only wore one prescription contact lens, just to give him "an edge." Ha-ha, it's funny when it doesn't happen to you, but when some idiot tells you this as he's driving you home it's a little scary! Mock the girl who eats cold Mini-Raviolis right out of the can for dinner because why cook? *It's only me!*

I feel like I'm the only one in the world who goes through this. Like I'm living this movie that shouldn't be a movie at all because it's so low budget and badly made, no one would pay to see it.

Yet even after saying all this, I still tell myself there's a chance I could end up with a movie star. Here these stupid married friends of mine settled early before they knew who they were or what they would become. I'll soon get discovered as the next Cameron Diaz and a Baldwin will beg me to marry him.

Or, maybe I'll end up with some old rich guy. I wouldn't have sex with him; he'd just want me around as a companion. I'd be nice to him, I like old people. He'll say I'm sweet and leave all his millions to me instead of the first wife he had for 26 years. Look who's laughing now, you married bastards!

But then again, maybe I'll grow old and die alone. No children, no stories that anyone wants to hear because all my friends are out with their couple friends, taking cruises to the Bahamas in groups of four and throwing non-alcoholic Christmas parties at their country-style suburban homes. And when I'm thirty-five and still unmarried, I'll run into two bitches I went to high school with. They'll be nice to my face, but when I leave they'll say, "I can't believe she never married."

"I know, she's not that ugly."

"Here she is, well into her thirties, not completely ugly, but alone. I hear she still lives in an apartment with a cat or something…"

"Eating frosting right from the plastic tub it comes in…"

"Green-mask facials every night with the hope that somehow it will make her look good enough for some man to actually marry her…"

"Chain smoking out the kitchen window…"

"Answering personal ads and placing ones of her own that say she's a rich tight-body with an insatiable appetite for sex…"

[Insert catty laughter here.]

"Going to movies by herself…"

"Cutting out pictures of wedding dresses in bridal magazines, hoping one day she'll be in the market to buy one…"

"It's sad isn't it?"

"Very."

In a way, I want to be married and go out for pizza on a Friday night. But in another way, I always want to go dancing on Thursdays. I've been trying to tell myself all day that everything happens for a reason. That people who marry young are settling. That truly interesting people never marry before the age of forty. That things that do not kill us make us stronger. And then I think, *"Fuck it."* I just want someone to call me Honey. It can't be too bad to be *Mrs. Somebody* can it?

I want to feel the way I did when I was seven years old. One of my favorite memories that I have so far in life is one that happened when I was seven. My brother and I were asleep in our bedrooms when my dad came home really late from work. I could hear the garage door open and my mom's voice greet him when he came up the stairs. I heard my dad talking and strained to hear what he was saying, but all I could hear was the gentle rumble of his low voice. He came down the hallway and stood so he could see into both our rooms.

"You kids asleep?"

"Yes!" I yelled (I always fell for that one).

"You want to go get some pizza?"

"Yes!" my brother and I yelled. I flung my covers off and started jumping up and down on the bed. My dad came in and turned on the light.

"Dad, I've got to change out of my jammies!" I said as he lifted me off the bed.

"Oh, just wear what you have on," he said, helping me put my coat on.

So, I went to the pizza place just like that. My brother wore his two-piece flannels and I wore my long, short-sleeved red and white checkered nightie, with a big white flower sewn right in the middle of the collar. I felt so wonderful sitting there in the crocheted slippers my grandma made me, swinging my legs, with a pizza slice in one hand, a Coke as big as my head in the other. I thought my dad was so cool. I felt like I was wearing a funny secret that no one knew because I had my coat on over it. It was probably nine o'clock at night, but I remember thinking it was much later and that the pizza guy probably had to open the restaurant in the middle of the night just for us. It was at least two in the morning! And I was wide-awake and eating pizza and drinking caffeinated sugar water!

I don't think I've experienced joy to that extreme since then. I don't know if I ever will. But I want to try. I will try my hardest to find someone who can make me feel like I did when I was seven, eating pizza in my nightie. I need someone who is enough like me to not want to bug me with all his differences. I'd like someone different enough but not so much that it irritates me. I need a man crazy enough to keep me interested, sane enough to give me a positive outlook, and smart enough not to make me feel ignorant.

Is that even possible? Is it too much to ask? Somebody tell me.

I guess this is what you would call a medium strength depression. I'm not suicidal but at the same time, I'm trying to figure out what it is that I have to live for. I'm sick of thinking about men; they're all I ever think about. I have no tangible life.

I got a new car three days ago so that's a good thing. That could actually be some sort of sign. Like maybe I should take this shiny new car and slam it into the side of a lovely brick building. But it has those damn safety air bags. Those aren't going to do me any favors. I'm asking for a face full of that powdery white stuff they pack those things in. Plus, that would really hurt. A huge latex bag popping me in the face. That's not going to kill me. A stiff neck maybe, but if I'm looking for sincere, hard-core death, this new car is not going to be the vehicle to do it in.

The other night, I tried lying in bed and holding my breath. *Death by Suffocation* had some sort of quiet dignity to it. And then there was the added amenity of mystery. No one would be able to explain my certain death and I would be this dead legacy, *The Girl Who Died without a Reason*; *The Girl Who Ran out of Breath*. I can almost see the well-produced story running on *Dateline* with a special video opening and this ultra dramatic theme music, complete with an audio sample of a woman getting the wind knocked out of her. This was all very appealing.

But I was so damn tired that I fell asleep and automatically started breathing again. Damn this body! This body with its own mind and stupid natural instincts! Everyone is against me, even the very pores of my own flesh! These bastard bones are too tough to break. I'm going to stop intake of dairy products of any kind, just to spite them. Down with cheese!

It's all very possible that death is not the answer. And when I really think about it, I don't want to die. If you ask me, people in comas are really getting a good deal. Obviously, time off work is the first plus. Secondly, you'd have people waiting on you hand and foot. Reading to you, singing to you, hell, you don't even need the strength to lift fork to mouth. They pump that food right in through your veins! Maybe I'd have a near-death experience, complete with a bright light, and I'd float around the room, looking down at all my relatives who wish they would have bought me the laptop computer I wanted last Christmas. Now they won't be laughing when they remember that I also wanted violin lessons.

If I could do something to myself to guarantee a coma, I would do it toot suite. But since it is not a guaranteed sort of thing, I'm just going to be a little more careless. I'm going to stop taking vitamins. No more exercise. Increase smoking by at least seven cigarettes a day. That should scrape a few days off this solo, mundane life.

I will drive my new car without wearing a seat belt. Who cares if I get sideswiped off a bridge? That way, I'm sure to die, or at least fall into a well-deserved coma. There's always a bad rap that goes along with actually doing the whole suicide thing. I don't want people talking trash about me when I'm dead in the ground.

I want people to say, "She was fabulous. It's a shame she died so young, before she had a chance to fall in love and get married. Why was she never married? All of her friends were married. What's with her, never being married! Her sexual talents were said to be considerable. She could have had two children by the time she died and yet, the fields were barren. Her poor parents will never have a grandchild. She was obviously very cold and selfish… depriving her parents of a grandchild. Instead choosing to live alone with a cat. Who was this loser? She should have never been born!"

All right, people! I'm dead, by accident no less, and you're still talking trash about me! Does *Rest in Peace* mean nothing to you? The RIP doesn't stand for *"RIP me a new one."* Let me be! I'm dead! You think that would be enough but, no! You have to stand over my grave and rub it in. Rub in the fact that I was as alone in my life on earth as I am in the Afterlife. And what's with those tacky carnations? I hate carnations. Nothing says *"I'm a big cheapo"* better than a bunch of stupid carnations. I'm making this rule now, No Carnations at my Funeral.

So here I am, dead in a pine box stuffed beneath six feet of over-fertilized dirt where still grass refuses to grow. This body is slowly deteriorating. Guess that doesn't matter now, not that it ever did. My body has always been a walking nightmare. I'm a blob, a thing, a clump of displaced DNA and a bad overbite. I'm no woman. I'm a caricature of a woman. All lips and hips, that's what I am... was.

And let's just talk about my body. I've been eating one meal a day for the past two weeks and I swear it looks like I'm eating twice as much. I know I should be exercising more, but with work and all the creative excuses I manage to come up with, I don't usually get around to it. Right now, I suppose I should go for a walk or a jog or something, but I just want to chain smoke and fall asleep face down on the carpet.

I've got to be the most unattractive person in the world. With clothes on, I'm not too bad. I can fit into a doorway without turning sideways and still only take up one seat in the theater. But I have the body of an old woman. I am an eighty-year-old woman that has had one too many Danishes and over-indulged in the Bridge Mix.

I don't know why I feel like this. Everything is basically OK right now. I have no huge complaints. Just huge legs and arms. I have man arms. If you were surgically to remove my arm from my body, lay it on a table and ask someone to identify if it was the arm of a man or a woman, they would say it was a man's. That's me, all big veins and sausage fingers.

I feel like I am the ugliest girl in the world. My features are so exaggerated and grotesque. I have a huge nose, huge mouth, huge eyes. I know I look female, but my face is all stretched out; like when you take Barbie's perfect pink face and bend it in half.

I don't have the desire to do anything at all. I don't want to go anywhere, but I don't want to sit here. I don't want to eat anything, yet I'm sure I could eat four gallons of ice cream. I'd like to go out somewhere with someone and do something, but I don't have the energy to move. And today is really a beautiful, sunny day. I should be out somewhere, doing something. Everyone in the world is enjoying the weather, being happy, doing happy things. Yet there is no happiness in me.

Maybe I should go for a drive. But where would I go? I don't want to see anyone. I don't want anyone to see me. And driving without purpose is so frustrating. All I can do is sit here and twist my hair. This will probably guarantee me early hair loss in various spots around my head, but I don't give a shit. I should be fat and bald, a cross between male and female.

There's no point in trying to sort this all out now. There's no way to get out of this emotional bog except to pass directly through it. I'm going to chain smoke and lie on the floor. There's nothing better to do. Except maybe to buy some carnations.

YOU'RE INVITED TO MY FUNERAL. [1:12 am]

I'm asking you now, check your schedule, are you free? To attend the event centered solely around me? You'll have to wear a hat and cry quite a lot, and dress all in black even if it is hot... I suggest you come early, no stragglers, no tardies... because this will be a *fabulous* party! I've the music all planned and verses to be read, I would have a great time... too bad I'll be dead, BUT DON'T LET THAT STOP YOU from dancing till dawn, and eat all the cheese and freshly chilled prawns.... get as drunk as you want and hit on my cousin, have a cigarette on me, hell, why not a dozen? Sing loud, break the dishes, and laugh till it hurts, in a few hours I'll be covered by dirt... BUT DON'T LET THIS HINDER a good time to be had! Macarana my mother, double dip my dad! Make loud obscene noises and propose a toast, to the reason you're there, the recent deceased host. Please mention my humor and make up sweet lies, say I was beautiful and a 4 was my size, say I was an angel and you miss my face, and forever you'll love me (if that is the case). Look in the coffin and touch my hair, even though you'll see me I won't really be there, I'll be watching from a far away corner, cursing you for not being an organ donor... but please try to come, it's you I want to see, and please don't forget to RSVP.

16. A Side of Fries and a Large Depression

I'm on a downward spiral to a place I know I don't want to be. There's no denying I'm there.

I had the worst day. I hate my job. I had my car towed to the shop today due to a recent bout of car trouble. Of course the tow truck was an hour late making me late to start on the foot trodden trek to work. Some yahoo was yelling the wrong name at me as I walked: "Beth! Hey, Beth!" That made me feel weird. Here I am walking around thinking I'm so distinctive when I'm easily mistaken for some chick named Beth. Who is this Beth? And who does she think she is, trying to be all me? Do I have a twin in the same city? That thought really freaks me out because she's probably oddly ugly… you know, her ugliness isn't all that blatant. But her nose is just a little too crooked and the bump on her forehead is a little too obvious to be a cute character flaw. Is she living a life parallel to mine? Does she sit at home on a Saturday night eating ice cream in a hot bath? Is one of her goals in life to be able to wear a sleeveless shirt without having people say, *"That girl should really not be wearing a sleeveless shirt"*?

I've truly given up on John. I thought he might call saying that he read the letter, but no. I think he's enjoying this. Here I'm the one who broke up with him and that obviously hurt him because every time I saw him for lunch he brought up how I dumped him. I'm always willing to play the game for a little while but now, I'm just too tired. He's in control and he likes that. I don't hate him for that. Hell, I don't even blame him. I would probably do it too. But enough is enough. I'm through. I'm packing up all my affections and really, really moving on.

I was about to stow the whole Bryan thing too. I called him a couple of weeks ago and he wasn't calling me back. I would write to him and again, nothing. Then last night he called me. It was a good and a bad thing. He is always so sweet. He said he missed me, that he thought about me. I just sat there listening to his words and his accent and felt sad. I know he isn't the one for me. He's not even the one for me right now. He is always so optimistic; I wonder where he gets that. I guess not enough bad things have happened in his life yet to make him jaded like me. He said that when I'm in this *"dark place in myself"* that I should remember he cares about me, all the way over on the other side of the world. Yeah, whatever.

This has not been a good year for me. I love my friends. I love my family. But now as the year draws to a close, I see the goods weighing up against the bads and the bads are entwining themselves to become this huge rope dangling over my head like a noose. It's just a matter of time before I slip my head in and end it.

I've decided not to speak for the rest of the evening. No talking on the phone, no talking to Pinkie the Cat; I'm going to live like a nun for the night. A nun that chain-smokes and wears a bright green facemask, because that's what I have on my face right now. I should at least attempt to have a good complexion. Who knew that acne isn't just for the pubescent. It's always so flattering to look into the mirror and see a big old pimple on your chin when you're well into your twenties. You feel so mature. I might as well move back in with my parents and put my WHAM! poster back up on the wall.

I don't know what the answer is or how I can force myself to be happy. I try to lie to myself and think that everything is going to be OK… nothing can stay this bad for this long. But I can't lie to myself. I don't know what to do next.

I could take a course on breathing. I read that everything is linked to how you breathe, your health, success, how much sex you get. I forget that I'm breathing at all. It's like blinking, once you realize you're doing it, it's almost painful and you can't keep up. Pretty soon you're over-blinking and hyperventilating at the same time, all in the name of good health. It's not worth it. I'd rather not know how many times I blink in one minute and keep breathing shallowly for the rest of my life. I don't care if bad breathing shaves a few years off the end of my time on this planet. I figure that's when you want time to be brief, when you're old and stuck in a pee-smelling retirement home. I want to check out as soon as possible. There are too many things in this world that annoy me to want to hang around longer than 80 or 90 years anyway.

Like the *Peanuts* theme song. Have you ever stopped and really listened to the *Peanuts* theme song? The one that the cruel people at CBS make us listen to every Christmas? Just thinking about it now, I can picture those stupid cartoon kids dancing around, and some of them on the piano. When I hear that song I want to strangle all of those kids, but especially that kid with the mangy blanket. And that Pig Pen kid, what's his story? There's no excuse for bad hygiene. Everything in the world today is antibacterial and sealed with a sanitized banner.

The *Peanuts* song breeds pure evil. You may think it's a cheerful, happy song, but let me tell you it's not. It's subliminal music. I'm sure this song is the reason I fight these severe bouts of depression. When I'm dead I'll be the center of this huge autopsy study and after years of searching for an answer to my incredible mental and emotional demise, the doctors will discover all my pain was due to listening to the *Peanuts* theme song every Christmas.

Another thing that bugs the hell out of me is seeing television commercials that feature food that talks. Who, in the advertising world, thinks that after I see an M&M talking to Halle Berry I will have the urge to eat one? And why would I want to ram a raisin down my throat after seeing one sing with back-up dancers? Maybe I would want to ram one in my eye, but I'm not going to eat one. In fact, seeing food that sings and dances make me not want to eat it because it's so great at doing the electric slide, that I like it now; I want it to be my friend. That food is more talented than I am. I admire the food. I want the raisin to take me dancing. If it can sing and dance, I'm sure it would be a great date to take to parties. It would probably tell jokes to all my friends and make people like me more.

One very sick thing I saw involving food with human characteristics was at the movie theater. The intent of the ad was to get you to buy some popcorn from the over-priced Snack Bar just within sniffing range. Here's this girl Pepsi that's on a date with a male popcorn box. The Pepsi leans over and whispers to the popcorn box that she wants a snack. The box goes into the lobby and gets the Pepsi a Pepsi. He brings it back to her and she sucks on this thing like there's no tomorrow. I'm sitting there, watching this scene, realizing how very cannibalistic it is. The Pepsi is gulping down the Pepsi and loving every minute of it. She's a freak! I know not one person in this movie theater is thinking, *"Ooh, now that I've seen a Pepsi drink a Pepsi, I want a Pepsi!"* In fact, I would think people would run, screaming. I'm appalled at this method of grossing people out so much, that they might have pity on the Pepsi and buy a Pepsi. *"It's better to have a person drink the Pepsi than another Pepsi!"* I feel like I should write a letter to someone about this, but I don't know where to send it. It's not like there's a Pepsi Protection Agency or something.

I wonder what kind of dancing food I would be—I mean if I had to be dancing food. I think I would be an ice cream scoop in a sugar cone. It's got a good shape, long "legs," nice round head. It's sweet, sinful, good in the middle of the night. But do I want to be something fattening?

I do know for sure what cartoon character I would be. Jem. People don't think of Jem because she's not exactly a superhero. People forget Jem because she was a short-lived, trendy cartoon in the 80s. Characters that have real reputations are cartoons that have been around for at least ten years, which is too bad. Jem was a real gem.

She was pretty, for starters. Secondly, she was in an all-girl band (very Go-Go's). Any cartoon that had a band involved in any way was cool in my eyes. Jem had really neat earrings that allowed her to talk directly to her magical friend that made holograms. Cool, yet high-tech. But the thing that made Jem really cool was that she was outrageous. Truly, truly, truly outrageous.

I'm not sure but I think she had a really cute boyfriend named Eric. She was always fighting the good fight with the anti-Jem band, the Misfits. And, guaranteed in every episode, there was an honest to God rock video featuring either Jem or the Misfits. The Misfits were a little more edgy then Jem; they were very Cyndi Lauper meets Joan Jett. Jem was a little more innocent Madonna combined with the Go-Go's, making it very hard for me to decide which band I liked better. It almost makes me sad to look back and remember a time when the most stress I would experience in a day was deciding who to vote for on those Battle of the Bands episodes.

I wish I could be Jem right now. Whenever something was bad or I wanted to change it, I'd just twist my earring and a little hologram would pop out and everyone would see things the way I want to see them. I try to be all Buddhist and chant and meditate, but all I really want to be is Jem. I want to have a cute boyfriend and to be in an all-girl band. I want to live in a cool house with no obvious means of employment. I want to end every day with a laugh over some stupid joke with all of my well-dressed friends.

I'm going to buy some new earrings tomorrow. At this point, anything is possible. And I'll try anything possible that could possibly lead me to a Jem-like lifestyle.

I've decided to spend the entire night in the bathtub. I think more people should do that. I talk on the phone in the bath. Lift my arm weights in the bath. Read a book on astrology in the bath. One of these days I'm going to sleep in the bathtub. It's just something I feel I have to do. I don't think you can successfully go through life without sleeping in a bathtub. You haven't truly lived.

I've become a pseudo-bulimic. The only thing that I don't do is throw up. I should probably take the next step and out all the extra calories, but I hate to throw up. The gag reflex is not my best reflex. I feel throwing up should be avoided at all costs. I would rather sleep on the cold bathroom floor with a washcloth as my blanket than vomit, feel better, and go back to bed.

I need to stop smoking. I've upped my usual one pack a week to a little over a pack a week, which is not good. I need to stop using so much salt. I'm a saltaholic. I salt everything except ice cream. All this salt and cigarettes cannot be good for the arteries.

I got a Christmas card from a girl I went to high school with. She's the same age as me. She has four kids. FOUR kids. What do I have? A cat, a tiny apartment, and an unhealthy addiction to salt. I feel like I have something wrong with me. Everyone else is on the right track, and somewhere along the line I got distracted. I don't know what I'm supposed to be doing. Aren't I too young to have kids, let alone four of them?

I've decided to get plastic surgery. It's gross though, trusting someone to rip off my face, scrape off some unnecessary nose cartilage, and then sew everything back into some desirable pattern. I just can't think about that part. I need to concentrate on the After part, not the During. If someone would just put a little staple over my right eye to revive my sagging lid, I'm sure I would have no problem meeting my future husband.

I feel like I need to vent something. What that is exactly I don't know. Just another day spent waiting for something to happen. But when will that thing that I don't know what will happen, happen? Forget it. Sometimes people shouldn't try to vent with wit or meaning.

God, I need a cigarette and some potato chips.

17. No More I Love You's

No one has said that they love me in almost two years. Except for my mother.

I've heard I Love You's from friends. But as far as the serious I Love You, said by a man that I am currently dating, then no. No one has told me they love me in almost two years. I miss that. I want that.

One time, during a roll-around with one of the more recent guys, I mouthed the words *I Love You* over his shoulder. But I didn't love him. I just wanted to see if my lips could still form the words. Then I wondered what it would sound like to hear my name followed by those three words in return. It would sound so foreign, like Chinese Pig Latin. My name would just seem to fall apart, each letter rolling off the tongue and falling to the ground, consonant by vowel, shattering into a million pieces.

When I was in my relationship with The Waste of Time, I was big time into the I Love You's. And there are about a million different kinds of I Love You's. There are so many different kinds of love, love for a sweater, a song, an aunt, there *have* to be different ways to say it to accommodate the various lovings.

My favorite I Love You is the tired, middle-of-the-night I Love You. It would just seep out and into the air without a thought. I love sleeping with someone I love. I mean for real, sleeping. When we were together, I insisted that He have at least one part of his body touching me at all times: an arm, a leg, what have you. At three o'clock in the morning, when He would change positions or move a leg, He would say, in the most tired, sleepy of voices, "I Love You, sweetie." It melted my heart, and I knew it was a real I Love You. It was like breathing, a natural thing He did without even thinking. In the morning I would tell Him what

He said in the middle of the night and He wouldn't believe me. But I knew what I heard. He loved me. He loved me so deeply that He wasn't even aware He was *telling* me He loved me.

I must say I'm also a big fan of the whispered I Love You, otherwise known as the I Love You Sneak Attack. For instance, you're at a party with your steady. All these people are around you, everyone's drinking, talking and then your person comes up to you and whispers in your ear, "*I Love You.*" Suddenly, everyone in the room has disappeared and it's just the two of you. You feel special. You feel pretty. Suddenly, you want to jump this person so bad, you're wondering if you can sneak outside to the back of the house and have crazy sex on the garbage cans. Lids clanking, milk jugs bouncing out of the dented receptacles, you don't care. This person just whispered that they love you and you are going to live in the here and now. It's inappropriate. Your mother would say it was wrong, but that's exactly why you're doing it.

Personally, I think the Hang up I Love You combination is entirely overused. It's too passé, too unfeeling. People get to saying it so often without meaning that when it isn't stuck onto the good-bye, someone's going to get mad. A fight will go on for days because someone forgot to slap it on the end of a sentence. It's ridiculous. It's not an afterthought, a routine! It's a declaration, an announcement, a proclamation that should be treasured, not trashed.

I do not hand out the I Love You's like Mormon reading material. The only I Love You's that escape these lips are the I Love You's that mean something. I don't think people should say anything without really meaning it. I'm not going to tell you I hate you until I want to erase your very existence off the planet. And even then, I may say that I'm "a little pissed."

Another bad I Love You example are the annoying people who love to use the multiple I Love You. These are people that call every hour on the hour to say that they *"love you, Honey. Can't wait to see you again!"*

A couple of times during the day and I'm set. Maybe more than one time a day would be nice, but I'm good after that. I get it, you love me.

I hate being around couples who use I Love You's like conjunctions in a sentence. To me that has *insecurity* written all over it. If you love someone, they no doubt love you back, and you are both very aware of the love. You can just stow the verbiage. We unloved folk really start to hate you after the third I Love You in three minutes. Less is more, my friend.

The same goes for public displays of affection. I'm all for them, I encourage them! But there is a time and a place for everything. Grabbing someone's face and smearing your lips all over them is perfectly acceptable on a street corner as you wait to cross, but during a funeral, I'm going to have to say no. I really don't mind if people kiss in a movie theater. I have always wanted to make out in a movie theater just because I think everyone *should* make out in a movie theater (while seated in the seats in the back, of course). Making out in an elevator is another one of my personal favorites, but if it's crowded, I think no. But if you're alone, a little drunk, and looking at 26 floors of travel time, I say go right ahead.

Handholding is a touchy subject. It's nice, but at the same time, I don't know if I need to hold someone's hand when walking down the street or just running into a store. I don't think I'm going to fall down without the support of someone's hand in mine. But when in the movie theater or riding a major mode of transportation (like a plane), that hand better be in mine or the boyfriend loses it.

The most irritating thing I see couples do is to have their hands in each other's back pockets, or to walk with one arm planted on each other's waist. People who are the fondest of walking with Hands in Pocket are either under the age of 17 or living in a car. Let me tell you, it is not comfortable to walk like that. If you love this person so much that you cannot help but walk in this fashion, I suggest you get the words *I'm In Love* tattooed across your face. It's less obvious. But let's not make an everyday thing like walking down a street into some sort of office picnic party game. Let's reserve the three-legged race for the heat wave and the BallPark Franks.

I do like the pressed-up-against-the-wall-of-a-club scenario. It's a bit trashy, but what the hell? You've had a few drinks, you're young, live it up while you can. Chances are in two weeks you'll be upset because that same Wall Presser hasn't called, and you'll be crying into a vat of cookie dough. Get it while the getting is good.

Making out in someone's car is borderline for me. I'm not for or against it. But when I do see some people steaming up the windows, I am not a High Beam Flasher. What does that mean exactly? *I see you?* Well, no shit, they're in a car. There are no curtains. That's why people make out in the car—it's a classic maneuver! People have been doing it since cars had wheels (and since young hormone sufferers often live with their parents).

If you happen to be a High Beam Flasher I beg you, redefine your ways. Let's all work together, shall we, people? Window Steamer to Window Steamer, haven't we all done it? And it's nothing to be ashamed of. We all should be doing it, and doing it more often! People on first dates. People who've been married for ten years. Elderly people too! I would love to make out in a car at a drive-in movie. Why haven't I thought of this before? Color me blonde and call me Sandy! That is one swell of an idea.

Personally, I've never had sex in a car. I don't think I would want to. There's no room to stretch out, not to mention that button marks and leather creases across your face are never classy. Having sex outside the car, on the car, and then getting in the car when you're done is probably your best bet. I'm putting that one on the list of things I must do before I die.

All these things, the I Love You's, the PDA, the hand holding all lead up to one big deed. The Business. The Nasty. The Bump and Grind. No matter what you call it, it's sex. My whole life, I figured I would only have sex with one man and that man would be my husband. By the time

I reached age 18 I knew that was a pipe dream. Practically all my friends had had sex by that age and I was beginning to feel a little itchy. But I always figured I was going to be older when I lost my virginity because I refused to have sex in a car or at my parent's house. It was just too creepy to have sex in the same bed that I once peed in.

And as far as having sex in my car, I got two words for you: Volkswagen Bug. There was no way you could fold up two bodies back there without snapping a ligament or permanently damaging your spine.

It finally happened when I was at Bible Summer Camp. I had been dating my boyfriend for about five months and we talked about doing it for a long time. He was very careful to cover all aspects of the business transaction before it happened. We got all dressed up and went to dinner at the nicest restaurant in town. We went for a drive, talked, had some wine, and then went back to do the hippy hippy shake.

It's so strange how you look forward to the moment, the very first moment that you leave the world of a child and become a woman, and years later you can't even remember what it felt like. Here I had read all those Judy Blume books about doing it, prepared for pain and did all the worrying, and now the only thing I can remember about my first time was thinking, *"That was it?"*

We dated for one year and one month and then broke up. I have no idea why. I don't remember being completely wrecked, but I probably was. It's funny how you forget something that at the time was so big you thought it would crush you. You think you'll never feel better and you'll never laugh or love again. Then one day you stop for a moment and realize you didn't cry that day, and the day before that, and the day before that. The rain of pain dried up and in its place is a new cloud that will probably downpour on your head when you least expect it. But why worry about that right now, when there isn't a cloud in sight?

I can't truly remember the pain I felt when my relationship ended on Valentine's Day two years ago. I think of it like a song I heard a long time ago but I don't know the words anymore. I can remember parts of it but not the chorus. Sometimes certain events in vivid color sneak back on me and I feel like the whole thing just happened. But right now the space it once filled up is filled up with other things. All the crap involving Shitbird got pushed to the back of the line.

But I do remember the I Love You's. It's too bad that He was basically a figment of my imagination. Sometimes I just try to figure out which parts of Him were real and which were fabricated. Did He really love me? Was He even talking about me when He said I Love You at three o'clock in the morning? Did He ever love me? Does He still?

I miss the I Love You's, and it will probably be a long time before I hear that again. No one will say that they love me on the first date. I'm looking at another, what? Four, five, six months tacked onto the amount of time I have to go through before I ever even meet this person before I ever hear the I Love You. It's a sad existence. In the meantime I guess I'll just keep going.

What else can I do?

DEPRESSION IS POLITE. [2 pm]

Depression doesn't talk
or eat between meals
It's considerate in how it advises sleep
and attracts distractions
and encourages you sternly
to see things as you see them.

It likes to hug you hard around the neck
and wonders if you consider death (as an option)
It is creatively literate
as It conducts and constructs
new and inventive ways to describe the pain
that is indescribable.

Depression doesn't want to be invited
and *wants* to be alone
It makes use of anxiety and welcomes the tears
It uses every ounce of your insecurity
applauds your incredible self loathing
and wants to hang around the house in black, baggy clothing.

It stays up late when others have left
And follows you to the movies without question
Complements your dark circles
turns out the lights
and strengthens the weakness you usually neglect.

Flattens the stomach and sinks the chest,
Depression is loss of weight
worry disseminates
When It shows you
you don't need to care,
and gives advice, "Simplify your life
for life, as you know, just isn't fair."

Other emotions may be funny, exhilarating or rude
But Depression is the most polite of all the possible moods.

18. Mitchy the Kid

In my apartment building lives the man who could very possibly be the man of my dreams. Tall, dark hair, painfully shy... when I see him on the street or in the elevator I want to press up against him and scream, "Take me NOW!"

Since this sort of behavior will either get you arrested or fitted for a straitjacket, I have tried to muster up the nerve simply to say hello. I have had a million opportunities to say something, each time coming up with a new and inventive way to avoid the task. I don't know why I put this off. I usually have no qualms about making a fool of myself. Some might say I go *out of my way* to look like a fool. But this guy leaves me breathless. I have no ability to speak around him.

When we're trapped in the elevator together and alone, all I can concentrate on is the irrepressible magnetic force between us. I should probably introduce myself or say "Hi" or something, anything; rather than stand there like a jerk, thinking about slamming him against the doors and kissing him like a mad woman.

I don't know what his name is but I just so happen to be very into *Gone with the Wind* right now, so I've named him Mitchell (as in Margaret Mitchell, the author). The Guys would call him Mitch. I would call him Mitchy the Kid.

Mitchell is obviously cute and shy, but he also plays the piano and is comfortable with ballroom dancing. He has traveled quite a bit but has yet to go to Venice. He likes to go to museums, read and see all different kinds of movies. His favorite food is Italian and he likes to cook it himself in his sixth floor apartment. He lives on the same side of the building as I do, which means he has the same beautiful view of Puget Sound. His apartment is clean, without being sterile, and he has *real* pictures in *real* frames on his walls, no motorcycle posters or Corona banners draped across the living room ceiling.

Mitchell has a quiet laugh but a huge smile, and his cheeks turn red when he's being shy or after he tells me he loves me. He enjoys all different kinds of music (but he's not too crazy about country) and he has a little sister who he takes to the mall on Saturdays.

All this thinking about him is completely unhealthy. Not only do I sound like a 13-year-old girl, I've created this movie star persona for him, making it so that I'm thinking someone this wonderful would never want me. He could have Christy Turlington, why would he want me? ... a freak who drools in the elevator, staring down at her platform shoes.

One night I was waiting for the elevator to take me down to the lobby where Scottie was waiting for me. I was all cha-cha'd out in black eye shadow and a hootchie skirt when the doors opened and there stood my sweet Mitchell. Next to him, a short girl that I knew was his girlfriend.

"Excuse me," I said as I stepped between them. The girl, being dumber than a doorknob, kept talking to him about the relevancy of cheese or something to that effect. I assumed the position of looking downward. Casually, I glanced in the Mitchell direction and he was looking back at me. He looked embarrassed. I wasn't sure if it was because this girl had invaded our private elevator time, or because I looked like a creature of the night.

I delicately stepped out of the elevator and tried to maintain my balance. I couldn't believe it. Never in one of my fantasies did I ever think that he possibly had a girlfriend. Every time I saw him he was alone, he was never carrying flowers or wearing a wedding ring or anything. He just seemed so perfect for me. Dating someone else? I never thought it possible.

But of course, it was all very possible. Here he is, with that fabulous black hair and blue eyes, there's no way this vision could be single. He obviously has a good job too, because when I see him in the mornings he's always wearing a tie, and believe me, I've looked for the button that says, *"Super-size it for 25 cents!"*

I was crushed. Here I'd been admiring him from afar the entire summer, if not longer, and the whole time he was seeing someone else. The very next morning, I saw him walking to the bus stop. I was walking about 50 feet behind him.

You can tell a lot about a man from the way that he walks. If he's a Toe Stepper, there is no way this man can flush the occasional spider down the toilet. If he walks heavily, it's annoying. There has got to be a reason he walks like a baby elephant and I don't want to know what it is. I favor a limp because there's a story behind it. Knee surgery after scaling a wall, football injury; something good and manly like that. The swagger is iffy. It could be he is too self-confident. On the other hand, he is more than likely a good dancer. Mitchell's walk was the product of a saunter meeting an off-kilter equilibrium. He walked with his body weight slightly shifted forward, like some little ghost was pushing him from behind.

Then I noticed his sunglasses—those stupid, wrap around gargoyle sunglasses, and yes, they were mirrored. I say wear gargoyles if and only if you're a sports star and getting paid six figures to wear them. Other than that, I'm going to say no. And mirrored! I cannot tell you how annoying those are. Unless you are a pro wrestler or a porn star, mirrored is usually not the way to go. I cannot trust a person whose eyes I cannot see.

The last strike was the goatee. Mitchell has a beautiful face. Why he would want to hide it behind the mask of a whisker, I will never know. It was a very thin goatee, but still prominent. Facial hair is a tough call to make. On Tom Selleck, give me the mustache. When I was younger, I was very much in love with TV's Matt Houston. My dad had a mustache throughout my entire childhood and I loved it. When he shaved it off, I cried for hours. (I was 15.) But facial hair on a young guy that is as hunkalicious as Mitchell, it's an unnecessary commodity.

The walk, sunglasses and goatee? I was beginning to think I was all wrong about Mitchy the Kid. Was he not the electrostud I thought he was?

I didn't see him again for two months. I worried that he moved out and I had lost him in the masses. Each morning I tried to be on that elevator at 8:30, looking cute and prepared to say hello; each morning he wasn't there. It was over before it ever began.

It's an odd sensation to mourn the loss of a love you never had. I didn't even try to explain any of this to my friends, in fear that they would think I was insane. Slowly, the healing process began and I went back to my old motto, *"If it is meant to be, it will happen."* Still, I missed seeing him and dreaming of what our first kiss would be like, or what the children would look like.

The other day I was driving the usual groove into work. Down Fifth Avenue I saw, on the corner of the next block, someone who looked a lot like my Mitchell. I squinted and tried to refocus, cursing myself for forgetting my glasses at home. Closer, closer… it was a tall, dark haired guy with camel colored pants and a white shirt, without a tie. It was The One and Only, Mitchy the Kid, in his Friday casuals, without sunglasses and without facial hair.

Mitchell stood on the corner and I could swear he stared back for just a moment before crossing in front of my headlights. *"Smile at him, you idiot!"* A voice cried out from somewhere amongst the amusement and wonder that was swirling around in my head.

I froze like dog shit in the snow.

He was there, downtown, just a few feet ahead of me, looking more ravishing then I remembered. That clean, close shave, the unbuttoned button-up shirt, and camel pants sent straight from heaven. If I could have, I would have jumped out of my car and clomped onto his leg. Each step he took would scrape my knees but I wouldn't care. It was

Mitchell and he was alive! My snuffed out passion was re-lit in a monumental way. I put him right back on the stove, in that same back burner position he had occupied for months.

Last night I saw him walking back from the bus stop at 5:30. I was attempting to parallel park on the street when he walked right past my window. I tried to whip my car right in there and sneak behind him in the elevator, but I am the worst parker. It took me at least ten minutes to park, and through the huge windows in the lobby, I saw him check his mail, flip through the bills and step onto the elevator. Another opportunity missed. But he still lives here! He must have just gotten a new job. *Moving up in the world*, I thought as I unlocked the lobby door. Maybe he's ready for a new girlfriend too.

I opened my mailbox with a drunken smile on my face. I still had a chance. This could still happen. But how *would* it happen?

I would be waiting for the elevator on a stormy Wednesday morning, looking irresistibly cute. The elevator doors would glide open revealing Mitchell, in those same camel pants and white shirt just slightly askew.

"Hi," I would say and step inside.

"Hey." With one perfectly manicured finger, I push the lobby button and the doors swoosh closed. I can smell his perfect cologne as he shifts his weight and moves slightly closer. I lean backward, letting one hand go behind me on the guard rail and the other adjusting the strap on my stiletto black heels. He exhales a slow, wanting breath and a smile draws itself upon my lips. Then, the lights dim and the elevator jumps to a halt.

"Oh my God," I say, as I grip the rail.

"It's OK," he says calmly, and moves to the buttons on the wall. "The storm must have cut off the electricity."

"Maybe you can push that emergency button," I offer. He pushes it, but nothing happens, just the *click-click* of the button going in and out. He bends down and opens the emergency telephone but it's missing.

"That can't be a good sign," I say followed by nervous laughter. He nods in agreement. "One time I was trapped in an elevator and I just pried the doors open. Maybe…" I push on the doors but nothing happens. I try to wedge my fingers in between the two doors but can't.

"That's not going to work. I think we're stuck between floors. I could climb up there," Mitchell says, noticing a cutout in the ceiling.

"Isn't that sort of dangerous?"

He looks at me in the dim light and smiles. "I like danger."

Just then we hear the manager's voice echo down the shaft. "Is anyone in there?"

"Yes!" Mitchell yells.

"Don't worry, I've called the fire department to get you out. They'll be here in 15 minutes."

"Fifteen minutes," Mitchell says to me. I shrug my shoulders in response. "Not a lot of time," he continues. "We've never really met. I'm Mitchell, and you are…?"

"Does it really matter?" I ask, taking his extended hand and pulling him toward me. "I've been watching you. And each time I see you, I wonder the same question."

"What's that?" he says, slipping one arm around my waist.

"How's it going to begin?" We kiss slowly at first, just discovering the softness of each other's lips. Then he backs me up against the doors, kissing me harder, his hands on the back of my head, and slowly circling the nape of my neck. I open my eyes just a little to see his blue eyes and the flush of his cheeks up close. There is a warm cloud around us, the smell of him mixed with my perfume, and the warmth of his hands as he slides one shoulder of my jacket off my arm and leans his body into mine…

The loud *ding* of the elevator brought me back to reality. I stepped inside and pressed three. I pray I will have the motivation and strength to really say something the next time I see him. I don't know why I'm acting this way. I usually am fine around men, good looking or not, but this guy, Mitchell, there's something different about him. Maybe I can too easily see us together and that scares me. Maybe I'm afraid of getting hurt. Maybe I know it will work out and I'm scared to be dependent on someone, it's so much easier being alone. But I'm tired of being alone.

I opened the door of my apartment, walked across the room and sat in my big green chair. Pinkie the Cat jumped in my lap as I looked out the window. Everything is temporary. This apartment is temporary. Being alone is temporary. I won't be single forever. Two years from now I could be married and pregnant and two years isn't too far away. Why Mitchell lives in my building, and haunts me on the streets of Seattle, I don't know, but I do know there are such things as omens and signs and if for some reason I can't breathe when I'm around him, that's got to be saying something. I made a vow to myself that I would say hello the very next time I see him, whether he is with someone or not.

CRUSHED BY AN ELEVATOR [7:07 pm]

I see him in transit
caught between lobby doors and private thresholds
side by side, we are motionless
in a vibrating clash of screws and pulleys
that moves us toward separate destinations
always always
a moment too soon.

Overcome by my
Everything
he communicates through stolen glances,
mentally measuring the length of my skirt
and he wonders if I go to the movies alone.

He dreams of me sleeping
in my home three floors down
and creates what I am wearing
underneath my night gown

Spoken in silent phrases, described in vivid verbs,
he says he wants to kiss me
when the old doors bounce shut
and we can finally steal time
from the routines that don't matter.

But 20 seconds later,
we have nothing to say
and he leaves me in the box
tossing that misinterpretal last look
giving me enough fluttler
to mastermind the next moment
I will one-sidedly share with my
Elevator Crush.

19. You Are My Fantasy

I have nights where I actually pass up going out to stay home and play *Make Believe*. I take a bone-scorching bath, pick out the best lip-synching songs and start the show. I get all dressed up in some getup, prepare myself with a glass of wine and the night of fantasy begins. I make up scenarios and dance in front of the glass framed pictures in the living room. I pretend I'm a combination of the 1980s Kelly LeBrock and 90s Elizabeth Hurley, without the English accents. I have a varied and extensive fashion sense that includes leopard-print pants and shirts made entirely out of feathers.

The music starts and I become a famous rock star, live in concert. Sixty-five bucks for a ticket to my show and these greedy people want every last dime of their money paid back in my sweat. I sing until my throat goes dry, the backup singers sing in black fringed dresses, while sweaty male dancers crawl around on the floor like hungry savages.

Then the CD changes and now I'm making a music video consisting solely of closeup shots of my mouth, eyes and upper body. The song is something grindy and oozy with sexuality. There's lots of biting my bottom lip and sucking on things. Upper body shots are tight and require lots of cleavage and a ton of glitter.

When the next song begins, I'm struttin' it on the catwalk. I'm a $5,000.00 an hour Supermodel and photographers line the stage. *Click-click, flash-flash.* I slowly smile at the media types who so want to be me. "*Over here! Over here!*" they yell, and I do a couple of slow three point turns in front of the lens. Whispers of *"fabulous!"* bite into the backs of my 12-inch heels as I walk backstage to down a $75 glass of champagne and force myself to throw up.

There are three special reserve fantasies that require much more background. They start in the bathtub, or should I say, the meditation in the bath before the show even starts. I forget the crap I usually worry about and transplant myself into a different lifestyle. I think of each detail, what smells would I be smelling, what the temperature is. This is how the first one goes:

I'm filthy rich with homes in Seattle, New York, Santa Fe, Paris and Italy. They are all personally decorated with lovely trinkets in each home; my purse collection in New York, and treasured tea pots in France. Of course, I have a pool man to take care of the pools in Santa Fe and Italy; he works alongside the gaggle of gardeners who tend to the manicured gardens and keep an eye on the vineyard. I will need someone to take care of the fish tanks in Seattle and New York. Of course, I have huge tanks of tropical fish with identically cute blowfish, for relaxation purposes.

Pinkie the Cat and Uncle Kitty, the future pug dog I will own, will travel with me to each home; I can't just leave them somewhere! Then again, the personal sushi chef, three spa technicians and a makeup artist would also have to follow me around.

They probably won't want to travel. The whiney Chef will go on and on about how he misses his family and *"doesn't get paid enough to be my slave."* The three spa chicks will eventually form an all-girl band and open for Madonna. The makeup artist and I would combine our talents in a book about makeup, hair color and how to make your nose look smaller.

I'll have men who will want me, maybe even stalk me. In two years I'll run into Mitchell in Tiffany's in Seattle. He'll say he was picking out rings that he'd like to buy for his as-yet-unmet fiancée. I'll say I was picking out rings that I'd accept. This all happens to take place around the holidays, and Mitchell and I have some Christmas cheer at a corner bar looking out on the huge tree downtown. It's busy outside: children trying to break free from parents, high school girls wearing too much lip-gloss, couples balancing packages and lattes. I'll look across the table at Mitchy and know, this is The One.

He'll get up from the table and bend down on one knee. He'll take my hand and say, "I know people will think we're crazy. They'll say it's too fast and how can we possibly know what we want. But let's live the wonderful story people always want to tell their kids. Let's get married."

"Mitchell, I don't know what to say."

"Make me the happiest, luckiest man in the world. Say yes!"

He will laugh out loud as I release some sort of cute-girl squeal and hug him. He'll fall back on the floor and I'll land on top of him. People will stare and smile, some will roll their eyes, but we don't care. We will just lie on the floor of the bar, laughing, hugging and planning the future.

"Mitch, I only have one question. What's your last name?"

OK, I'm not too sure about that one. There's always Fantasy #2:

I've just had my first book published and I get an obscenely huge check in the mail. The first thing I do is buy a perfectly Pottery Barn-ish home on Queen Anne Hill in Seattle. I start to plan the most extravagant party ever.

The party is held in some secret-secret ultra-posh location, with champagne fountains and presents for everyone. The food is fabulous and the drinks are free; the nice mix of disco, '80s and modern music beats through the sound system.

Feeling extravagant, I fly Cher in to sing her latest hit song. At the last minute, she'll cancel because she's having emergency liposuction—so Prince comes in her place. Everyone is dancing and I look ever so cha-cha in my high fashion new dress created by some up-and-coming designer who's already asked me to be his featured model.

Of course, I invite my publisher to the party and she'll tell me she's launching this huge book tour for me. I'll go on local TV shows, radio programs and even guest star on *Friends*. But the biggest gig of all is the *Today Show* and Matt Lauer is going to interview me.

While in the makeup chair, Matt comes up to me and says he wishes he would have met me before he married that dim-witted former model. We'll move out to the set and then it's live on the airwaves. I come off as confident, clever and extremely talented. Matt says he's honored to tell me: my book is #1 on the New York Times Bestseller List and three movie companies are interested in developing it into a film starring Sandra Bullock.

"Is there anyone you'd like to thank?" Matt asks.

"Actually, yes." I'll turn and look directly into the camera. "I'd like to send this out to a trailer park in Seattle… that's right, Mr. Loser, this one's for you. Thank you for cheating on me and deserting me on Valentine's Day years ago. Your selfish and assholish ways have led me to this chair I sit in today, here, on the *Today Show*. You stopped me from becoming something I was never meant to be, a waste of space like you. To you, I send my eternal thanks. Look for your signed copy of my book in your P.O. Box today. Without you…" I take Matt's hand, "none of this would have been possible," then I plant a big old kiss right on Matt's face.

At that exact moment in Seattle, The Man Formerly Known As My Boyfriend sits, jaw open and eyes wide. Next to him, in an identical Laz E Boy, The Waitress sits, along with the 85 pounds she gained while carrying the forbidden love child. She pulls up her pink socks, takes off one of her clogs. "That foot powder sure ain't working. Honey, do you know that girl or something? Isn't she the new Victoria Secret model? Sweetums?"

Shitbird will close his eyes and slam the generic beer can into his huge forehead. He'll open the shredded screen door, kick the mangy dog asleep on the porch and yell across the parking lot, "I'm such an idiot!"

Now that's a keeper! That's a special occasion fantasy. I don't use it too often because it is just too wonderful. It would be like having Christmas twice a year, it loses its magic.

But my most commonly used fantasy is the one where I'm the lead singer of a band (that's the influence of Josie & the Pussy Cats sneaking up on me). The setting: a dark bar, bordering on a trouble spot. It's junky chic with a raised stage, round tables boarding the dance floor, and booths lining the back. It's a Friday night and the joint is packed.

It's almost midnight and the crowd is licked. An ultra-cool stud saunters on stage. He raises one hand to quiet the crowd and says, "OK, everyone, thanks for coming. Tonight we have a special treat, live music by one of the great local bands led by a gorgeous lady. Let's give her a big hand..." The crowd musters up modest applause and I step into the spotlight.

Depending on my Make Believe mood, I vary my outfit from something very Audrey Hepburn to something completely trashy. Tonight I'm in a dark blue long skirt with a huge slit up to my thigh, some very stylish strappy navy heels, and a sleeveless, very low cut, dark blue shirt with only one button toward the top, no foundations underneath. My hair is long with metallic gold streaks, and I push a few strands away from my black eye-makeup'd lids and run my tongue over pale colored lips.

The light glints off the subtle sparkles on my face, chest and legs. I start to move when the band begins to play *Send Me Someone to Love*. No one makes a sound as my velvet voice is expelled, mixing with the smell of whiskey and cheap cigarettes. During the guitar solo, I sit on the tall stool placed on stage and the flash of my leg makes all the men lean forward. I pull a cigarette out of nowhere and the guitar player lights me up. I take a drag and blow blue smoke out in one steady stream.

As the last notes of the song are pulled out of the bar by the ceiling fans, men explode with mass applause and catcalls. All their dates get jealous and walk out in one solid chorus line. Now it's me and 77 men, packed in one alcoholic, smoke-filled room. I tell the band to play *Turn to You*, the best song by the Go-Go's, ever.

Somewhere in the middle of the song, I notice a guy toward the back standing still and staring. It's The Blue Eyed Devil. He looks like hell and at least 100 pounds heavier than He was two years ago. The flashing lights in the bar reflect off His bald spot while black circles and blotchy chicken skin swallow His dead eyes. He starts to walk toward the stage, and I subconsciously dare Him to come forward.

Now He's directly in front of me, trying to get my attention, but movie star Jeff Goldblum has just sent a drink up on stage. I nod thanks and down the shot of Jagermeister, not batting an eye. Brad Pitt is smoking at a table to my left and is looking me up and down. Yeah, he wants me. Dylan McDermott gets up from the bar with a vodka tonic and steps on stage. He hands me the drink, pulls me close and kisses my neck. I laugh and push him away. Dylan puts his hand over his heart, as if I'd broken it, and falls to his knees. I pull him up by the shirt collar and slowly kiss his open lips.

The Loser reaches His scaly hands toward me and I step back. Two security guards rush the stage and grab each of His jiggly arms and drag Him toward the door. He yells out my name and tries to fight the bouncers. I simply blow Him a kiss. The Man Formerly Known As My Boyfriend starts to cry like a little girl as the heavy doors slam shut.

My set lasts about an hour and somehow all of my ex-boyfriends have wandered in and spread out around the bar. I can hear one of them say to the other... "I dated her, you know."

"So did I!"

"She was the best kisser I have ever kissed."

"Tell me about it. I still have dreams about her body..."

"Her *body?* How about how great her hair smelled?'

"She was the smartest girl I was ever with."

"She was the funniest person I've ever met."

"The sexiest woman on the planet."

"My family loved her."

"*One of the Guys* but all woman."

"A fantastic dancer. God, could she move."
"The guy that gets her is one lucky man."
"You can say that again."

The envious bastards beg me not to stop when I say my final good night. "You're very kind, thank you…" I say in a raspy voice, exhausted from singing. I float off stage, leaving behind a glittering, perfumed cloud, teasing the nostrils of the hot and horny men who are sure to have a restless night full of sex dreams, about me.

20. "Look! Up In the Sky! It's the Powerfully Unbearable *Boy Annoy!*"

When I was in college, I started to compile a list of annoying things that men do. At that point in time I was 19 years old and already had 130 annoying habits clearly identified. Now I'm 26 and that list has multiplied like a thousand worms cut in half. I still have the list of The Dirty 130 buried somewhere beneath the masses, but have yet to have the energy to tackle the monster. I'm reduced to just having this specialized List of Horribles saved in my head. While the realization and identification of these male faux pas may have grown, my tolerance has too. There are only a handful of general characteristics that annoy the shit out of me.

Right off I have to say that grown men with God-given names like Tim should always be called Tim once they are over the age of 30. The name Timmy expires after 30 years, I'm sorry. You can't get on the kiddy rides at the Fun Forest once you pass 4'7", and once you turn 30, you're stuck with the single syllabled name your mother intended for you.

Then there are names that aren't ever meant to end in an "eeee" yet they somehow morph into them. Examples: Paul = Paulie, Stan = Stannie, Craig = Craigie. There *are* exceptions. Like, you happen to be a drag queen, or you're an eighth year senior in college and a diehard Frat Rat. Of course, you could also be a member of the mob. I don't think they'd let anyone in named "Tom." It's gotta be Tommy. But then it wouldn't just be Tommy, it would be "Tommy the Fist."

The next blazoned DON'T is the use of the most mispronounced word in the English language. For years people have tried to figure out if the correct pronunciation of the word is "supposEDLY" or "supposIBLY." Women waver back and forth between these two words too, but for some reason it's more irritating coming from a man. According to your dictionary, the word is "SUPPOSEDLY". I hate to toot my own horn, but... toot toot. I have always favored and used the word "supposedly" rather then succumb to the dark side of mispronunciation. I always thought supposiBLY sounded a little too *Fat Albert* to be legit.

Pay attention when you're talking to a man. Listen to hear if they are a "supposedly" or a "supposibly" speaker. Try and tell me you won't hear fingernails on the chalkboard when that nasty B slips from some guy's lips. You'll have to fight the urge to strangle harder than anything else you've ever had to fight. I'm thinking of having a Supposedly Campaign. I'd run PSAs encouraging the D and eliminating the B. Posters would be plastered in airports. That way the word would travel with the people and cover unimaginable geographical areas.

There would be radio ads, TV jingles, mass mailings... banners dragged behind planes in air shows! There's no way a single user of the English language could dodge the message, and before too long all the people in the world would know: the word is supposedly.

Another verbal annoyance is the extreme overuse and irrational abuse of the word "literally." An example of this is: *I was literally drinking a glass of water.* No, you weren't literally drinking a glass of water, you were drinking a glass of water. Throw in a "literally" when saying "I was literally shitting my pants, there was shit in my pants, for real." OK, now that is literal.

I worked with this one guy that would use "literally" like a verbal crutch. *"Sorry I couldn't talk to you when you walked into my office but I was literally on the phone for an hour. Literally! Then I had to get something to eat, because I was literally hungry. Then, I had to literally go to a meeting that lasted about an hour, literally."*

I think this guy liked to use the word "literally" because it sounded like the word "literature." And if you know anything about literature, you must be pretty smart. But the use of this word didn't make him smart. It made him dumb. A word derived from the word "literal" isn't a magic portal into the World of Witty. I wanted to stab Literal Man in the ear with a pencil; he drove me insane... literally.

The next one down on the List of Annoy is the use of too many condiments. I'm referring to the gross addiction of one condiment on everything. I really have no problem with someone who likes salt on this, pepper on that, salsa on the side... this is no problem. It's the use of one condiment on everything! Ranch dressing on fries, the baked potato, hamburgers, fish, onion rings, salad... oh my God, I can hardly even talk about it! Just stop it already! No meal should be constructed around the consumption of Ranch dressing.

Once I broke up with a guy because he used too much Ranch dressing. I'm not kidding, it came down to putting up with his addiction or dumping him. I opted for the latter. I couldn't take it! We would go to a drive-in burger joint and tubs of Ranch dressing would have to be rolled out from the kitchen so he could dip this, dunk that. I suggested to him that he see if a surgeon could sew little packets of Ranch dressing to the inside of his cheeks. "Why not have a Ranch dressing dispenser installed on the dash of your car, like those things you see in athletic club showers that hold shampoo? Now there's an idea! Ranch dressing in the shower! How about that?"

I broke up with him two days later. Don't feel too sorry for him. I mailed him a bottle of Ranch dressing with a note tied around the bottleneck: *We're through. Bon appetit.* It was the best thing for the three of us.

The one thing that will push me to the brink of insanity is stupid watchbands. I once heard you can tell a lot about a woman by the shoes she wears. For men, it's the watchband. Describe the man that would wear a plastic-banded plastic watch, equipped with a mini calculator and a little alarm that goes off every hour. Again, there are exceptions, but I would guess this man as a nerd. At first sight of that plastic band, you know you're in trouble. It's all very possible that he has to wear this band for the type of work he does. But when he's out with me, is this necessary? We aren't going scuba diving, it's dinner and a movie. There is no deep sea diving or calculating involved.

I am very pro leather or metal watchband. Leather is the more telling of the two. Is it worn out? Rugged? Well kept? Braided or flat leather? Brown or black? The metal watchband is a little more sentimental to me because my Grandpa wore a metal watchband and I remember thinking it was very cool. Not too binding, you know? Gently, it slides over the big wrist with grace and style. But the metal has to be silver. A gold watchband? Very *Godfather*, very *Good Fellas*. It's too flashy to be real gold, so that guy is a big faker. And if it *is* real gold, this person is some sort of idiot for spending that much money on a piece of jewelry he will no doubt tire of in a few years and get something newer, more shiny. Do you get what I'm saying here? It's all about symbolism, sister; beware.

Let's talk for just a moment about the element commonly referred to as one's personal style. It seems to me that men are so much more style impaired than even the women who wear white flats, stirrup pants and kitty sweatshirts. Men have no thought in their head as they pull together a red crumpled-up shirt and a green pair of pants. Come on. Even Stevie Wonder can see that this is a bad combination. Are you a man or Santa Claus?

I'm at this point that I don't even care what style a man's personal style is, just as long as he has one. Want to be a nerd? Be a nerd! I want to see that pocket protector and tape in the middle of the glasses. Are you a jock? Wear those latex bike shorts and a tank top, throw in the essential sporto earring and change your name to Dion. I don't really care. Just be *something* (other than stupid).

I went on a blind date with this one guy and I swear the fashion police had thrown up all over him. He was wearing a shiny, latex mock turtleneck complete with the Nike swoosh (jock), a choker-type, leather-stringed, single-bead necklace (hippie), Dockers (yuppie), tennis shoes (adolescent), little girlie bootie socks (cross dresser), and a black overcoat (secret agent?). This guy was all over the map. I didn't know what to make of him, but I knew that I would never make out with him.

I can see a totally unattractive freak-show and totally be attracted to him if he dresses with style. I have turned my head for the radical after-sex haired, pierced generation X-er. They have style and they are committed to that style. But nothing turns me off quicker than a man who has no style.

I have style. I cannot be with someone who doesn't. Hanging out with someone who is not as stylish as I am takes away from my own personal style and I start to look bad. The Unfashionable One starts to suck the style out of the Fashionable One. If I hang out with someone like this, before I know it I'll be wearing white flats, stirrup pants and a kitty sweatshirt. I cannot let that happen. I refuse to look bad by choice.

I'm not asking for much. You may say I'm picky but these are minor, minor details! I'm not asking for a Sagittarius, fluent in three languages and who enjoys salsa music. These few little items are common sense items, crucial to *my* personal laws of attraction. They're not for every woman, they're for this woman. I think it's important to know what you want.

So, if you're in a restaurant and sitting next to you is a guy named Dan who passes the salt and says he's "supposedly meeting a client in twenty minutes" *[insert smile here],* and you ask him the time and see he's wearing a silver watchband that goes well with his stylish outfit, and he is literally the cutest guy in the place, give him my number.

THE PERFECT MAN. [8:12 pm]

   will walk into a room and immediately have me.

have my heart
have my lust

   He Will Have My Attention.

At the bar, he'll ask for his usual whatever
and I'll reach for my extra limed vodka,
searching every corner of my mind for a name that would or could possibly suit him… impossible.

I want him to see my eyes
and the look in my eyes
and experience the moment,
this indescribable, long awaited moment
that's been unable to be defined by a simple emotion or single syllabed word
until now
until just now when we created it.

And his eyes, an unmattering color
will widen and stare…
those eyes that care
that will explore the body and enrapture the mind…
the eyes that will let me in
size me up

I Only Smoke On Thursdays

sex me out
and look me over

pulses race as begins the chase
and what will our first kiss be like?
The slide of his hand on the usual first date
will put such rush in me that floods and flexes my insides with a heat
I've never felt before.

Later I'll laugh about how many times I wondered
how it would happen
when would it be
that he finally would come to find all the things I've been missing
and instantly upon hearing the sound of his voice say my name
all that I've been looking for would suddenly be found and
I never knew why I was in such a hurry.

Everything about you is what I wanted
and I thought I never wanted
captured in such a way that when I look at you
I always
want to cry.

21. Blah, blah, blah

My friend Kenzie likes to use the term "dead wood" when describing men who will not go away. No matter how hard you try to sink them, they pop back up like bobbling corks. Fighting the currents and shunning obstacles, they resurface, like a bad female itch.

I argue with her that these unfortunates can be better described as an alligator attack. I saw this show about alligator attacks on the Discovery Channel. There was this sweet little gazelle having a cool refreshing drink from a river. Slowly, a wicked alligator floated closer to the shoreline. The poor gazelle didn't even look up. *Sip-sip*, the gazelle's lips delicately grazed the water's surface and that nasty alligator, cleverly disguised as an everyday average log, snuck right up practically right under the gazelle's nose. All the other gazelles ran. No one bothered to warn the thirsty gazelle, and that nasty alligator clamped its big jaws around her neck and dragged her out to the middle of the river. That poor thing screamed and that stupid alligator waved its tail at the camera and even had the nerve to wink.

I am that gazelle. I experience an alligator attack about once a month. The alligator usually comes in the form of three different people: Bob, Dustin or Spencer.

Bob is an alligator I met when I was 21 and he was 47. We developed a friendship that is hard to describe. It was a mutual using. I used him for free meals and he used me to make people think he was a stud. We never did anything physical or had a commitment, but this strange sort of ownership soon developed.

If I didn't call, he got mad. If I told him anything remotely personal, he would tell me what I should or shouldn't do about it. If I told him I was interested in a guy, the alligator made a dive for my jugular. He was the originator of the hour-long lecture on how crappy men were and I should just settle and be with him. I would sit there and not say a word. I figured the verbal assault was in exchange for the meal, and at this point in my life I was starving. I couldn't live on tuna fish alone. But one day I got sick of him and ended it.

I didn't see him for almost a year. When I finally did see him again, I was in the relationship with Shitbird. The next time I saw him I was single. He wanted to start things up again and I said no. That's basically where this relationship is now. I have met him for dinner approximately three times over the past two years, thinking things would be different but I could still get a free meal out of the deal. Yet that's impossible. The lectures continued, with me not realizing I signed up for the class.

He's very orchestrated in his mannerisms. We will go to a restaurant and he'll sit there, squint his eyes while gazing outside, trying to look deep and ponderous I guess—I never quite figured it out. He has never tried to kiss me (which I very much appreciate), but he's a fan of The Talk, how he wants me, how beautiful I am, blah, blah, blah.

Bob has a way of making you feel sorry for him so you'll go out with him. Sometimes I bite, sometimes I let that little wiggler go right on by. If I wanted to do charity work, I would join the Make A Wish Foundation. Maybe he should do the same.

Dustin is a young alligator from the past who is not at all welcome in these waters. This was the one that stood me up at the dance club and since then has been trying to persuade me to take him back. He floats right in like a camouflaged log, smiling his toothy grin.

Dustin and I dated for maybe three weeks, a whole year ago. No business mergers. A few Roll Arounds but nothing more. Yet he continued to call me and ask me out. He'd say that I was so special and that he'd never met anyone like me again, and probably never would. "You're right," I said and hung up on him. I've had about six conversations with this dreamer outlining the fact that I did not want him calling any more and was not interested in him. Each time, the man momentarily loses his ability to hear. He swims back in, saying he is so sorry he let me get away… blah, blah, blah. I bet that's what the alligator said to the gazelle before he snapped her in two.

I translate his words of undying affection as a declaration of desperation. Dustin let it slip that the ex is definitely out of his life, meaning he's not getting any. He tried to tell me that he is so different now, that I was so special and "The brief time we spent together was so wonderful."

"Get over it." *Click.*

Spencer is the alligator who is forever lurking. We went through our entire length of school together. I love Spencer very much. He has always been there for me and he leaves me messages that always begin with "Hey, Beautiful…" Anyone would love that. He has adored me my whole entire life, throughout the two years of rubber banded braces and frizzy hair in junior high, black bat-caver hair and red lipstick in high school. He has always thought I was beautiful. But he attacks. Just like the other two. Calm waters for months, and then all of a sudden he'll call and put me on a guilt trip that you would not believe. I never see it coming.

Spencer has a few personality quirks that have made him not all that attractive to my specific tastes. He likes to insult people on the street. He calls cultural events *stupid*. And this is our relationship. He'll say something stupid or inappropriate and I lay into him about his immaturity. Why this man insists he loves me is beyond my realm of comprehension. He's a man-child.

Spencer has always dressed like a slob and been a tad lazy. But since we've graduated from high school, he's changed. He got a good job, dresses nice…let me tell you, he's hot stuff. At the reunion, people are going to shit their pants when they see that this GQ money-makin' stud is the new and improved Spencer, of Smoking-behind-the-Bleachers fame. My parents saw him after seven years and encouraged me to consider him as a suitor. (Spencer is very talented at parent wooing.)

Because of this prompting, I asked Spencer out on a date. I had gotten tickets for a concert at an outdoor theater and asked him to join me.

"Is this a date," he asked, "or a friend thing?"

I considered this question carefully before answering. "It's a date."

"It is?" he asked, noticeably shocked.

"Yes."

"It is?"

He picked me up in new threads and in a very clean car. We went out to dinner at a fabulous waterfront restaurant. The conversation was pleasant, there was no burping or any insulting comments at all. We walked to the concert on this beautiful night and sat underneath the stars. I hadn't felt that calm in a long time. He put his arm around me. It was nice to feel someone's warmth around my shoulders. I'd forgotten what it felt like.

He took me home and that's where it fell apart. I did not want The Lean. I tried to scream out in body language and subconscious subtleties that I did not want any part of The Lean.

So here we are, on my doorstep and I was doing everything but screaming, "*I do not want The Lean!*"

I got The Lean.

And I did what girls do when The Lean is unwanted. I turned my head. I didn't even think I did it. I thought that I *thought* about doing it but I didn't actually do it. But I did it. He ended up getting a slice of ear lobe and a mouthful of hair. He pulled away from me as if I had slapped him.

I kissed him on the cheek and thanked him for a wonderful time. But it was too late. The venomous Turn Away was working its way through his nervous system. He quickly walked away and I knew. He was pissed.

He was pissed for a long time. He didn't call for two months. Finally I called him and he told me I was always so mean to him: "Here I devote my life to you and you treat me like shit."

"What are you talking about, 'you devote your life to me'?" I said.

"I treat you like a queen, and you treat me awful."

"Spencer," I said, "I do not treat you awful. I just didn't want you to kiss me. I just wanted to have a good time and here you force The Lean on me!"

"I did not force The Lean on you," he said.

"You did. Whether or not I wanted to reciprocate isn't even an issue with you. You're pissed at me because I wouldn't give you what *you* wanted. You don't even consider what I wanted. I do what I want to do, and I'm a bitch or something."

The conversation went silent for awhile and then he presented the worst question ever.

"Why don't you love me?"

I would have done anything to have suddenly fallen into a huge crack in the earth. But those cracks are rare.

"Spencer, do you like pickles?"

"Pickles?"

"I love pickles," I said. "Ever since I was a kid. Sometimes I just have one of those huge deli dills for lunch and I'm satisfied all day. I *crave* a good pickle, I can actually make my mouth water by thinking about a pickle. Do you like pickles?"

"No."

"Why?"

"I don't know."

"There you go," I said.

"I don't get it."

"Why some people like pickles and others don't is beyond me. People just like the things they like and that's that. There's no reason, no explanation. You're either a pickle person, or you aren't. I obviously think you are attractive, I like you, I love you, but I don't *love* you. I don't know why."

I felt like the meanest person on the planet. But after 20 years of him "devoting" himself to me, it would be pretty mean if I allowed it to continue. There would never be a chance of us getting together. People say, "Never say never," but this is pretty much a sure thing.

I have no idea why I continuously push away this person who basically has been pretty decent to me for the past 20 years. I think deep down he is a wonderful person, but he hates that part of himself so he acts like a jerk and says stupid things to push people away so they won't discover he is a peach in jerk's clothing. He's afraid of his true self. Maybe he doesn't think it's manly to care, or he believes the lie that women like men who are jerks.

Spencer is not the same as the other gators. I want him to be a part of my life, but he couldn't be my friend. He wanted something I simply could not give. I decided the best thing was not to have contact with him. His devotion wouldn't stop and he refused to look for anyone else as long as he thought there was the slightest chance with me. It was easy to love me, I had known him his whole life. It was scary to go out and meet new people. I was his safety net.

I haven't talked to Spencer in months. I recently heard through old high school friends that he's telling people that I'm truly mentally ill. He's probably right. I thought about talking to him about his rumor of choice but decided it wasn't worth it. What do I care what high school people think of me? It will make the 10-year reunion even more interesting. I've always wanted to be a rumor.

While I'm all for saving the wetlands and I oppose cruelty to animals, these are three alligators I would not miss. Float on down to some other gazelle. All I want is a little sip of water.

Does anybody else ever wonder what the point of everything is? I mean, why make your bed when it's just going to get messed up again? Why work out? You'll just become an exercise-obsessed freak who talks about jogging all the time and no one wants to hear about that because you'll make them feel fat because *they* aren't jogging all the time. It's not like they can ignore the topic, you talk about it all the time! If you didn't exercise you'd be talking about something interesting, like art or architecture, and people would no doubt be impressed and instantly want to hang out with you. So you see, exercising is bad for your social skills and may even work to the detriment of several long-standing relationships that you truly cherish.

I'm sick of trying to succeed in anything at all, even weight loss. I am by no means fat, but almost everyone could afford to lose seven to ten pounds. I'm no different. But do I have the motivation to get my ass mobile? No. Because what's the point? I looked pretty good when I was wasting three years with The One Who is Jerk-like, and look what happened there. Even top models get dumped, so I guess it doesn't matter what I look like. And why should I do anything good for this body that's not looking out for me? What has it ever done for me? Constantly reminded me that I could use 20 laps around an Olympic-sized pool. Depressed me. Infected me with a cold or forced a wicked smoker's cough on me that I don't want. I'm going to smoke two packs a day just to spite my hack attacks.

I see no point in trying to have a boyfriend either. I'm cute and interesting. You hear all the time that men are looking for a *cute and interesting girl*. Right here, boys! But do they come running? Hell no. They run in the opposite direction. I have a pretty realistic view of myself. I know when I look good, I know what my best features are, and I'm not too shabby. I would love to have me as a girlfriend. I have girlfriends that I would love to have as a girlfriend. Of course, that would entail a lifestyle change and I'm not quite willing to take up western line dancing at this point in time.

I'm beginning to notice that all attractive guys are dating ugly women. It's like some sort of sick phenomenon has spread through the entire attractive male population. Suddenly these men are struck blind, and they don't care who they're dating. I ask you, why does a dog go for Alpo when he could have a steak? The only reasonable answers I can come up with are that the whole population has been cursed by a really ugly chick, or they settle for these women because they are security blankets. The Alpo is not stupid. She will be forever faithful and make cookies for him until he pops. And this is what every man wants: a mother, someone to take care of him. My problem is that I would say something like "Why don't you try making *me* cookies?" and that's where the interest in me would stop and I would get passed by for Alpo.

I don't know why I try to be a better person. For awhile I was on this whole Better Yourself kick. Each day I would do something that would make me smarter or more attractive, like learning a new word or using moisturizing cream at night. Forget it. I'm going to get wrinkles, there's no avoiding that. Learning a new word every day is not going to make me smarter, and who cares if it does? No one is going to know what the hell I'm talking about with these multi-syllabled words.

There is no reason to get out of bed. I have no money. It's not like I can go shopping or something. It's not like I have a date to go on. The only good reason for me to get out of bed is that I hate my bed and the apartment it's located in. I can't stay in there for too long or I start to shake and consider locking myself in my closet, where I would make odd, high pitched squeaks and eat saltines like a gerbil (little bites, little bites).

I'm sick of being a guest at other people's events. I have been to so many weddings, showers and engagement parties. I'm sick of it. It's nice that I'm included in all these events, but I'm irritated. I have no events of my own. I can't even throw a dinner party because I only have two chairs to my kitchenette. I would rent a room at a restaurant and throw a party there, but you need to make a deposit for the room, and I just know someone is going to stick me with their $200 bar bill. It's not right for the hostess to be charged for someone else's Bloody Marys.

When will it ever be my party? Will I ever get to pick out invitations? I doubt it. Sentenced to a life of solitude, I will rot in my apartment, solo. No one will notice. There I will slowly decay into dust and lint that eventually gets sucked up by a vacuum cleaner. No one will remember me. Sure my mom will be sad, but she'll start drinking and soon all her memories of me will be replaced by new memories of getting drunk at family gatherings and falling down steep stairways. I'm not leaving behind any children, so all my genes and rare, good traits will never be revived and live on to give the world new hope for a better day. It will be the end of this exact shade of blue eyes. My love for Gene Kelly and black olives will die with me.

Why do people die? Is the point of living simply to die and it's then that we really start living? Each day I try to understand why bad things happen, not just to me but to the world. Why do buildings get bombed or children die of leukemia? What's the point of that?

Sometimes I wish that I could go back in time and stop bad things from happening. Like right when someone is about to kill themselves, I would knock on the door and take them out for a vodka tonic with extra lime. Who knows how this one drink would change everything? This person could go on to be the President of the United States. This person could be the eventual mother or father of some talented artist who would create wonderful art that will generate happiness and celebration for decades to come. I could stop important people from being assassinated or stop someone who will eventually die of a drug overdose the very first time they try drugs. I would be the girl who provides distraction so some person wouldn't get on a plane that will crash, leaving their family in horrible pain for the rest of their lives. I wish more than anything that I could do this.

But maybe someone's already done it. Someone could have seen what *really* bad things were coming and went back in time, time that we are living in right now, and caused something else to happen that we think is awful, but in the long run, it's for the best. Maybe the way things are now is the way things should be and are meant to be. Maybe we need homeless people and tornadoes. Maybe the bad things that happen are so much less painful than the big thing that would come if the first thing didn't come at all. Maybe someone is looking out for all of us after all. Maybe there is a point to senseless tragedy.

I don't know what to think any more. All I want to do is listen *to I Got You Babe* by Sonny and Cher over and over, until I am forced into happiness by its pleasant melody and tender lyrics. I don't want to think about losing weight or what I'm doing right or wrong to get the perfect boyfriend—who, by the way, is probably as real as the Loch Ness Monster. I don't want to wrestle with my theory of time machines and saving everyone. It's too much to think about. And I can't take too much more of anything.

22. Always a Bridesmaid

So I'm wondering why I just don't replace every outfit in my closet with a damn bridesmaid dress. Get rid of the jeans, the black pants, the white shirts. Just replace them all with yellow afternoon sundresses and huge, ugly straw hats.

I have been a bridesmaid in ten weddings over the past two years. I was even a grooms-woman when one of my best male friends got married. Is it just me or does that seem like a lot of crab stuffed mushrooms? I have no idea why this unnatural phenomenon has happened to me. It's like getting repeatedly struck by lightning.

I guess I should be flattered that I have friends who feel I'm special enough to be in their wedding party. But in another way, it seems that with each wedding, I become more and more of a spinster.

Why is it some people get married when they are 22 and others when they are 42? This is the question I ponder while enjoying a frosty mug of Boones Strawberry Hill and building cigarette chain out my kitchen window. I can't figure it out. For the most part, I've done everything right, in a dating aspect. I always have lipstick and eyebrows on. I shave my legs every day. I lift weights so I won't have jiggle arms. I make sure my hair always has a shiny sheen and smells good.

I know there is more to the Laws of Attraction than just physical traits. But ask anyone and you'll find I'm a peach of a girl. I'm not bitchy, even when it's that time of the month. I try not to complain about things. I have the ability to act really interested in something a guy is saying, when I'm really thinking about how cute my new shoes are.

I meet a lot of men. My friend Richard thinks the reason why I'm not picking out china patterns is lack of exposure. Nothing irritates me more than when he says this. I meet people through work, friends of friends, in bars, at parties. I even had one guy ask me out when I was walking down the street minding my own business. So exposure is not the problem. I've narrowed it down to two things: the men, or me.

I meet guys, date them for some insignificant amount of time, and then get bored. This last guy was dull as dishwater. At first he was great and no doubt the best looking guy I've ever dated, but he had the most annoying habit of always hitting me on the arm. I would come home from dates with my left arm swollen twice the size of the right.

I would get a jab if I said something funny. A poke when I was quiet. A tap when something funny happened. A thud when he wanted me to look at something. I'd get home and would try to figure out if it was a date or Assault and Battery.

Let me also say that he was totally into Hasselhoffing. Hasslehoffing comes from the root word Hasselhoff, as in David Hasselhoff of *Knight Rider* and *Baywatch* fame. He was good looking but a total poser, a nerd in babe's clothing. Hasselhoff had the right look, the big muscles, curly hair (though I thought it was screaming Olgolvi), but he was a nerd trying to be Hot Stuff. I'm sorry, no sale.

This last guy I dated, the Assault and Battery man, *majored* in Hasselhoffing. Who can stand to be around that for more than a few hours?

Maybe it's not the men. They are just there, being men, doing what they do. What man could tell a story that would possibly hold my interest? Maybe it's just too much to ask. Could I be asking too much from men?

It must be me. Who could possibly care to join me in a conversation on the idiocy of Tupperware parties? Who would think buying Barry Manilow's Greatest Hits is exciting? Who wants to eat Italian at a place where they pass out tambourines and encourage you to sing along with some lady the waiters call Mama? Maybe I'm crazy and don't know it yet. I'm a crazy person in denial, the worst of the worse.

Isn't there a non-Hasselhoffer who isn't always slugging me in the arm, who would enjoy a gem like me? Someone who enjoys the occasional ball game and beer, and likes to go dancing? Who wants to rent movies and order greasy pizza with me? Wouldn't you like to go sailing and eat sushi? Who wouldn't want a sex kitten that your mom would actually like?

But let's remember what we're talking about here: the fact that I am not married. Really, I don't think I'm ready. I don't want to depend on anyone right now. I don't want anyone to depend on me. I'm scared to get attached to someone who will eventually leave me for a waitress. The plain and simple truth is, there's no one in my life to get too attached to.

It's hard when almost all of your friends are married. You feel like such an idiot calling them with your dumb boy problems, asking them if you should call the latest guy tonight or wait three days. These people can't relate to you any more. They're worrying about house payments and children. Why would they want to talk about the huge undergrounder you have coming in on your chin?

Then why is it that these Marrieds still have me over for dinner? I can't help but feel like the odd man out. I get in my car and drive home afterwards and realize that I am the definition of Alone. There's no one sitting in my passenger seat, laughing about what my friend's husband said over the salmon loaf.

When my best friend JJ got married, I wasn't too emotional. She always had boyfriends, so I just thought of this guy as her perma-boyfriend. When she asked me to be one of her bridesmaids, I didn't give it much thought. I never sat down and thought, "I am standing up with my best friend as she gets married." I was thinking, "What am I going to wear?" It wasn't until a week after she got back from her honeymoon that I realized life was different.

"Wanna go shopping?" I said.

"I need to spend some time with my husband today."

"Why? Target's got their winter stuff out!"
"I'm sorry but I need to spend some time with my husband."
"Oh God, J, he's not your husband!"
"Actually, he is." And she was right.

I never thought of him as her Husband. He was just going to hang around for awhile. It was stupid for me to hide from the truth, but it was The Truth. He was The Husband. The Husband comes first in the life of the wife. When children come into the whole thing, then it's The Kids, The Husband, and then the friends. Before I knew what was going on, I was Number Three.

My whole life I've known J and was in the Number One spot. Now I'm Number Two. Before I have time to recover from the dizziness, I'm looking at me as a Three. How was this going to work? J is still my one, but now I'm her three. Do you average the two numbers? Drop the one and multiply by four?

This was the end of Girls' Night Out and talking for hours about hair color. Now she had to spend time with her Husband. And that term "husband"—what is that? I hate titles: Boyfriend, Husband. Do these people have names? Do people lose their first names once they get engaged?

I can take a title if someone says, "*I met Sam for dinner last night*" and I say, "*Who's Sam?*" Then it's OK to say, "*My fiancé.*" But to use it so loosely like that, it's bragging!

"I have a husband," "My husband called today," "My husband and I had sex last night." I am all too aware that you have a husband and I do not.

I think *Husband* really is just a code word for Sex on a Regular Basis. *Boyfriend* means Sex on an Irregular yet Pretty Consistent Basis. *Just Seeing Someone* is Occasional Sex and a Free Dinner.

A few months after the bouquet wilted, J started to tell me a few annoying things her Husband did. Not that he was all that terrible of a

Husband, but obviously he is still male. There are imperfections aplenty.

I would have a hard time coming up with a rational answer to the haunting question, "Where's dinner?" I will not deny the fact that I will probably take command of most of the dinner duties. But when I work late, don't get home until 8:00, and he's watching television and this question comes out before a simple hello, someone is sleeping on the sofa.

I do not want to do all the laundry every week.

I don't want to haul all the groceries up the stairs by myself if the person inside the house watching TV plans on eating the food.

I think marriage is 50/50. I will take on the decorating duties, naming the children, buying the presents, occasionally cooking, and throwing fabulous dinner parties. The Husband is responsible for the killing of bugs, washing my car, reaching the top of the cabinet, getting up in the middle of the night to investigate noises, and buying me flowers.

I guess marriage happens when it happens. There's no way to speed up or slow down the process. JJ got married when she was 26. My other friend Jessica got married at 19. I will probably get married when I'm an old crazy lady and committed to an insane asylum. I'll fall in love and marry some drooler I met in the crazy cafeteria.

But that's OK. His multiple personalities will keep me from ever getting bored.

HATING DATING.

Ritualistic ceremony,
"The Dating of Men"
a guy named "Guido"
a Swede named "Sven"
"… *met at a bar*"
"… a friend of a friend"
Chatting with the girls
and shirts they will lend
You set a time
6, 7, 8:30?
plan the evening
get dressed in a hurry
nervous, distressed
"What next do I say?
this guy is a jerk
I'm sure he's gay
he hates spicy food
slurps when he drinks
he hates all kitties
a moron in think
worships Jerry Springer
no belief in fate
loathes foreign films
and sushi he hates
points at fat people
hates all cheeses
he insults the old
and laughs at Jesus
he cannot dance
and hates the arts
loves pro wrestling
and releases all farts
never seen a play
no need to travel
declares all women
should be treated like cattle
asks stupid questions
never read a book
is one eye wandering?
I'm afraid to look!
His hands are pudgy
Skin is chafed
His eyes are dead
and unevenly spaced
He smells like soup
and talks like a chick
His nose is crooked
and front tooth chipped
No ass to speak of
No shoulders at all
He's 5'5"
and claims that's tall
Loves old sneakers
and Metallica shirts
Wants me to wear fringe
and red leather skirts
Calls me "Babe"
and "Kumquat Head"
I try to be sweet
But wish he were dead…"

He grabs my knee
and licks my ear
blows on my neck
and pulls me near
"Tonight I'm yours.
I'll treat you right…"
"OK, Pal
that's it,
good night!"
I leave the place
and hail a cab
Just looking for a guy
a little like dad

Pull out a smoke
start to wonder
how long will this last
can it be much longer?
I want to go home
and get into bed
close my eyes
and clear my head…
When will I find him?
The one that won?
It's the ritual of dating
it just must be done.

One day I realized that I have a lot of gay friends; not that there's anything wrong with that. But when you have a lot of gay friends, you tend to frequent gay bars and nightclubs. I had begun to find it incredibly depressing... water, water everywhere and not a drop to drink. Not only that, the water ain't even interested in me. And can I tell you a not-so-little-secret about gay men? They are perfect for women. They're rarely overweight, they're well-coifed, use the appropriate amount of hair products, always smell good, dress well, and are very giving with the compliments. It's so easy to go to these gay bars and convince your straight female self that these gay men are somehow available to you. Never have I been referred to as *Gorgeous* as many times as I have in a gay bar. Gay men always love my eyes and big lips. A straight man may enjoy these traits as well but the difference is, the gay man tells you that he likes them. The straight man clams up, afraid to compliment. And here I thought a man wasn't supposed to be afraid of anything.

Hanging out with gay men was fabulous, but the depression became too much. These weren't my people, they had their own society, their own way of behaving around one another. I didn't fit in. I made a conscious choice to hang out with straight women more often. Here all my gay friends hung out with their gay friends (with the exception of me, the token straight girl). Scottie told me, "Gay men like to hang around their own kind." I decided to seek out my sisters. I was a single girl, I should be with my peeps.

In the past, I never really got along with women. Let's face it, women are hypersensitive. They dissect every single sentence to come up with the actual, alternate and possible meaning of every conversation, and they want to have long discussions about it. Women fight over men. Women steal each other's men, and date their best friend's boyfriend. I've done it, you've done it. We're all guilty victims. I can think of at least four friends who were once close to me at some point and now we hate each other because I dated her boyfriend, or she had sex with mine.

That's how I got into the whole gay man scene. I get along better with men, gay or straight. The gay man likes to see cheesy movies and go dancing, yet you can still hug or kiss him and people think you're dating. The straight guy friends I have are all married and their wives are pretty cool about letting us hang out. I'm no threat anyway; it's like hanging out with their sister. We play video games, watch movies, or play air hockey (where I humiliate their macho-ness by kicking their wimpy asses!). I can talk to men about men and get their perspective.

Being around gay or straight men has made me wise. It's research. All these conversations and late night outings… I find it truly educational. It's made me comfortable around men, and I know how they think and what they want. When I finally do find a man with potential, I will know exactly how to relate to his side. I've been brushing up on my conversational skills my whole life. I'm constantly doing research of the ins and outs of a proper kiss. I watch those love scenes in movies and take notes. I have evaluated each man I ever kissed, starting with the first kiss back in kindergarten, and narrowed it down to exactly what it means to be kiss-worthy. I have perused *The Joy of Sex* to learn how to get things done. Free education is all around us, girls! We just have to pay attention.

So here I am, embarking on a straight girl venture where my guides are fellow sisters. I turned to the few women I knew for guidance down the path of heterosexuality.

I worked with Ally for about three months. We got along great, right from the start. She is a little bit quieter than I am and has got the greatest laugh. We talk about everything over our occasional dinners. If I were to divide up my personality, she would be the quiet, shy side of me. We talk about going out some Friday or Saturday, but she usually just wants to stay in.

CeCe is the *get drunk and stay out till five in the morning* part of me. Her sentences usually begin with "I was naked and totally drunk…" I laugh at first, then give her a pseudo lecture later about rolling with randoms. CeCe is very no-nonsense and has the admirable ability to cut people off and not think twice. She is very hip and fond of sparkle makeup, something right up there with tiaras and sushi on my list of favorites.

Maleka is a combination of Ally and CeCe. She can talk for hours on the phone about anything, and then will want to meet you for a drink at the Amigo Bar at Denny's. She's been dating a guy for almost five years so she's not officially in the Club. He isn't around too much so I let it slide. She's very much an Outdoor Girl, totally unlike me. I knew I would love her after our first conversation. She said, "My idea of a good time is cooking up a pound of bacon and just eatin' it." You gotta love a girl like that.

Then there's Jill. I met her through Scottie. He got a new job almost a year ago and that's where he met Jill. He told me she was just like me, so of course I hated her. Who was this girl? Thinking she was all… me. The nerve! I met her a couple of times at the parties Scottie had, each time trying to get a read on her. The first time I met her she gave me The Lookover, a common characteristic among women, but not the women I like. If you're going to do The Lookover try to be discreet. It's like yanking up your nylons when you're in a crowded room; it probably shouldn't be done.

The third time I saw her at one of the parties, we sat outside, smoking and talking for hours. We had a lot of things in common: past relationships, lack of a current boyfriend, high fashion and too many gay friends. She said she had a few straight girl friends but hated them. "I guess we'll have to be friends then," I said, and we embarked on a new friendship.

Jill likes to have a good time and go out, but I've never seen her drunk. She is totally hysterical and loves any item of clothing with feathers on it. I've never met anyone who admits their faults so openly and easily but makes no effort to change them.

She told me about one of her many vacations in Vegas. In a three day period she rolled around with a guy who told her he was in Vegas for a bachelor party, later learned it was *his* bachelor party, made out with the Best Man poolside at the Tropicana, got busted by a security guard for disorderly conduct, won $500, got her belly button pierced, and saw Tom Jones. We are currently planning a trip to Vegas together.

Not that I want to have my way with some groomsman, or to get arrested. We just both think it would be fun to get up at 2:00 in the afternoon, lie by the pool with umbrella'd drinks till eight, get dressed for dinner, go out at ten, catch a show, go dancing, have an all-you-can eat brunch at 6:00 in the morning, and head back to the room, only to do it all again the next day. Throw in a visit to a tattoo parlor somewhere in there (along with the mandatory shopping for tacky trinkets to hand down to our grandchildren), and we're talking about a severe good time. I definitely don't think Vegas is the cultural hot spot of our great nation, but sometimes you have to experience things just for the hell of it. It's amazing; just a few short years ago I thought I would have been married and pregnant by now. Instead I'm planning hangovers in Vegas.

My years as a beard to the gay man and a sister to the straight man have made my friendships with females easier. There's not so much competition for men. I know what I'm looking for and I'm not going to compromise. If one of my friends has it for some guy, I will stay away. The friends I've lost due to The Boyfriend Swap are sadly missed. Plus, men are like buses: another one will be along in 15 minutes.

I realize jealousy and competition will never truly die out between women. I can honestly say I have girlfriends I'm envious of: their jobs, their looks—but I don't hate them for it. I'm grateful that I'm lucky enough to have such wonderfully successful and beautiful friends. If I were as canine as I often feel, these beauties would not hang out with me. People hang around their own kind, so I must be just as blessed as they are, in some capacity.

·

I see now that women are the stronger of the two sexes. Do you think it's just luck that women are the ones with the ability to give birth? That shit was planned out. God (or whoever) knew we could take the pain, whereas men would collapse at the first inkling of a contraction. One menstrual cramp and a man would be bedridden.

I saw on TV that the female spider eats the male spider after intercourse. Haven't we all wanted to do that! Look at the Queen Bee, now there's a bitch to be reckoned with. The Queen of Sheba, Cleopatra… these women were terminators in blue eye shadow. What about witches back in their day? Witches were killed because men were frightened by their unexplained strength. The only thing I can't figure out is if our strength is in our ovaries or our heads. But it's there. I've seen it, I've felt it, I am it.

When I'm with The Girls, it isn't just fun. It's reassuring. There's a connection there that isn't there for men. Women can talk forever, or not say a word and know exactly how the other is feeling. We are the creators of life and the makers of homes. That's more important than knowing who won the Superbowl in '86.

Women are survivors. Women are thinkers. There are more male criminals than female criminals. Women rarely beat the shit out of their husbands (not because they don't want to). It's purely ironic that the physically weaker of the sexes is actually the stronger. No one ever said God didn't have a sense of humor. We've always been warriors in underwire bras, and now Glamourina is reclaiming her position.

Don't ever underestimate the power of a woman.

Only our skin is soft.

23. JJ Is Pregnant

Three days after Christmas, JJ told me she was pregnant. I was shocked. She had just gotten back from her Honeymoon on Christmas Eve; how could she possibly know already?

"I was pregnant when we got married. Almost three weeks along."
"You didn't know?"
"No," she sighed, "But remember how I felt sick at the wedding and everyone said I was just nervous?"
"Yeah?"
"Guess I wasn't nervous."
"Shit, J, what are you going to do? *Did you tell your mom?*" I whispered.
"We're married. There's no reason not to have it."
"I keep forgetting that you're somebody's wife. You're somebody's mother!"
"I know. In a couple of years a kid is going to say, 'God, I hate my mom, she's driving me crazy,' and he'll be talking about me!" she said.
"You think it's a boy?"
"I think I think it's a boy."
"What are you going to name him?" I asked.
"Jack. What do you think?"
"I love Jack."
J started to cry, "You're going to be an auntie."
"Are you ready for this?'
"I think so. We can handle it. It's time."
In no time at all, it had become time. We went from one summer of drinking electric ice teas on the beach to a summer of planning baby showers. I couldn't even picture her as mother. She was like me and I

couldn't picture myself as a mother. All of a sudden there would be someone there, with her, all the time. Who was this baby? What if he was a little shit? What if J and I stopped talking because she was so busy changing diapers and pumping her breasts?

Was I falling behind in life? All of a sudden I was hearing how all these girls I went to high school with were having babies. I didn't even have a boyfriend. These girls had husbands and were starting families. I heard that one girl I knew from high school had four children. A mother of four, and here I was eating mini raviolis out of a can and steam cleaning cat hair out of my carpet. While these people had house payments, I was ordering Wonderbras from Victoria's Secret. They were saving for their kids' educations and I was selling CDs for cash at the used record store.

I was way behind everyone else, even though I went to college three months after high school graduation. I was the only one I knew who did that, and the only one who graduated from college in four years. I moved out of my parents' house four months after college. But somehow, everyone was beating me. Either they skipped college and worked this whole time and got married, or they met their husbands in college and got married after graduation. Four years later they started having kids. Where had I gone wrong? While I was living in an apartment, they were throwing candle parties in their family-style, four-bedroomed suburban duplexes.

I don't want to have kids, right now anyway. Kids, for cryin' in the night! There were times I thought about getting rid of my cat; what kind of mother would I make? Maybe I don't want kids at all. Who thinks like this? Am I a frigid bitch, the kind that you see out in public, tripping small children and scolding the parents for not controlling their children? I'm a freak, a reject… all women want to be mothers don't they?

JJ said it was her time to be a mother. I wonder if it would ever be my time. When would I be prepared to say, *"It's time, now I want to have* kids"? I feel like I just graduated from high school; I still get zits and watch *Saved by the Bell*. I even contemplated buying a New York Style Barbie a few weeks ago... for myself! This person is not mother material. And let's talk about the pain of childbirth. I've heard it's about a million times worse than cramps, and I've had cramps that bring me to my knees. A million times worse than that and I think that every bone in my entire body would shatter.

JJ being pregnant was all very scary and hard to believe. This coupled with the fact she didn't even show for five months. I saw her almost every day and each day she would ask me if she looked different.

"No, you look exactly the same."

"I look bigger and you know it."

"I do *not* know it, I can't even see it."

Then one day I saw it.

She was meeting me after work at a restaurant. I got there early and was leaning against a brick wall, smoking. I saw her familiar walk from two blocks away. It was hotter than hell that night and she was wearing a green maternity tank top and stretch pants. She hadn't seen me yet and was waiting to cross the street. She put one hand on her stomach when a group of undesirables stood next to her, as if her motherly hand were somehow protecting her unborn child. She started to cross, led by her protruding stomach. The wind blew against her thin frame and that green shirt plastered against her midsection, revealing the child I was trying to deny was there.

Tears welled up in my eyes. By the time she approached me I was in full-fledged tears. My best friend was going to have a baby.

On the Fourth of July, J went into premature labor. I was waiting at home, waiting for her to call me so I could go over to her apartment for a rooftop bar-b-que. I sat in my green chair and looked out the window. I was by myself on the Fourth, a holiday that I established as a romantic holiday; I always wanted to have some man wrap his arms around me as we *oohed* and *awed* at the lights in the sky. But alas, again I was boyfriendless and the dream of my romantic Fourth was pushed back to maybe next year.

In the distance I could hear people yelling, drinking and shouting out that they wanted their burgers medium rare. I started to cry and Pinkie jumped in my lap. I had no idea where JJ was. She had forgotten about me already. The baby was due in a month and I was already a second class citizen. At least I would have a good view of the fireworks.

The phone rang. "J, I'm sitting here waiting for you to call. The fireworks are about to start."

"I know."

"Why didn't you call? You better either be dead or in the hospital."

"I'm in the hospital."

I sat up, "Oh my God! Are you all right? How's the baby?"

"I started bleeding around three o'clock. I checked into the hospital this afternoon. I was going into labor."

"Where's your permanent boyfriend?"

"At home," she sighed.

"Why?"

"I don't want to talk about it."

"OK. Want me to come see you?"

"No."

"Why not?" I asked.

"I feel like shit. I just thought we could watch the fireworks together."

"You want to come over?"

"I have a TV in here and you can see them from your window. Let's just watch."

"OK." I leaned back in the chair. After about three minutes of silence I said, "Look at us."

"What?" she yawned.

"It's the Fourth of July and you're all pregnant in the hospital, and I'm sitting here with a cat in my lap and we're both completely alone."

"You're not alone," she said. "Jack and I are with you."

Thirty days later, Madeline came into the world. There was no Jack all along; it was little baby Maddy fooling all of us by crossing her little legs. I said she was either very ladylike or a practical joker. I had already helped J paint the nursery blue.

The night Maddy was born was one of the hardest nights of my life. Not only was my best friend in some serious pain in the room at the end of the hall, my whole life was changing. There was no reason why I wasn't the one in that room, trying to push some child from my loins. It could have been me. I was mother age. I was 26, a very acceptable age to become a mom. Already I was one year older than my own mother was when she had me. I was five years older than my mom was when she got married. That shit is really freaky when you think about it. I recommend that you don't.

It was the end of our childhood. She was a mother and I *could* be a mother. Somewhere along the way we crossed over a line of maturity and I didn't even see it. Now J had to think of someone else, she had to feed and clothe someone else. For the first time in both of our lives, she was different than me. We'd always been the same. We were always in the same grade, lived in the same sort of house, we had the same life. Now she had one blaring difference, and it was a biggie.

It's not like this child was going to go away. She was here. And nothing would ever be the same. I felt sick for almost two weeks after Maddy was born. I had absolutely no urge to see the baby. JJ would call and invite me over and I would make up some excuse not go. Somehow the birth of Maddy made me realize how alone I really was. J had a family, a husband, a child. I had a cat and a strange rash on my eyelid. All of a sudden she jumped at least five years ahead of me and I blamed it all on the baby. If she hadn't come along, things would've stayed the same. So what that J was married? It wasn't all that different. Maddy was what made things different. I called J and told her we couldn't be friends any more.

"Why not?" she said, with Maddy crying in the background.

I started to sob, "Because I can't relate to you any more. We're completely different, everything's changed."

"It has not."

"For fuck's sake, J, you have a kid! I have a rash! Let me just point out to you that one is pretty different than the other!"

"You'll get used to her."

"I will not. Am I just going to forget that she's there? People change, things change. You're a mother; I'm a loser. I don't even have a boyfriend and you're breastfeeding."

JJ started to cry. "Don't do this to me. I need you. Maddy needs you. You don't know it yet but she needs you. You think that all of a sudden I'm so different? I'm exactly the same! But now I have a daughter. It's scary as hell. You think I'm so different from you? How would you feel if all of a sudden you were responsible for a child?"

I blew my nose. "I don't know."

"How would you feel?"

"J, I don't know! I don't know the first thing about babies."

"Neither do I! I need your help. Don't leave me now." We were quiet for a long time. All I could hear was my own breathing and the sound of a brand new baby crying.

"I have to think about it," I said, quietly.

"Well, I'm not giving up on you after 21 years of friendship."

She called me five times a day. I tried to be cold when she held Maddy up to the phone so I could hear her little cooing noises. I tried not to smile when she showed me the tiny pink shoes she bought for her daughter. She convinced me to paint the bookshelves in the nursery and help her put the crib together. Each time I saw Maddy, I tried to ignore the fact that she was getting cuter and cuter every day.

"Can you hold Maddy while I take a shower?" J asked, handing her to me.

"Well, I guess."

"I'll be five minutes."

I sat in the rocker in the nursery with Maddy in my arms. She was asleep. I looked down at her little face and listened closely to her baby breath. She was so tiny; her red hair was starting to come in. I touched her little nose and she opened her eyes. She looked right at me. I swear that kid touched my heart with that one look. Her pale lashes framed her big eyes and I realized Maddy didn't represent the fact that I was alone. She was my hope. She made me see outside the stupid world I created. There were other things in life than going to the movies with some guy. Not everything was about having messages on your answering machine.

When I put my finger in her tiny hand, she clamped onto it with surprising strength. I knew then that I would do anything in the world for this child. If she needed a leg, I would chop mine off and give it to her. This was half of my best friend, the friend who was there for me almost my entire life. The friend who wouldn't let me ruin our friendship with my own selfishness.

If J had a baby, than I probably will too one day. After all, we've always been the same our whole lives. She was always one step ahead. She should have a child first; she got a bra before I did.

LITTLE MISS MADS. [8/25/98, 11:55 pm]

You came in by a whisper
an unexpected truth
crawling into a world
& a room full of people
who never knew
they were expecting you.

Created from his bluest eyes
& her most beautiful smile
you grew
& I knew
that this baby was not only theirs
but mine.

Before I ever heard your beating heart
You already filled mine.

24. Cake

Dear God,

I'm probably not the type of person you want to hear from. I'm the kind of person who never prays until they need something.

I'm guessing you favor those who go to church and actually give up something for Lent. I try to be your devoted servant but I get wrapped up in my own stupid things and forget you're there. I do try to pray every night. I get in bed, press my palms together and start something to you, but I doze off. I hope you recognize my nightly efforts as true, serious intentions to be the good Catholic I so desperately want to be. I've just got a lot on my mind right now, which causes excessive exhaustion. I know you understand. You're probably the busiest person in the universe. I don't know how you fit it all in: listening to everyone's prayers, keeping an eye on the angels. It's no wonder the occasional natural disaster gets past you.

I'm a good person. I've never intentionally harmed anyone or stolen anything from a department store on purpose. I feel like I don't ask for too much. I take a lot of things on myself, like knowing it's up to me to get a good job and keep my apartment clean. So that's why I'm hoping you can help me. What I'm asking for is really quite simple.

I like to think of my life as a cake. It's a good cake—moist, delicious; I really like it. And I thank you for it. I have wonderful friends who've helped me make this cake. My good health is a big slice of it too.

But what I'm asking for is just a little *frosting*. I don't need fancy flowers stuck on the cake. I don't want birthday candles, sprinkles, shavings or marshmallows. Just a simple layer of frosting that will make the cake just that much better. The frosting equals (in this rather confusing and stupid equation) a relationship with a man. A *good* relationship with a *good* man.

Now I understand why you allowed the whole shitty experience to happen to me those years ago with What's His Face. At the time, I couldn't understand why you allowed it to happen. But I get it now, I get the joke. I see that I was weak and trying to navigate my life on this narrow little path, not knowing that you were in control the whole time. I appreciate the last few years of my life. I've lived on my own and enjoyed being single. God knows I've gone through several meaningless relationships with members of the opposite sex, but now I know exactly what I want.

Two and a half years ago, I thought I knew what I wanted but I didn't. I just wanted what was easiest. I feel like I've not only learned from your lesson, but I survived it in a most successful way. I've spread the word about the things I've learned to women everywhere—that lesson being that women need to be independent and happy with themselves before they can be happy with someone else. A fulfilling relationship with someone else should not be the main focus of one's life. The relationship should add to what's already good, *like frosting on a cake*. Cake is OK without the frosting, but it's the frosting that makes the whole thing really damn good.

I've let go of the hate and hurt feelings caused by events that happened years ago. Hate is like acne. The more you focus and pick at it, the worse it gets and eventually you'll have a scar you can never cover up. If you let go of the hate, everything will eventually go back to normal and you won't have any red splotches.

I'm no saint and by no means have acted like one the past few years. If you truly know and see everything, then you know what I'm talking about. Sorry about that. But lately I've made some sincere changes in my life. I know who I want to be and what I really want out of life. I want to be a true friend and a good person. I want to be proud of everything I do.

But what I really want is to sit in a grade school auditorium and watch my daughter act as one of the Wise Men in the annual Christmas pageant. I want to sit in there and laugh at the baby Jesus who's making silly faces at Mary. I want to turn to the fine man sitting next to me with tears in my eyes and say, "I love you."

I want to glue a million stupid feathers to my kid's peacock outfit and take her to piano lessons.

I want to chop carrots in my very own kitchen and have my husband hug me from behind and say I'm the most beautiful woman in the world.

I want to get flowers on major holidays.

I want to hold someone's hand in a video store and argue about what movie we're going to rent.

To show you how serious I am about these wants, I've made a decision that in the past has been unthinkable: I'd rather never have sex again for the rest of my life, than have sex with some guy who doesn't get excited when I walk into the room. I call this my "Snack Cake Vow."

I would rather starve than have a little snack cake here and there (a "Ho Ho" on some drunken Saturday night; a "Ding Dong" at a random party.) I'm going to hold out for The Big Meal. I want the wine, the appetizer, the salad, bread, soup, sorbet, main course and dessert.

I want to know what it's like to love someone, and to be with someone who loves me more than life itself. I want to know what it feels like to have someone who loves me kiss me passionately. In order to get these things that I want so badly, I'm vowing to give up all snack cakes forever. That's my promise to you as your humble servant.

I hope you will consider my request, God. If you grant me this one wish I will be happy for the rest of my life. It's not like I'm asking for something that people don't normally ask for. You probably get a million requests a day for the love of one's life to suddenly appear, but I hope you'll help me out first because I just feel like I'm more serious about this than other people.

I'm ready, God, I'm prepared. I can handle an adult relationship now. I've put my faith in the idea that you make things happen when they're supposed to happen, but if you could just push me up to the front of the line, I'd sure appreciate it.

I'll be on the lookout for any kind of sign if you should choose to operate in that fashion. I'll search my dreams for symbolism and your acknowledgment of my request. I'll even say my nightly prayers standing up so there won't be any chance of falling asleep in the middle of a Hail Mary.

Thank you, God. I appreciate your time, especially when I know there's got to be a volcano somewhere that needs cooling off. I hope to hear from you soon.

Amen.

25. Why Girls Are Stupid

Advice columnists really have it made in the old proverbial shade. Here they are, dishing advice like hashbrowns chock full of onions at a diner, with people picking out the advice they don't want to hear like the unwanted onion.

Why do people trust columnists? Who knows what kind of training these people have, yet they are trusted enough to guide people like ships through the night toward uncharted waters. It's all very possible they have no idea what they're doing. I think people in the advice giving business are the ones in need of counseling and/or psychic healing.

If you ask me, there is no real difference between advice givers and fortune tellers. I usually believe in all that metaphysical stuff, but lately I've been entirely pessimistic about the whole occupation. Luck counts for about 50 percent of everything in life, so getting 50 percent of someone's past, present or future right doesn't seem too tough. If anyone sat right in front of me, I could guess what kind of person they were. If some fortune teller happens to be somewhat logical and level headed, they'll say something moderately intelligent and you'll get some sort of direction out of it.

There are tons of generalities that apply to everyone: You're headed for a new job, Focus on your inner child, You're an extremely talented person, all that crap. It's pretty much applicable to any person with a heartbeat.

Some Head-Shrinker will make it possible for you to wear a thimble as a hat with all the bogus advice they pass out at 90 bucks an hour. It's funny how when we were little we didn't want anyone to tell us what to do, but when we're older, we'll pay someone to do just that.

Based on the fact that anyone with half a brain and an ounce of sensibility has free range to give advice, I've decided that I want to become an Advice Columnist. I can bullshit with the rest of them. The only difference between me and the other Crap Talkers is that I know what I'm talking about. I'm not going to sugar coat anything for you, even if it means I have to admit there are definitely some severe, deep-seated problems with every human with a uterus. True, I'm one of them, but that doesn't blind me to the things I see wrong with women. And it is to women that I would like to speak.

Women give women a bad name. Women are a bad name. Women can think of tons of bad names to call other women.

I would like to tell women that they can answer every question with the answer to this one question: *What Would Audrey Hepburn Do?* So many mishaps would be prevented if women used this question as an emotional ruler. There would be no more roller skating in string bikinis. No one would wear kitty sweatshirts. It means the end of all clothing that has been Bedazzled.

Say you meet some guy at a bar, and he says, "How 'bout we go back to my place to knock boots?" Audrey Hepburn would not go to the Den of Sin. She would flick the ashes from her cigarette holder and walk away—after saying something entirely brilliant and clever.

Audrey Hepburn would not call a guy over and over at two o'clock in the morning.

Audrey Hepburn would not send some man a raunchy e-mail. Everything in life must be based on what Audrey Hepburn would do.

One of the many mistakes women make is acting desperate. This involves calling a man too often or being at his sexual disposal at any time. It all goes back to caveman days. Men want to go out and hunt something, club it over the head, and drag it back to the cave. If you act like you've already been clubbed and dragged, what's the point? There is none. It's like having sex with a piece of furniture. It's always there so you might as well use it, but it's not all that exciting, and it's kind of sick.

Jumping from man to man is a mistake women make so often it's almost inbred into our chemical makeup. Audrey Hepburn was single in *Breakfast at Tiffany's*. Why shouldn't you be single? Are you too good for Audrey? Is Audrey any less of a person than you are? Hell, no!

If being married and washing out some guy's undies were so exciting there would be at least one hit movie made about it. But when a movie does involve the characters being married, it's always about some bitch trying to steal the husband or shrinking children to the size of ladybugs. Hi, I'm bored. If being single were so bad there wouldn't be so many movies, TV shows and songs about it. It's more exciting than cooking a chicken potpie for some guy you have to beg for sex once a week.

Sleeping with a man too soon is another no-no that I would definitely advise against. Generally, the One Month Rule is a good one to go by—that is, if you see this person once or twice a week with the every-other-night phone call rotation thrown in there. Sleeping with someone on the first date is not a very Audrey thing to do. If every woman were being logical, she would agree with me. It's like impulse buying; it's great to snatch up that item at a moment's notice, but there's just something exhilarating about buying that jacket you've had your eye on forever.

Another thing women do is put requirements on themselves as to what they should have by a certain age. For instance, I recently ran into this girl I went to high school with and she's been dating this guy for three years. She said to me, "I have got to be married or engaged by our 10 year reunion." Why? So these idiots you went to high school with, who you didn't give a shit about 10 years ago, who don't give a damn about you, can be impressed? Audrey Hepburn wouldn't care about these idiots! Let them burn! Go to your reunion looking like hot stuff and that is it. Is someone who has four kids, a beat-up station wagon and looks like hell, better than you? Better than someone who is single, knows what they want, and looks fabulous? No, says Audrey, and I raise a glass to that.

Please don't think there are no good men out there. First of all, saying this out loud to your girlfriends while you're out having drinks will not lure men over to your table. Don't even say it when you're alone in your apartment. Bringing these words to life is like jinxing yourself. There are good men out there; this is something I can assure every woman. Thinking this about men is the same as men thinking this about women, when obviously that's not true. Look at me: a perfect example that good women do exist.

This world is huge and full of good men. You've encountered such a small amount of men, it's almost comical when you really think about it. Relax. If you want something bad enough, you'll get it. But don't focus on it. It always amazes me when people complain about the weather here in Seattle. I never even notice it, unless of course it's 90 degrees or snowing. I figure if you have time to notice the weather and it affects you that much, you need more things to do. I think the same thing about women who focus on the fact that they are without a mate. Get off it, honey, it can't rain forever.

Don't settle for some loser just because you don't want to be alone. You would rather have some jackass around who drives you crazy? Being single, and waiting your turn, is not that bad. Look at it this way: there's no one to question the $80 you spent on a hot rock massage and no urine stains to clean up next to the toilet. Now, that ain't so bad.

This is what I say to women, with the ghost of Audrey Hepburn whispering in my ear: Do what you think is right. Say something when you feel like saying it.

Treat men the way you want men to treat you.

Let go of your requirements, like they have to be this tall or make that much money. Love can come in any package and maybe you've never been receptive to it because you're wrapped up in silly prerequisites.

Visualize what you want and you shall get it.

You deserve all that you desire.

No one is better than you.

Be who you were when you were little, before you got all jaded and wicked like me. You just wanted to be happy, and found that happiness in the little things. Like movie previews or a chip that was stuck to another chip so you got a double chip. These are important things in life, the things you will think about when you think your last thought. All the rest just makes for a bleeding ulcer.

Sit back, have a cigarette, and a vodka tonic with extra lime. Don't let some shrink or palm reader predict your future. You can make your life go any which way you want. What a wonderful opportunity you have: the destiny of your own life is right there in your very own hands.

26. Brave New World

I've started having massive anxiety attacks. In the past, when I heard people say they were having anxiety attacks, I always pictured a cat hanging by its claws from the ceiling. I am that cat now.

It's hard to describe what these attacks feel like. I can't stand or sit in one place for too long, and I constantly have the mild shakes in both hands. My stomach feels like I've eaten too many Pop Rocks and I can sweat on command.

I'm not sure when the attacks started but it seems as if they were always there. I blame it on a traumatic birth. I was a C-section baby and had the umbilical cord wrapped around my head. That can't be a good sign for sound mental health, my poor little brain getting squeezed during those vital, formative months.

When I was a kid, I would get wildly nervous the night before school began. I can remember my brother snoring away in the next room, and I'd be in the bathroom throwing up with my mother consoling me through the door. I'd be upset that I was one year older, or I didn't have homeroom with any of my friends. I'd worry about what I would wear and if any boys would like me. I was nervous about the math class I knew I'd have to take and the fact that things were different from last year. The only thing that would calm me down was eating a peeled orange and drinking water out of this really cool coffee cup my mom had.

Now I hate oranges and the cup broke. I don't think those tricks would work now anyway. Being upset about a math class and being upset because your thirtieth birthday is three years away are two different things.

It's the end of me. The Beginning of the End. The other day I swore I could see smog and toxic fumes floating through the air as I was driving down a major interstate. I honestly considered getting one of those surgeon/Michael Jackson masks to save my lungs.

And my dreams lately have been so weird. Last night I dreamt I went to Hooters for breakfast, where my toast and chocolate milk cost $16.00. All the Hooter girls thought it was great that I came to their cult restaurant alone. I tried to escape but all the doors were locked. The girls in their orange shorts and super tan nylons grabbed me and threw me into this empty room. There were no chairs so I sat on the floor, when this woman suddenly came in and started to teach me makeup tips for winter.

Last week I had a dream that I was six months pregnant and still trying to fit into my normal clothes. I was trying to hide my pregnancy by jamming myself into my regular jeans and JJ said, in this heavy New York accent, "You can't even tell, sweetie! You just look bloated."

This dream really freaked me out because it was one of those really real dreams that you can actually feel happening. I was standing in front of this full-length mirror, running my hands over my stomach, and I could feel my pregnant lower half, plain as day. Talk about a nightmare.

The next night I had a dream that Shitbird wanted me to go to a family reunion with Him. The Waitress couldn't make it and He wanted me to pretend I was His wife. My subconscious left out why I decided to go, but I went. Some long lost cousin asked me, "Where are your kids?"

"Kids? More than one?" I said, glaring at Shitbird.

He nodded slowly and these children come out of nowhere yelling, "Mommy! Mommy!"

I passed out. I remember seeing nothing but darkness while the in-laws circled around me.

"Is she going to be OK?"

"My God, what's wrong with her?"

Then I heard His voice so clearly. That whispery voice that sent a chill through me each time I heard it, and He said, "Doesn't she look beautiful?"

I also dreamt that I was at a party wearing these gray sweat pants that were at least 10 times too big. I looked like a perfect gray elephant. So I'm at this party, sucking up peanuts, and someone tells me that Shitbird is there. Here I am, uniformed in these awful sweat pants and He's there. He comes over to me and says I look great. Then all of a sudden, Scottie (who I didn't even know was at the party) starts making out with me. I push him away and Scottie introduces himself to The Blue Eyed Devil as my boyfriend. After that, I don't remember much except that there was this murky pond in back of the party house that had alligators in it. The next thing I know, I was standing in a doorway with Him.

"What have you been up to?" He asked.

"You are not a part of my life anymore, so you aren't privileged enough to *know* anything about my life."

"Fair enough." He took a swig from His beer bottle.

"Can I just ask you one thing?" I said.

"Sure."

"Do I ever cross your mind?"

"How can I not think about you? I think about you all the time." I woke up in a cold sweat with my heart racing like a cheetah.

The wacked out dreams are not the only things adding to my personal hysteria. A simple trip to the post office last week led to an obscenely huge freak out. I was standing in this huge line getting self-adhesive holiday stamps for my Christmas cards. Looking around at the usual gaggle of characters who frequent the P.O., I notice this huge reader board counting down to the year 2000. It showed how many years, months, weeks, days, hours, minutes and seconds were left in this century. I stood in this line that went on for days, and stared at that damn countdown. I could feel my pulse quicken and my lower back started to ache.

I just lost one minute. There! I just lost two seconds! Two seconds of my life that I will never get back! This reader board has always been there, not counting down to the year 2000, counting down to the day I die! Never again will there be this day, this year and this moment, and I'm wasting it in this stupid post office line. I don't have much time left, how am I going to get it all done? Go to Europe, get a good job, meet a good man and have kids… I'm on a schedule here, people! What numbers are on my board? I don't even know how many years I have left.

How many eggs do I have socked away in those ovaries of mine? How many more seconds do I have left until I start to develop a double chin? Oh my God, it's happening now. As I stand here and watch the seconds go by, I'm that much closer to growing excessive facial hair and getting saggy elbows. At this moment I'm aging and losing my youth. Seconds go by so fast—in the amount of time I just spent figuring that one out, I lost 21 seconds!

I had to leave. I didn't wait for my 42 self-adhesive holiday stamps. I don't know how people can work in that environment, what with the major countdown happening right in front of their eyes. No wonder Postal Workers go nuts. I better write a letter to the Human Resources department of the United States Postal Service. If they're trying to calm down those postal people, they need to get rid of that sign and install an indoor fountain. Maybe paint the walls an earth tone or pump aromatherapy into the heating system. The reader board from hell isn't giving anyone any breaks.

Because I'm so stressed, I get really irritated with people. If the person driving in front of me leaves their turn signal on while driving in a straight line, I am fully irritated. A checker at the grocery store who is too slow is guaranteed to suffer the wrath of one of my gypsy hexes.

The other day I was riding the elevator up to my office on the eighth floor. The elevator was completely crowded when I got on, and this man was standing right next to me, about a foot into my personal space. What can you do? It's a packed elevator. But as we're going up, making the stops, people are getting off. By the time we stop at the fourth floor, the Personal Invader and I are the only ones left. He does not move to the opposite side of the elevator or budge one small inch. I rode up the remaining four floors with him sticking himself in my space the entire time. It took all that I had not to shove this man into the opposite wall and yell, *"Outta my space, Jackass!"*

Why was it that this moron could not step away from me? Now, if it were someone desirable, I would have no real problem. But this was a fifty-something, balding man wearing cheap plastic shoes and a Members Only jacket. Move your ass, pal! Is it too much to ask to simply ride an elevator? Do you have to stand right next to me when the entire elevator is empty? The only thing that prevented me from acting on my anxiety-filled instincts was thinking that this person could have been a new guy at work or a potential client. I can just see myself tearing into this man and later he introduces himself as the new work counselor.

I'm sure all of this anxiety is not only brought on my bad experience at birth, but because I'm still carrying around the anger and sadness caused from getting my heart broken. I need to concentrate on the future. Not my future of getting married or not getting married, but *my* future. Concentrating on what makes me happy. This is probably the only time in my life I will only need to think about me and that's it. There are no children to feed or husband to entertain. It's all about me. I don't have control over the past, but I can control the future.

A couple of days ago I had the urge to drive by the apartment that I lived in with Him. I hadn't been there in two years. It was always so beautiful at this time of the year: the huge Christmas tree in the lobby, the white lights around the roofline. I just wanted to see if I could remember what it felt like to pull into the drive and to smell the hallways. I wanted to see if I could recognize the sound of the fountain in front of the building, and remember what I felt when I walked into our apartment and saw Him.

"Hi, sweetie."

"Hi," I said, kissing Him.

"I have a surprise for you."

"You do?"

"Yeah. Sit down."

He jumped up and put on a CD.

"What are you doing?" I asked.

"I'm doing something for you, something I haven't done in awhile."

I sat as the familiar sounds of the Rolling Stones floated out of our speakers and I slowly smiled.

We'd only been dating for about two weeks when He came to my apartment for dinner. He was helping me chop and grate something when a Rolling Stones song came on. He put down the knife and proceeded to do the funniest Mick Jagger impression I'd ever seen. Tears jumped out of my eyes and I stood in that tiny kitchen, my whole body shaking with laughter. He hadn't done it for me since then.

But I sat on the couch in our apartment two years after I had seen it the first time, and I laughed at Mick Jagger. As He stood there with His lips pouted, one hand on His hip, I fell in love with Him for the millionth time. I thought it would be like that forever.

Now I sat in my car, looking into the lobby of our old building. I started to cry. Nothing stays the same. Nothing lasts. I was so naive, so young. I can't even remember what it's like to sleep next to anyone, and I was crying because there was a time when I couldn't remember sleeping alone. I appreciated every day with Him, every moment; not knowing those moments were little gasping breaths.

Everything was so different now; I was different. I don't look the same. I don't like the things I used to like. I live in a different apartment with different furniture. I drive a different car. He was someone I never really knew. Just someone I wanted Him to be.

When I think of the relationship, I'm not sad or mad at Him. I think it's too bad it didn't work out. He was the only person I have met so far that I could see spending my life with. I knew His thoughts before He even thought them. I loved watching Him play golf. I loved that we were a couple. I loved showing Him all the goods I bought at the grocery store and telling Him I was going to make Sloppy Joe's for dinner.

But He wasn't real. I think He saw what I wanted and made Himself into that. In return, He got everything. I paid for everything. I made Him a part of my family. I loved Him for as long as He allowed me to love Him. He cheated on me, He was out of work for a year and didn't try too hard to find a new job. It was all Him. I did nothing. No, I did everything.

I wiped my eyes with my fingertips and looked in the rearview mirror. *I need to move on.* Dating other people doesn't mean that I've moved on. Here I've been telling everyone I didn't give a shit about Him any more and that I was over the whole thing. But when I was alone, I'd still remember what it was like. And I'd miss it. I wanted it again.

I don't think I should erase the whole thing from my memory, but I can only think about something for so long. It was completely out of my control and yes, it happened. I can think about it, cry about it, and do this self-torture thing over and over again. But what really matters is me and what I *can* control. Blaming someone or something is a short-term cure. The true cure is realizing that it happened, and moving on.

Maybe I hadn't met anyone good since the whole incident because God was waiting till I was ready. I thought I was ready, but I wasn't. Thoughts of what was still lingered. I didn't give everything to any relationship since Him because I was afraid of The Waitress; she had to be there somewhere, lurking in the shadows.

If someone was the tiniest bit boring, I dumped them. Look at the Ranch dressing guy. Everyone has their quirks. Maybe dating someone with an appreciation for condiments would have been rewarding. OK, I still think *no* on that one. I'm not going to compete with salad dressing.

There is a very thin line between settling and having unrealistic standards. I refuse to date some loser just to say that I'm dating someone. I'd rather go to the party alone. But just because I've never been attracted to a blond man doesn't mean that I can't be attracted to a blond man. All this time I've been looking for these ultra specific characteristics like hair color and height, but there is not and shouldn't be a physical description of the perfect man for me. Maybe brown eyes are just as beautiful as blue.

I pulled around to the back of our building and looked up at our place. I could see an old woman walking around inside. It was time for me to let go. No matter how hard I try to stop it, I will always love the man I thought He was. I will smile when I hear a Rolling Stones song and remember what it felt like to hang my leg over His when we were sleeping. If I ever make Sloppy Joe's again, I will no doubt think of how much He loved it when I made them. I will probably always look into the interiors of cars like His to see if it's Him. But this was the end of the ending and the new beginning of a new beginning.

I drove home and lit a bunch of candles around my apartment. I stretched out on the carpet and breathed in and out very deeply. It was strangely quiet in the building, and the moon was especially bright that night. It bounced off the glass of the TV screen and reflected around the room. I took it all as a sign. Good things were yet to come.

And I deserved every one of them.

THE NEWNESS STEPPED IN [10:31 pm]

Something new
that shines in the light and glows in the dark
has caught my eye
and wrapped me around Its finger.

Uninvited
It stepped inside with an unexpected purpose
Pulled up a chair,
and made Itself comfortable.

It stayed awhile and made me smile,
forgetting the insecurities I always remembered.

It made me nervous
and laugh in high pitched squeals
as I tried to let go
of the familiar
of the similar
While Loneliness got up and slammed the door
on its way out.

And as I look into the unseen eyes
of this familiar stranger
I see my own eyes are blue
my head is strong,
that I am me
and that's…
pretty good.

I shared a cup of tea with no one
on a verandah in Santa Fe
while The Newness put Its arm around me
and protected me from the past
yet vulnerable to the future.

It whispered in my ear
"Everything is yours,"
and stepped back, into the darkest corner of my world,
to see
what I
would do
next.

27. Thursday

So, that's where I am right now. I have all the hope and aspiration in the world. I'm going to try not to think about things so much. I don't want to care about stupid things any more. Stupid things like Shitbird. Like John or alligators. I don't want to worry if I'm going to get married someday.

I figure if you want to get married, then you'll get married. When I see all my friends' husbands, I really wouldn't date any of them. I'm not attracted to them. But they're not for me; they're for my friend. I just haven't met anyone so far that I would want to be around for a long period of time. I haven't met anyone who could make me laugh. It's funny, but I can honestly picture myself with someone, someday. I see myself sitting on the couch with someone, having kids, kissing in the dark. Could be Mitchell, could be not. Could be someone I haven't even met yet. Could be someone I already know. The possibilities are endless!

How many people do I know right now? I mean, in comparison to how many people there are in the entire world? There are millions and millions of people that I haven't even met yet. The person for me could live in a completely different part of the world. Like Bali. I haven't even been to Bali yet.

I've decided to live like a Mormon. Well, actually I just want to live by the Mormon idea: *The body is a temple.* I'm not going to start wearing special underwear or anything, but I'm only going to eat healthy food. No fried food that will clog my pores, arteries, or soul. I will be like an old Inca woman and grow my hair long and do yoga on a mountaintop. I'm going to get one of those dream machines that play ocean sounds or raindrops when I'm sleeping. I'll meditate twice a day. I'm going to drink the proper eight glasses of water a day. I've decided to be healthy.

"But you're still smoking," the counselor said.

I looked down at my right hand, holding a cigarette. "Oh," I took a puff. "That's true."

"When is that going to stop?"

"Well, that's why I'm here. I've been trying to quit for awhile now."

"Have you tried the patch?" The counselor crossed his arms in front of his chest and looked very bored.

"No. I don't like the idea of adhering something to my body. It's a little too *X-Files* for me. But I've cut down. I used to smoke two packs a week. Then I moved it down to one pack every two weeks."

He yawned.

"See what I did? I swapped it. Two packs one week; one pack two weeks." I stubbed out my cigarette.

"Yeah, I get it," he said.

Rita, a fellow Smokers Anonymous member, raised her hand. "Are you done? I mean, you talked the entire hour we were here." She motioned to the other nine people sitting in the gray folding chairs, each with an ashtray balanced on their right leg. "Every week we all come and you monopolize the entire meeting. We just sit and listen to you read from your lame journal or drone on and on about this stupid, meaningless shit…"

"Rita, let's be supportive," the counselor said. "The purpose of these meetings is to share the feelings that lead to our smoking habits. The stories she tells each week are indications of why she cannot quit smoking."

"I think her stories are interesting," said Jesse, the shy chain-smoker who always sits a few feet away from the group.

I smiled at him and fumbled around in my bag for another smoke. "I've been drinking a lot of coffee lately. It makes me go off at the mouth pretty severely, I guess."

Old Woman Betty snapped her gum. "Quit guessing. You're a chatter box."

"You could have interrupted me at any time. You all obviously have mouths… and opinions," I said under my breath.

The counselor interrupted, "Why don't you try the Step Program? Try smoking one pack every three weeks. Cut it down even more than you have been?"

"Well, I've started this thing of limiting myself to only smoking one day a week."

"Which day?" Jesse quietly asked.

"I only smoke on Thursdays."

"Why Thursdays?" Rita spat out.

"Seemed like a good day," I said, leaning toward Al, the guy with the worst body odor on the planet, as he lit me up.

"That's the dumbest thing I've ever heard," Betty said, shoving a handful of grape-flavored Big League Chew into her big mouth.

"If it works for her, then it's working. We're all trying to move toward health," the counselor said, looking at his watch.

"You're a freak!" Rita whisper-yelled in my ear.

"OK, so we'll all meet next week, same time, and let's try to hear someone else's stories, all right people?" the counselor said, looking at me. "Have a good week, and remember *Nicotine Is Awfully Mean*. Say it with me now."

"*Nicotine Is Awfully Mean*," we all repeated.

"OK. Please fold up your chair on the way out, and don't forget to dump your ash." A few people started to clap, and we all stood to gather our belongings. I pulled on my gloves.

"I really like the way you tell a story. It's entertaining," Jesse said, taking a drag off his Camel Light.

I looked up. "Oh, thanks. I thought I was going to get the hook there for a minute. I think Rita was one cigarette away from chucking chairs at me."

He laughed, "It's a rough crowd—chain smokers and habitual gum chewers."

"I know!" I laughed and picked up my bag. "Well. See you next week."

"You want to get a cup of coffee and a smoke or something? It is Thursday, you know."

"Thanks but… I really have to go."

"OK. Maybe some other time?" Jesse asked.

"Maybe." I smiled and walked out.

The cold air hit me in the face as I pushed open the heavy door. I tightened my collar around my neck as I walked the few blocks to where my car was parked. I'm really going to try to make this a good Christmas. I've never been much of a Christmas person. The lights are pretty and all, I just think everything gets going too fast and then it's over. My favorite holiday? Valentine's Day.

I remember making those little mailbox things in the third grade and spending hours picking out the crucial card to that one person I had a crush on. What message did I want to give this guy? The little puppy with the heart on its head that said, *You're Cute!*, or the bunny card that read, *Be Mine*? During lunch I would go through the valentines that I got and try to decipher exactly what that one boy meant by *Hope your Valentine's Day is filled with love.*

I think it's rather funny that I like that holiday. The one holiday where most women cry and eat boxes upon boxes of heart shaped candies. Strange. After all that's happened, I still love Valentine's Day.

I got in my car and started home. The tree lots were packed with husbands holding out the perfect tree, wives rejecting it, later heading to the Chinese restaurant and to watch *It's a Wonderful Life*. It *is* a wonderful life. I've made severe progress. And progress is never a bad thing. Progress is progressive. And I am so very progressive.

I am what I want; therefore the person I want will want me right back. Comparing what I've got to the girl who has four children is simply not fair. Different lives, that's all. One life isn't better than the other. I know I wouldn't want four kids right now. And the woman with four kids probably doesn't want to go home, climb into a hot bath, and listen to vintage Cher music, but I do, and that's what's waiting for me when I get there

I parked my car and walked toward my Mary Tyler Moore apartment building (I always thought it looked like a place she would live). I had an urge to toss my hat into the air but stifled the inkling. I put my key in the lock and twisted it open, dropping my bag in time to see Pinkie jump from the spot where she isn't supposed to sit. I picked her up and walked toward the windows reflecting the Seattle skyline. I am truly blessed. Good family. Great friends. The ability to dance better than anyone in any given dance club. I can be anything I want to be. I can be whoever I want to be. I'm someone people notice, and that's a good thing. Choose any metaphor you want, but life is a bowl of soup. It should be good without the crackers, but if the crackers are there, then have the crackers. If not, enjoy it and move on. You may not have wanted soup in the beginning, but you got it, and surprisingly, it's not half bad. In fact, it's just what you wanted all along.

I gave Pinkie a squeeze and put her down. *Where did I put that Cher CD?* I walked over to the table and sorted through the stack of cases, when, out of the corner of my eye, I saw two quick, red flashes. I put down the cases and walked over to the answering machine. With my breath coming slowly, the sound of Clarence's bells ringing through my neighbor's walls, I looked down at the machine. It looked back at me, displaying the number, one.

Flash-flash.
Flash-flash.

I'm 27 years old and have picked out my wedding dress.

It looks great on me. As I walk down the aisle, the small gathering of family and friends will smile at me and my dad, who's doing his best not to cry. The reception will have crab-stuffed everything and my mom's famous hot mushroom dip. Everyone will be required to drink at least one vodka tonic with extra lime. The cake will be chocolate decadence with a small replica of me and my husband standing with our tiny feet in the chocolate.

My husband will be very good to me. The dance floor will be filled with everyone I love, dancing to all my favorite songs. My husband and I will stand on a staircase before we leave the reception and I'll read something emotional that I wrote to our friends and family, thanking them for their love and support. Then I will turn to my husband and tell him that I went through a lot to find him, and had times that I thought we would never meet…

"… but now I know that everything happened as it should have, because I'm here with you, and I promise to love you more and more every day of my life."

As we drive away in our car, fireworks will explode in the sky, illuminating the smile on my face. He'll turn to me and say…

"I love you."

With a sigh and a feeling I've never had before, I'll look at him and say,

"I know you do."

And we'll laugh like idiots.

About the Author

Georgie Nickell is from Seattle, Washington and enjoys photography, travel, and of course, writing. She is currently working on her next novel.

0-595-23646-4